STICKS AND STONES AND A BAG OF BONES

STICKS AND STONES AND A BAG OF BONES

A MERMAID BAY CHRISTMAS SHOPPE MYSTERY

HEATHER WEIDNER

Author Photo Credit: Joy Pfister and her wonderful crew at Studio FBJ

First edition

ISBN: 978-1-68512-258-4

Cover art by Level Best Designs

This book was professionally typeset on Reedsy.
Find out more at reedsy.com

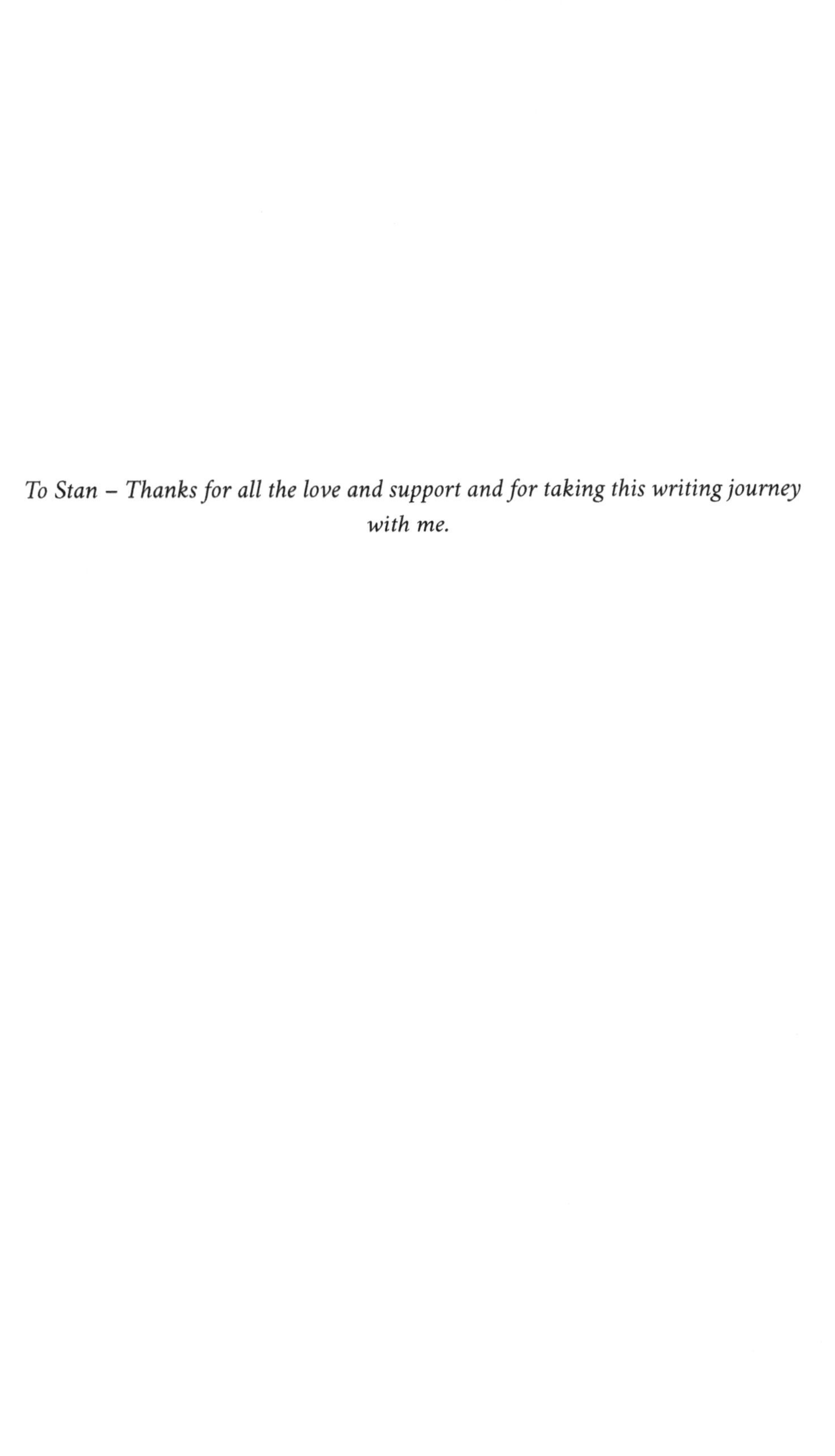

To Stan – Thanks for all the love and support and for taking this writing journey with me.

Chapter One

Escaping for a few minutes from the constant grind of living and working in a beach community, Jade Hicks and Chloe, her French bulldog, walked near the water's edge and breathed in the tangy, salt air. Chloe, a white ball of spunk, spent most of her time chasing the advancing and retreating water and the occasional fiddler crab.

Ambling across the wet sand toward the pier, Jade made to-do lists in her head for things she needed to finish this morning at 'Tis the Season. She loved the Christmas store her grandmother created but trying to keep it viable in the tiny community of Mermaid Bay, Virginia, was a full-time job and then some. Jade felt as if she spent every waking moment finding new ways to keep the business solvent year-round.

A shrill scream pierced the quiet morning, and Jade's thoughts of the store evaporated like the sea mist. She looked around for the source. A second, longer scream drowned out the caws of the seabirds. Scooping up Chloe, she trotted toward a blond woman in hot pink and black athletic wear. The woman waved her arms like she was swatting bees and hopped around in the sand.

A male jogger and his chocolate Labrador retriever reached the woman first. Both stared at an open sandy, wet suitcase. Bernie Nash, Jade's occasional handyman and part-time Santa, waddled over with his metal detector.

The woman took several deep breaths and pointed at the suitcase. "I tripped over something, and when I got my footing, I saw that...those..."

Several long bones and some seaweed had spilled out onto the sand, while a lone skull sat inside a suitcase filled with wet sand and dregs of seawater. The male jogger snapped several photos while his dog sniffed the contents.

"It was open like that?" Jade asked.

The woman shook her head no. "I peeked inside to see whose it was. I didn't expect someone to be in there."

"Stuff washes up all the time. You never know what you'll find out here. So far this morning, I've found a belt buckle and thirty-eight cents." Bernie jingled the change in the pockets of his khaki cargo shorts. His curly white beard almost touched the second button of his flamingo, Hawaiian-print shirt. "This tops it all. She's got me beat with the finds today." Bernie's eyes widened as he stared at the suitcase.

Jade pulled out her phone and dialed 911. "This is Jade Hicks. I'm on the beach near Suggs's pier, and a bag of bones washed up on shore."

"A bag of bones?" the dispatcher asked.

"Yes. In a black suitcase. We can see bones and a skull. You know, human remains…" Jade's voice drifted off.

"I'll send a unit by. Is anyone in any danger?"

"No. It was just not what we expected to see on the beach this morning." Jade adjusted the wiggly Chloe under her arm to keep the little dog's curiosity about the suitcase's contents and the other dog contained.

"The unit is about ten minutes out. Make sure someone directs him to the location."

"Will do. We'll be here waiting." Jade disconnected and looked at the others. "Police are on their way."

"I'll go stand near the road to see if I can see them," the male jogger said. "Come on, Oscar." The man whistled, and the lab followed him to the parking lot near the pier.

"Are you okay?" Jade asked the female jogger who'd plunked down in the sand.

She rested her head in both hands. "Just a little surprised. I thought I tripped over driftwood or something buried in the sand. I was humming along on this perfect morning, and wham. Where in the world did these come from? Who puts bones in a suitcase? This is beyond creepy." She wrapped her arms around herself and shivered.

Jade stared at the grayish, brown bones in the sand. Some of them looked dented, with chipped ends. She shuddered and stared out at the ocean to keep her mind from dwelling on what might have caused the bones to be so damaged.

Jade and Bernie watched the waves while the woman tapped on her phone. Chloe wriggled to escape, knowing she was missing all the action on the sand. Jade tucked the little dog like a football in the crook of her arm to keep her from damaging the bones any further. The last thing she needed was to wrestle one of the bones from her dog.

The sounds of rolling waves and the occasional squawk of a gull filled the air. In the distance, a handful of fishermen cast their lines from the wooden pier, seemingly unaware of the unusual activity on the beach.

The jogger's lab barked, and all heads turned toward the road. The man bounced up and down, waving his arms wildly as a black-and-white police SUV pulled into a spot facing the bay. Deputy Sebastian Sanchez put on his Smokey Bear hat and trudged down the incline. Jade grinned at what looked like an animated conversation between the man, the deputy, and the spirited brown dog as they approached the suitcase.

Sebastian said, "Morning, y'all. What happened here?" He pulled a small notebook and pen from his front pocket.

"Like I told you. Oscar and I were jogging, and we heard this woman scream. When we got closer, we found this spooky mess."

"And you are?" Sebastian looked at the man.

"Tripp Baskins. This is Oscar. We live down the beach toward the overpass at Sunset Palms in Seaport." The rail-thin man pointed over his shoulder. "I moved here from New Jersey last month to get away from all the crime."

"Thank you, Mr. Baskins. Anything else?"

The man shook his head.

Sebastian looked at the woman seated in the sand. "And you are?"

The woman stared at Sebastian. "Char Nichols. I tripped over this. I guess I knocked some of the contents out. Sorry. I was listening to my music and jogging. I had no idea body parts washed up on beaches. Do you think you'll be able to figure out who it is? Or where it came from?" She gulped and turned her head away from the bones.

"Are you hurt?" Sebastian asked.

Char hugged herself again and shook her head. "I'm fine. Just startled." The woman batted her eyes and smiled coyly when she looked at Sebastian. *She went from horrified to flirty in less than ten seconds.*

"We'll send the contents to the lab in Richmond. They're able to uncover all kinds of things. Bernie, Jade, you notice anything unusual?" Sebastian's short-sleeved uniform stretched almost to the limit of its tensile strength around his biceps.

Char continued to stare at the deputy.

Jade shook her head. "Chloe and I were out for a stroll before we open the store this morning. We came over when we heard her scream."

Char smiled and jumped up, scooting closer to the deputy. "I've never seen anything like this. Such a shock." She covered her mouth with her left hand and wiggled her fingers, void of any third-finger rings.

Sebastian turned his attention to Bernie. "And you?"

The older man shook his head. "I was out detecting. It seems this lady found way more than I did."

"Anything else?" Sebastian snapped pictures of the suitcase and its contents with his phone. He pulled out a pair of gloves and returned the loose bones to the suitcase. Picking up the skull, he turned it around several times. He paused and stared at it. "Something's not right." He tapped his finger a couple of times on the side. Then, without saying anything, he returned it to the suitcase and zipped the lid. "If y'all think of anything else, call the station. Thanks." He picked up the suitcase and trudged through the sand to his vehicle.

Char dusted sand off her shorts and watched Sebastian until he climbed into his SUV. "Hopefully, the rest of our day will be quiet. *Ciao*, y'all." She stretched and continued her run.

"Oscar and I are headed out, too." Tripp jogged off after Char in the opposite direction of Sunrise Palms.

"Chloe and I have to get ready for work. It's good to see you, Bernie."

"You, too. I'll be over later this week to look at that squeaky front door. Lorelei left me a message it was acting up."

"'Preciate it." Her aunt Lorelei, her mother's sister, was always a step ahead of her with the daily store tasks. Lorelei insisted she loved keeping her fingers in the business world, but Jade knew down deep her aunt was there to support her like she always had been since Jade's parents were killed in a car wreck. And it didn't hurt that 'Tis the Season kept Lorelei in the thick of Mermaid Bay's grapevine of news.

Bernie pulled out a pair of sunglasses and turned on his metal detector. "Let's see if I can uncover anything interesting before I pack it in for today. Uh oh. Looks like someone is monitoring the police scanner." He pointed toward the parking lot.

Nell Jones, social reporter and gossip monger for the *Beach Comber,* bustled across the lot, watching the taillights of the deputy's vehicle. By the time Jade and Chloe approached, Nell stood with both hands on her hips, staring at the SUV as it disappeared around the corner.

She made a harumphing sound. "Morning, Jade. Hey, Chloe."

The little dog sniffed the reporter's lemon-yellow Crocs.

"Deputy Sanchez had no comment. What's going on this morning?"

"You're here early for the Christmas in July festivities." Jade gave an impish grin.

Nell maintained the weekly paper's events calendar and covered puff pieces. The tiny paper was a favorite with tourists for its coupons and with the locals for the latest rumors in Nell's "Around the Bay" column. Jade knew Nell was well aware of the town's weekend festival to boost the local economy and didn't need reminding. She just felt like poking the bear a little. Jade couldn't remember the last time the local paper had a hard news story.

Nell snorted. "Very funny. I heard all the activity this morning and decided to pop by. A mysterious find would be a great cover story. Murder, hidden treasure, and a pile of bones." The reporter's eyes widened at the thought of an unexplained death in Mermaid Bay, one that might get picked up by a larger news outlet.

"Not sure it was that exciting. Just a wet suitcase. The deputy is probably the best one to talk to, or one of the joggers. Bernie and the joggers were there before Chloe and I arrived."

On cue, the little white butterball let out a long woooo.

"Okay, sweetie. I know it's getting warm out here. We need to head back anyway. See you around, Nell."

Nell nodded and pulled out her cell phone. She furiously punched away on the screen.

Jade and Chloe picked their way across the parking lot, filling up with sun worshippers and families with wagons full of beach gear. When the coast was clear, they crossed the street and walked down the block to the former beach cottage with the wraparound porch, home of 'Tis the Season, where it's Christmas every day.

Jade paused and glanced at the rustic front porch filled with rocking chairs and country holiday decorations. Mermaid Bay held so many fond memories for her. She left her interior design job in Richmond after her grandmother's death two years ago to return to the tiny beach community. Determined to keep the store her father's parents had poured everything into, Jade constantly looked for ways to expand offerings and create multiple revenue streams. Shaking off the melancholic feeling of missing her parents and grandparents, she climbed the porch steps and turned to watch the waves roll across the bay. Gulls drifted gracefully across the blue sky, dotted with cotton ball clouds, and a large gray trawler inched across the horizon on its way to the open waters of the Atlantic.

Chloe joined her and sniffed the white rocking chairs as she waited for Jade to open the screen door. The little dog trotted inside behind Jade.

Minutes later, the bells on the front door jangled, and Patti Hall, known to everyone in the neighborhood as Peppermint Patti, swooped in and picked up Chloe for snuggles and kisses.

"Did you hear? The town's abuzz about what drifted up on shore this morning." The thirty-something's cheeks were rosier than normal against her porcelain skin and shoulder-length blond ringlets.

"Sorry we're late. I had planned to be here to open early this morning.

Chloe and I took a walk and ran into a couple of joggers and Bernie."

"And you saw that suitcase full of bones," Patti whispered, setting her phone down.

Wow. The Mermaid Bay gossip mill was on fire this morning. "That didn't take long. It just happened."

"I saw photos on Facebook. Ewww. That's the last thing we need during tourist season. And Bernie called a minute ago. Where do you think they came from? And who is…was it? It could have been someone killed in a gruesome way, like a mob hit, and the suitcase was thrown off a bridge or a boat in the middle of the night. Or maybe it was the result of a lovers' quarrel." Patti took a breath and smoothed her oversized holiday sweater.

Jade shrugged and opened the Dutch door to the back room and kitchen area. She unclipped the dog's leash and filled a pink and white polka-dotted bowl with water. Chloe snorted and slurped her appreciation.

Stepping back into the store, she pulled the door behind her, not knowing where Neville the Devil Cat was. The tuxedo cat, a black-and-white stray that she inherited with the property, usually pranced around like he owned the joint. The cat tolerated Jade and Patti but had sworn an oath to torment Chloe every chance he could. Fortunately, Chloe stayed in her fuzzy bed next to Jade's desk, giving Neville free rein of the store. He often treated visitors to occasional cat sightings under and around the trees and displays.

The front door's bells jingled, and Patti turned on her best holiday smile as she greeted a pair of women. "Welcome to 'Tis the Season. If you're interested in something in particular or you have questions, please let me know."

"Thanks," the taller of the two women said. "Our concierge told us about this place, and my sister Dot and I had to swing by while our husbands are golfing."

"This store is adorable." Dot glanced around at all the trees and sparkles.

"Enjoy your visit. I have some cider and gingerbread cookies on the counter if you'd like a snack. And we have an entire room to your left filled with handmade ornaments from our local artisans. How long are you all going to be here?" Patti asked.

"Until next Thursday. We're at a timeshare in Williamsburg. It's really nice around here. I've never been to Virginia before." Dot fingered a tiny Christmas tree made with green and red glass beads.

"Then you should come back this weekend. The town's celebrating Christmas in July. We'll have many of the artisans here on Friday and Saturday. There will be holiday-themed events and lots of food trucks. There's also a fun run and a parade of lights on Saturday." Patti handed a flyer to each woman.

"Sounds perfect. And it smells so good. I could get lost in here for hours," the taller sister said.

"Here are two of our shopping baskets to help you keep your purchases together. Just come back when you're done, and we'll ring you up. We do have a Christmas cat who naps under the trees. Just wanted to give you a warning so Neville doesn't startle you."

"Aww. Come on, Martha. We need to see if we can spot Neville." Dot grabbed a pine green shopping basket Patti offered and wandered into the next room. "Do you have any animal ornaments?"

"They're in the Toyland room," Patti said. "Go through this doorway, and it's the third room back. You'll know when you're there. If you see an ornament you like on a tree, they're in the peach baskets right below it."

"Ooooh, this is too much fun. It's like a treasure hunt." Martha followed her sister through the open doorway to the cottage's former living room. 'Tis the Season, originally a large cottage built in the late 1940s, boasted seven display rooms and a multi-purpose room Jade added last year for events and classes.

When the guests were out of earshot, Patti leaned forward. "I heard there were human remains in that suitcase this morning. If it wasn't a mob hit, do you think it was some other chilling murder where someone thought the sea would take care of the evidence? You know, dead men tell no tales. Those bones could have been out there for years. Just floating along."

Jade hoped she didn't roll her eyes. Someone watched a lot of true-crime TV. "The suitcase looked pretty modern." Jade straightened a stack of brochures on the counter. "They were definitely bones. Nell showed up, but Sebastian didn't stop to talk to her. I'm sure she went looking for the joggers and Bernie after I left."

"Nosey Nell won't let it rest. She's like a dog, well, with a bone." A sheepish grin crossed Patti's face as the bells on the front door tinkled, and she snapped into greeter mode. "Welcome to 'Tis the Season. Please let Jade or me know if we can help you with anything," Patti said to the couple and their three children, who blew in the front door like a whirlwind. She handed the adults shopping baskets. "There's a schedule inside with all the events for this weekend's Christmas in July festivities."

"Sounds like fun," the woman said. "And, kids, this is a look with your eyes, not your hands kind of place." She gave them a sideways momma-bear glance that was almost as scary as hearing your mom yell all three of your names.

The children, who ranged in age from about four to ten, put their hands obediently behind their backs.

"Enjoy your visit. We have snacks up here on the counter if you're interested. And be on the lookout for Neville, our Christmas cat. Sometimes he makes an appearance under the trees," Patti added.

The smallest girl's face lit up, and she was immediately on the hunt for the elusive cat.

When the family disappeared into the next room, Jade said, "I'm going get some coffee. Want anything?"

Patti shook her head and pulled out a feather duster from behind the counter. "I put the mail on your desk. Our hunky delivery driver should be here soon with the morning boxes. I put the bin from yesterday out for him." Her eyes sparkled like one of those cartoon characters with hearts for pupils, and a slight flush crossed her apple-round cheeks as she hummed and busied herself with the trees in the lobby.

Chloe jumped into action when Jade closed the bottom of the Dutch door. "Hi, puppy. I missed you, too." She slipped the pudgy little dog a treat from the stash on the counter as she popped a pod in the coffee maker.

Her phone dinged with a string of texts as the coffee machine sputtered and spit out a blast of steam. Her coffee dribbled into the mug.

The text that caught her eye was from Bernie. **I've been Googling. Something's not right about those bones.**

Chapter Two

Frustrated that Bernie didn't respond to her question about the bones, Jade pulled out her phone and left a voicemail for him after his quirky message. Waving off thoughts of the creepy find, she opened the list of overnight online orders.

For the next hour, she filled and packaged orders. Jade's first investment in the store had been to create a website with easy online shopping and ordering from anywhere. It had been a huge expense at the time, but it saved her business during the pandemic and provided a steady stream of sales in the off-season.

After ensuring all the internet orders had mailing labels, she put them in the bin and carried it to the front door.

"We had thirty-two online orders waiting this morning." Jade slid behind the counter. "They're all ready for your favorite driver."

"Good job. And it's been steady out here, too. I'm excited to see what the festivities will bring this weekend. I peeked at the schedule. I'm glad you added Lorelei and Tori to the calendar. We'll need the help, especially with the booths outside."

Jade brushed a stray red curl from her face. "I'm hoping the weekend brings in a lot of tourists. The business owners have been blasting it all over their social media accounts, and the council did a great deal of advertising to the tourists in the Historic Triangle."

"It's the perfect little excursion for the folks who come to visit Jamestown, Williamsburg, and Yorktown. Mermaid Bay, land of fun and sun, our little quiet corner of the world."

"They need to put you on all the brochures," Jade said.

"Just sharing the love. We have the perfect job…Christmas every day and a beautiful beach. I wouldn't live anywhere else."

Interrupted by another string of texts and her vibrating phone, Jade glanced at the screen. **Emergency meeting at the library at 1:00 Need you there. Need to make plans now. Must avert crisis!!!!**

Jade let out a breath she didn't realize she was holding. Vivian Turner, the town librarian and Mermaid Bay Business Council President, could fret as well electronically as she could in person.

Of course. See you then. Jade responded.

"I'm going to take Chloe home for lunch in a bit and then pop in at the business council's emergency meeting. Tori will be in at two. Do you want to go to lunch before I leave?"

"You can leave Chloe here. She's napping. Don't disturb her. And thanks for the offer, but I brought a snack. I'll wait until Tori gets settled before I go for a little walk. Just let me know what's going on at the library." Patti winked.

"Will do. I'm hoping there's no drama, but that may be a lot to ask for after Vivian's crisis text. Be back after the meeting."

"Can't wait to hear about it, especially if it's juuuuu-ceeee." Patti's voice rose several octaves, and she added jazz hands for effect.

After a quick lunch of leftover ravioli and some applesauce she found in the back of the fridge, Jade picked up her purse and messenger bag. Her cottage seemed empty without Chloe's little nails clicking on the hardwood floors.

Jumping in her lime-green Jeep Wrangler, Jade rolled down the windows and drove the half-mile from her place to the town government center. The name sounded bigger than it was. The library and sheriff's office took up most of the space in the office complex.

Leaving her windows cracked, she hightailed it inside. Somehow, time had gotten away from her, and the meeting was about to start. Jade hustled through the front doorway, and the arctic blast from the AC hit her in the face. She shivered and dodged bookcases and carts on her way to the meeting room near the children's section.

Slipping in, Jade zeroed in on one of the few remaining seats facing the lectern. The flags stood tall in the background. She plopped down between Todd Brickman, owner of Hot Diggity Dogs, and Ruby Ellis, proprietor of the town's only bed and breakfast, the Pearl.

"How're things in your neck of the woods?" Todd asked.

Ruby moved her purse to make room for Jade and said, "Quiet until this morning."

"Did I miss anything?" Jade whispered.

"Just Ms. Perfect Tish sashaying in with that developer, Jared Carswell, like they own the place. What's he doing here anyway? He's not part of the council. He tries to insert himself everywhere. He's determined to figure out a way to develop our little community." Ruby raised one eyebrow.

"He and Tish are always trying new ways to get their fingers on beach property. The market's hot now. I've told both of them not to come on my property again, unless they're there to order food. I'm tired of their barrage of pitches. The hotdog stand's not much, but it's been in my family for generations," Todd said.

"It's like most of the buildings around here. They give the area its history and charm," Jade said. *And your place sits on a corner lot with an ocean view.*

As Jade glanced around the room, her gaze landed on Tish St. James in her champagne-colored slacks and matching blouse. Her angle-cut bob looked like something out of *Vogue*. The model-perfect realtor stood next to her buddy, real estate developer Jared Carswell. The tall man in a tailored gray suit whispered something to Tish. Her overexaggerated laugh rang through the room. She seemed to notice people staring and covered her fire-engine red lips with perfectly manicured nails.

Vivian banged her gavel on the lectern, and conversations halted in midsentence. "Shhhhhhh! I now call this emergency meeting of the Mermaid Bay Business Council to order. An unsettling event occurred this morning, and we need to decide what to do with our planned activities for the weekend."

A collective gasp emanated from the crowd.

"I've already paid for advertising and decorations. Whaddya mean? Are you proposing that we cancel?" Claude Simpkins yelled from the third row as the buzz from the crowd increased.

"Order. Order." Vivian pounded on the oak lectern with her gavel and glared at Claude. "In case you haven't heard, this morning beachgoers found a suitcase full of bones on our fair shores. It washed up from who knows where, bringing with it an ill wind." Vivian, as wide as she was tall, stared out into the audience. "Sheriff, do you have anything to add?"

All heads turned toward the door. Nick Driscoll leaned casually against the metal doorjamb. He cleared his throat and made his way to the front of the room. He winked and pinched Jade's arm when he passed. She swatted at him and then smiled at her childhood friend. Growing up, he was always the goofball. She never picked him for a career in law enforcement, and she was even more surprised when he left a job in a bigger department to return home to fill the shoes of the retiring sheriff.

Standing next to Vivian, Nick looked like a giant. "Good morning. My deputy responded to a call this morning. It appears some remains were found in a wet suitcase. The evidence is en route to the lab in Richmond. We'll release a statement as soon as we have more information."

Tish St. James stood and turned toward the audience. "Is there any immediate danger?" Her eyes widened, and she licked her plump lips and ogled the sheriff.

"We always need to be aware of our surroundings, but no, I don't think this incident is related to any threat to our residents or guests. Right now, it looks like it washed ashore from a boat or other means. The state forensic authorities are assisting with the investigation."

"Thank you, Sheriff. So, I open the floor to discussion about our plans for the Christmas in July celebration," Vivian said. "What do we want to do?"

Ruby Ellis stood. "Should we cancel? I mean, is it appropriate to have a celebration when there's a dead body on the beach?"

"There's no dead body, just some bones and we don't know where they came from," Claude said. "A lot of us have invested time and money into this. If we cancel, people like me will be angry." He glared and crossed his arms across his white rumpled oxford and red tie. He looked around at the faces near him. "And I hope this isn't some kind of ominous warning."

"I agree with Claude. We've been planning this for a while. This could be some kind of publicity stunt or joke. It's better not to make a big deal about it. I vote we carry on as planned," Emory Jessup, owner of Mermaid Books, added in her Boston brogue.

"Any other comments?" Vivian scanned the room and paused for a few seconds. "Then can I have a motion to continue with our weekend festivities?"

"I motion," Claude yelled. "Or move, or whatever the term is."

Emory and Tish quickly added their support, and Vivian banged her gavel.

"Okay then. We'll vote. All in favor." She paused. Hands went up around the room. "Any opposed? Then we'll proceed with the festival. Any media requests about the festival need to be directed to me, and any questions about the unfortunate, uh suitcase, need to be directed to Sheriff Driscoll's office. Any updates or news from our committee chairs?" Vivian glanced around the room.

"The vendor booths and food truck spaces are all rented. We have a variety of interesting wares that don't compete with any of our existing businesses. Oh, and the committee has collected quite a tidy sum of fees from vendors for future projects," Emory added.

"We have over five hundred people registered for the fun run," Todd added.

"And we're all set for the lighted boat parade. The Coast Guard will lead off. We have close to sixty boats and jet skis. The flotilla sails from the pier at eight," Bernie added.

"We've got a jam-packed weekend. Any other business?" Another brief pause. "Then we're adjourned. Eat your Wheaties. And be ready to start at the crack of dawn on Friday. Let's show them our beach hospitality."

After several more gavel bangs, the audience stirred and gathered their belongings. Jade waved to friends and wended her way through library patrons and bookcases. She rounded a corner near the biography section and almost ran into the back of Nell Jones, who was hunched over her phone and blocking the aisle.

"Oh, excuse me," Jade said.

The reporter turned toward the voice. Seeing it was Jade, she held up her phone. "Hey. You never know when a lead will pan out. I have to constantly monitor my phone. Word on the street is the bones are what's left of a murder. The sheriff shouldn't be so quick to dismiss it. The big city ills have arrived in Mermaid Bay. Hope it's not an omen like Claude said." She turned before Jade could respond and bustled through the stacks.

Chapter Three

Jade shook off Nell's negative attitude and slipped into her Jeep. She had invested too much time and energy into this weekend to worry about things that hadn't happened yet. Blasting the AC to dissipate some of the hot air, she drove through town and parked behind her store.

She barely had the door open before Patti and Aunt Lorelei rushed into the office. The humans wanted news, while Chloe wanted hugs. Picking up her little dog, she kissed her on the head.

"Well?" Lorelei tapped her shiny red flat on the wooden floor. "What's going on?"

"The council decided to move forward with the events. Most of the business owners thought the show should go on. Nell's convinced Sheriff Driscoll and others are sugar-coating the story of the bones so people won't worry."

Before Jade could continue, the bells on the front door alerted them to guests.

Patti zipped through the doorway, "Ber-neeee! It's great to see you."

"Thought I'd stop by and check on that squeaky door. Is Jade in?"

"Go on back. She and Lorelei are in the office."

The Santa look-alike in cargo shorts opened the bottom of the Dutch door. "Hey, gals. And salutations to you, too, Chloe." He leaned over to pet the wiggly dog, who greeted him with puppy licks.

"Everything okay?" Jade asked.

"Nothing a little oil on the hinges can't fix. No real issues with the door."

A half-smile crossed Jade's face. "I meant your last text. I never heard back from you. And I didn't get a chance to talk to you at the meeting."

"Can I get you something to drink?" Lorelei asked, smoothing her silk tunic.

"I'm good. Thanks." He winked at Lorelei, who busied herself with straightening items on the spare desk.

Jade watched her handyman Santa.

"Oh, I was doing some Googling after this morning's adventure." He pulled out his phone and held up a picture of the bones scattered on the sand. "These aren't human bones. Well, at least most of them." He pointed to the longer, thin bones with a brownish, gray tint.

"What do you mean?" Lorelei leaned closer to get a glimpse of the picture.

He pointed to the bones again. "I did some research and sent this to my friend Mac. He's a retired butcher. These are from a cow or large animal. See the knicks in some of them. I'm guessing they came from a butcher or processing plant."

"So, no creepy murder victim?" Lorelei asked. Her hand shot up and covered her mouth. Her diamond and emerald rings sparkled under the overhead lights.

"I don't know about the skull. That could still be something hinky, but these bones are from an animal. Could be just a weird prank. It's a good thing we didn't cancel the festival. We would have looked silly."

Before anyone could comment, he continued, "If I know Vivian, she's trying to keep all this under wraps. Can't have something like body parts on the beach ruining her festival." He snickered and pocketed his phone.

"She likes everything to be harmonious. Anything spontaneous sends her into a twitter. Vivian probably won't sleep until this weekend is over." Lorelei pulled a bottle of water from the refrigerator and headed for the store.

"Have you told Sheriff Nick yet about what you found?" Jade asked.

Bernie shook his head. "I'm pretty sure they know already."

Jade furrowed her brow and side-eyed her Santa.

"Okay. I'll let him know. I got a couple more errands to take care of…" Bernie muttered.

Jade pursed her lips.

"See, I'm texting him now as I walk out. See me text."

"Thanks, Bernie. I appreciate all you do," she yelled to his back as he shuffled out the doorway.

"Mail call." Patti bustled through the doorway. She handed Jade a stack of envelopes. "Got anything for the afternoon delivery pickup?"

Jade shook her head and flipped through a stack of bills. A manila envelope with no postage caught her attention. When she slit the flap, what looked like a folded invitation on thick, cream-colored paper with gold edging, fell on her desk. The pretty paper contrasted with the hurriedly cut-out magazine letters that seemed to scream at her, "Stay home. Mind your own business," she read. It looked like a ransom note from days gone by.

"You okay?" Patti asked as Jade reached for her phone.

She snapped a few pictures and texted them to Nick. "I'm fine. I think we have a prankster around." Jade pointed to the note.

"Oh, my stars!" Patti's hands fluttered on her cheeks. "Do you think we should heed the warning? This isn't the beachy holiday vibe we were going for when we started planning Christmas in July."

Lorelei glided in to check on the chatter. Her eyes widened as she read the note Jade handed her.

"Is this for real?" her aunt asked.

"I'm hoping it's a stupid joke." Jade's phone binged.

Put it in an envelope. Be over soon. Nick responded.

About twenty minutes later, the front door slammed. Chloe yipped as Patti, Lorelei, and Jade hustled to the lobby.

"Can you believe this? What's going on here?" Ruby Ellis waved a cream-colored piece of paper in the air.

"You got one, too?" Patti's voice rose several octaves.

"Someone's trying to send us a message. Jade, you have to help me convince the council this is serious. I think we need to heed the warnings." She opened her card for them to read,

"'Beware! Something's going to happen this weekend.'" A gloomy pall settled over Jade as she looked at the mix-matched letters and a skull and crossbones at the bottom of the page.

Before Jade could comment, heavy footsteps moved across the wooden porch. Sheriff Nick Driscoll stepped inside and took off his hat. "Afternoon, ladies. Jade, you have something for me?"

She held up the card and envelope. Pulling on disposable gloves, he took it and turned it over in his hands.

"Sheriff, I got one, too." Ruby waved hers in the air. "Ominous and spooky, just like those bones. What should we do?"

"Nothing for now. Let my guys look into it. Just be careful and be aware of what's going on around you. But go on with your normal routines."

Ruby scowled at him. "I still think we should cancel this weekend. Especially with some crazy person sending anonymous warnings. Emory got one, too. She was more upset it was addressed to 'Mermad Books' than receiving the note. She ranted for ten minutes about the need to proofread."

"Let me have yours as evidence, too. I'll stop by and see Emory. If you hear of anyone else with one, have them call the station."

Ruby nodded and reluctantly handed her card to him. "But what about the bones? Somebody washed up in a suitcase."

Nick cleared his throat. "This will be out later in the afternoon news cycle. The bones were from a cow, and the skull was a cheap plaster Halloween decoration."

"Somebody's idea of a sick joke." Ruby planted her fist on her hip and frowned.

Lorelei's platinum blond head bobbled in agreement.

"Thanks for letting me know about these." Nick held up the cards. "Call if you notice anything else."

"I'm on high alert. And you're on speed dial." After he left, Ruby continued, "I still think we need another emergency meeting. Like the card said, something's gonna happen." She turned, and her sensible shoes squeaked on the wooden floor. "I hope we're not sorry."

"Do you think we should warn the vendors or cancel?" Patti asked. "It would be terrible if something happened. We can't afford the bad press. What if it scares people from coming to the beach? That could ruin our season."

Jade's jaw stiffened. "I'm hoping it's only someone with a twisted sense of humor. It feels like a prank. Why would a community Christmas-themed festival cause this much trouble?" Her hands curled in indignation. "This is our town, and I'm not going to let somebody sabotage our hard work with cow bones and Halloween decorations."

"Go girl!" Patti patted her on the back. "I'm going to check on our displays on the floor while Lorelei watches the till. Need me to do anything else first?"

Jade shook her head and winked. "I'll get any new online orders ready for your favorite delivery guy."

Patti giggled and disappeared into the store.

As Jade printed shipping labels, she tried to shake the foreboding feeling the notes caused. Should she be more worried about the warnings? What if something tragic tainted Christmas in July?

Chapter Four

Jade and Chloe took an extra-long walk on the beach at sunrise. "It's set-up day, and we're in for a long weekend. Let's enjoy our quiet time while we can."

After sniffing a shell, the Frenchie dug in the sand.

Following the path from the beach to her cottage, Jade noticed a sign flapping in the morning breeze on the first telephone pole. These served as Mermaid Bay's old-school form of social media to announce yard sales, lost dogs, and concerts. The one that caught her attention this morning was at eye level in bright red letters, "Stay Home This Weekend." At first she thought it was a concert announcement, but the warning had blood dripping from the words onto a skull and crossbones. Jade snapped a picture of it and texted Nick.

She pulled it down and hurried to her cottage. Gathering her purse and work gear, she stuffed the warning in her bag and locked the door behind them. "Come on, Chloe. It's time to get a move on."

On her walk to the store, the ocean breeze ruffled Jade's hair. Chloe paused every few feet to sniff the air. Somehow the tranquil morning didn't feel peaceful anymore.

She rounded the corner to the main drag, Neptune Road, and stopped in her tracks. Every telephone pole on the block sported copies of the same sign. She took pictures and sent another text to Nick. She Googled "Stay at Home," hoping it was the name of a band.

A noise put Chloe on high alert with several low growls. Vivian and Emory bustled down the street, pulling down the signs.

"Jade, can you believe this prankster? Someone went to an awful lot of trouble to post these." Emory pulled down two signs and stuffed them in a shopping bag.

"Someone is trying to ruin us." Vivian wrung her hands and looked down the street at the warnings. "They stuck one on every spot they could find. This is too much. Do you think we need another emergency meeting?"

"No, don't be silly." Emory glared at Vivian with one hand on her hip. "We settled this yesterday. We're having our celebration. No good-for-nothing is going to control us. We'll clean this up, and no one will be the wiser."

"But what if something bad happens?" Vivian whined.

"Then we deal with it. We can't live our lives trying to avoid what-ifs. I'll do that side of the street, and you keep going on this one. We should be able to have all these down before most folks are even up."

Vivian pursed her lips and swallowed whatever comment she was going to make. She let out a sigh and continued to remove the unwanted signs on her side of the street.

Jade tugged on Chloe's lead, and the dog reluctantly followed her to the store's back door. Dropping her bag and the leash on her desk, Jade made a beeline for the coffee maker. Caffeine was a must this morning.

After checking her email, she fired off another text to Nick with a picture. **Signs were all over town this morning.**

He replied, **Thanks. Received a bunch of calls already. Busy morning.**

Busy weekend, she replied with a smiley emoji.

After draining her coffee mug and filling all the orders that popped in overnight, Jade yawned and did a few yoga poses to work out the kinks in her neck.

Chloe's ears shot up when she heard a shuffling outside. Patti opened the door, and Bernie trailed a few steps behind. The dog yipped and greeted her friends.

"Good morning, y'all," Jade said. "Thanks for coming in early to help with the set-up."

"Not a problem. I'm looking forward to this weekend. Got the boat all decorated, and I'm ready to go Saturday night. I'm going to be Captain Santa of the Mermaid Bay fleet."

"The marketplace on Friday and Saturday will be such fun and a boon for our local craftspeople. I'm so excited. Jade, it was a great idea to have them at your shop. How do you want the outside booths arranged?" Patti asked.

"I was thinking maybe in a 'U' shape around the front of the building. I have eight canopies and long tables. I told the folks there would be two people to a table. They're going to be responsible for their own sales. The big red canopy is the one for the store. Tori is going to staff that with sale items."

"I have my outfits ready for both days. I also made cookies and gingerbread. Bernie, I made some of your special orange treasure cookies. They're perfect for any occasion," Patti said.

Bernie's eyes sparkled, like the jolly old elf in beach attire.

"I ordered a collection of Christmas candy, and I have apple cider and a fruit basket for the lobby. I think we're ready to go. I've taken care of all the burning tasks this morning. Anybody want coffee or tea before we start?" Jade asked.

Bernie shook his head as Patti flitted around the office. The trio spent the next several hours hauling tables and canopied tents to the front parking lot and arranging them for the sidewalk sale.

"There." Jade taped the last artisan sign to the table. "All the spots are labeled and ready to go."

The weather report looks perfect for this weekend, so I think we're good." Bernie stood under one of the small tents to catch his breath.

A red Fiat buzzed into the lot and screeched to a stop in front of the tents. Patti sighed as Nell Jones hopped out of her car.

"Morning, all. Seen any oddities this morning?" The entertainment reporter asked.

"Besides you?" Bernie muttered and coughed. He cleared his throat.

The three women stared at him.

"Jade, looks like we're done here. If you need anything else, give me a call." He shuffled down the sidewalk toward the pier.

"Just some weird posters," Jade said.

"I heard they were all over town." Nell stepped closer. "Are you worried about all the warnings and strange stuff?" She pulled out a small notebook and a purple pen.

"Not really. We've planned a fun weekend, and I'm excited to celebrate Christmas in the summer. Nobody else has events like this, so it should be a good time for all our visitors. I hope the prankster doesn't ruin it for folks," Jade said.

Nell scribbled in a notebook. "Anything else? Are you taking any special precautions to protect your business?"

Jade squinted. "No more than normal. We're following the sheriff's suggestions."

"So, you're not worried?" Nell's glare locked in on Jade.

"We're open for business and excited to welcome people to 'Tis the Season."

Nell smirked. "Anything else?"

Jade shook her head. "Make sure you stop by. Patti has some homemade Christmas sweets, and we'll have a lot of amazing decorations."

"I'll be around. Call me if you notice anything out of the ordinary." She returned to her car and zipped out of the lot.

Patti shrugged her shoulders. "It's a beach community. There's always something weird." She chuckled and dusted her hands off on her jeans. "It looks good here. I think we're ready."

"I'm going to do a walk-through of the store and check on the comments on our social media sites," Jade said.

"I didn't pack a lunch today. I'm going to run over to the Busy Bean and grab a sandwich and iced coffee. Can I get you anything?"

"That sounds good. How about one of their pimento cheese croissants and an iced white chocolate mocha. My purse is inside."

"Don't worry about it. We'll settle up when I get back." Patti walked across the street to the large brick building that housed Mermaid Books and the Busy Bean coffee shop.

By the time Jade had checked her social sites and the inventory in the themed rooms, the bells on the front door jingled. Neville darted out from under a tree covered in polar bears and made her jump.

"Howdy, Neville."

The cat ducked behind a tree covered in cat ornaments.

Patti's voice echoed through the store. "Whooo hooo. Lunch is here."

Jade made her way to the office after a quick stop to wash her hands. "Thanks so much." She pulled out her wallet from the desk drawer and handed her a twenty.

"That's way too much, and I don't have change."

"Delivery fee." Jade unwrapped a pimento cheese croissant and a side of pasta salad. "Mmm. This is good."

"James was working the counter this morning. He said they're adding more breakfast items to the menu. And they have a whole line of holiday sweets ready for this weekend." Patti plopped down at the other desk and pulled out a tuna sandwich on a ciabatta and a fruit cup.

Jade wiped a dab of the orangey cheese spread off her lips and smiled. James and Sophie Fournier, the brother-sister team at the Busy Bean, were always good business partners. It was Jade's go-to spot for boxed lunches when she needed catering for special events and workshops.

After more munching than talking, Jade picked up the empty containers and drained the last of her iced coffee as the bells sounded again.

"I'm done. I've got this." Patti hopped up and pulled the bottom half of the Dutch door closed behind her.

Before Jade could comment, her phone dinged with a series of rapid-fire texts.

Not again!!!

Can you meet me at the library?

Not sure what this means????

Jade let out a sigh and replied to Vivian, **Be there in a sec. Are you okay?**

When no response appeared, she stepped into the store, where Patti doled out shopping baskets and information to four women in brightly colored T-shirts and capris.

When the four wandered through the store, Jade whispered, "I got a text from Vivian. I'll be back in a bit. I need to run down to the library."

A dark look crossed Patti's face. "Everything okay?"

"It was hard to tell from her cryptic texts. Hopefully, it's nothing."

Patti pasted on a half-smile. "Chloe, Neville, and I will keep everything around here humming."

"Thanks. I've got to run home and get the Jeep," Jade yelled from the office as she grabbed her purse.

A few minutes later, she found a parking spot under an ancient cypress tree next to the building that looked like something from the 1960s, with its brick front and wavy metal awning over the front door.

Before Jade climbed out of her Jeep, Vivian flew out the front glass entrance and waved her arms like some kind of large bird as she galloped toward the parking lot.

"Vivian, are you okay?" Jade climbed out and shaded her eyes with her hand.

The breathless librarian stopped in her tracks and pointed to the Jeep's front bumper. "That's funny. I never noticed that before. NO GRNCH is the perfect license plate for you and this green machine."

The moment of mirth passed as a bleak look crept across Vivian's face. What kind of storm was brewing behind her deep blue eyes?

Before Jade could comment, Vivian continued, "Jade. It happened again. Look!" She thrust a padded envelope toward her.

Lifting the flap, Jade found another note on the same cream cardstock. A doll with a teal dress and crazy silver hair sat at the bottom of the envelope. Jade pulled it out, and large hat pins stuck out in all directions. "Beware," it read. "Danger is ahead for those who don't agree and keep their promises."

Jade squinted. "I don't even know what it means." She stared at the red-gemmed hat pin stuck in the doll's heart.

"It's a voodoo doll," Vivian whispered. "We've upset someone."

"Why would someone send this to you? Was there an angry patron or someone who fussed about a fine?"

"No, it's not mine. I was over at Mermaid Books this morning, and Emory was ranting about bad online ratings, and she pulled this out of her desk drawer."

A lightbulb flashed in Jade's brain. The little doll did look like a homemade rendition of Emory in her brightly colored wraps, bangle bracelets, and crazy silver hair. "Did she call the sheriff's office?"

"No, she poo-pooed it as another prank. When she tossed it in the trash, I salvaged it. I knew you'd know what to do. This stuff is nothing to fool around with."

Jade reached for her phone and punched in Nick's contact. After a couple of rings, she heard a brusque, "Hey, what's up?"

"I'm at the library with Vivian. She has another warning and a voodoo doll that was sent to Emory."

"Be there in a sec. Just finishing lunch at Hot Diggity Dogs." He disconnected.

"Nick'll be here in a few," she said to Vivian.

The librarian's glance darted around the parking lot, and she fidgeted while they waited. "This is too much. I hate this wondering what will happen next. It's crazy." Vivian fiddled with the ring on her hand. "This is a peaceful little community. We don't have problems like this."

Nick's police SUV pulled into the lot, and he climbed out before Jade could respond to Vivian. "Afternoon, y'all. What did you find?"

"This. It's another one of those stupid notes. This is the second one left at Mermaid Books. Emory threw it in the trash," Vivian said.

The sheriff pulled out a pair of gloves from his utility belt that rivaled Batman's. "When did this arrive? With the others?"

"No. This one arrived sometime last night. She found it this morning after we cleaned up all those nasty posters someone tacked up all over town."

"No camera footage of anyone dropping it off?" Nick asked.

Vivian shook her head. "Emory doesn't believe in devices that can track her or her customers."

A slight frown crossed Nick's face. "I'll go talk to her. Let me know if y'all find anything else."

Vivian cleared her throat. "Uh, do you think we should still go ahead with tomorrow? This seems to be escalating."

"Be safe. Be vigilant. I've upped the patrols this weekend. You'll see us and our partners out in full force. Call if you see anything suspicious."

"I think the tension and the anxiety are part of the thrill for this person. He or she is enjoying striking fear and being disruptive," Jade said.

Nick nodded. "A voodoo doll. That's new. Haven't seen one of those around here." He returned the doll and note to the envelope. "Anything else on your minds?"

Both women shook their heads.

"Thanks, Nick," Jade said. "I hope you got to finish your lunch."

He grinned. "See ya. Don't hesitate to call in any problems."

"Oh, don't worry about that. We won't," Vivian yelled as he headed to his SUV. "I still don't know about this. This doesn't make any sense. I don't like all the creepiness."

"It'll be okay. Nick and his guys will figure this out. I'll see you tomorrow. We'll be up and out bright and early." Jade waved as she opened the door to her Wrangler to let the summer heat escape before she plopped down on the black leather seats. Voodoo dolls in Mermaid Bay. Who was trying to scare everyone? None of this made any sense.

Chapter Five

A double espresso and a yogurt helped Jade mute the morning groggies after a fitful night of tossing and turning. Vivian's anxiousness must have seeped into her subconscious. She shook off the feeling of dread and led Chloe to the shop. She wanted to have everything open and ready for the vendors when they arrived. Chloe, usually excited for an adventure, needed a little prodding this morning, too. "Come on, baby. Let's go bye-bye."

A few minutes later, they climbed the steps to the store's porch, and Chloe did a little French bulldog jig until Jade opened the door. Neville paraded by, and Chloe made sure he knew she was there with several woofs and a growl for good measure.

"Good morning, Neville. You hungry? Breakfast will be served momentarily."

The cat meowed and wandered toward the country Christmas room.

After turning on all the lights and filling food bowls, Jade settled in at her desk to peruse the overnight orders. She smiled at the two full pages that popped up on her screen. It took about an hour to print receipts and package the requests.

As she put a pod in the coffee maker for another jolt of caffeine, the front door bells jangled. Chloe zoomed to the dividing door.

"Whooo hoooo! Happy Christmas in July." Patti's perky voice echoed through the store.

"Good morning. Can I get you some coffee?"

"I'm good and juiced up this morning. Can't wait to see all the fun today.

It looks like some of the vendors are starting to roll in. I'm going to add my stuff to the snack table, and we should be all set. Let the holly jollies begin!"

"All the orders are ready for pickup. I'm going to head outside if you need me." Jade pocketed her phone and ducked out through the store before Chloe noticed.

Jade strolled through the lot, where fourteen of the sixteen vendors decorated their tables. A lemon-yellow Volkswagen Beetle zoomed into the lot and kicked up a mini-sandstorm with a sudden stop.

Tori hopped out and jogged toward Jade. "Sorry I'm late. I'll have the table set up in a jiff." The teen pulled her long, brown hair up in a messy bun and secured it with the elastic tie she wore on her wrist.

"The red and green bins are in the back room. I'll help you get set up," Jade said.

"I've got it. You've got other stuff to worry about. Be right back," Tori yelled over her shoulder.

Jade continued her stroll through the little tent village of craftspeople. The booths overflowed with glass items, Santas, wood creations, and all kinds of jewelry. She greeted friends and checked out their wares. Tori hustled out with the store's bins and set to work at arranging the table under the tent closest to the store's entrance.

After two complete circuits and no questions to answer, Jade moseyed over to where Tori had set up two small Christmas trees and spread out colorful ornaments. "Looks good. Do you need change or anything?"

Tori shook her head, and her bun bounced from side to side. "I'm all set. Patti gave me the iPad with a scanner and some change. Thanks for the extra hours. I appreciate it. I told all my friends and blasted your memes out on all my social sites."

"Any buzz on our weekend activities?" Jade picked up a pink feathery flamingo and an angel made out of seashells.

Tori arranged the items by size and color in neat rows under the tabletop trees. "Everyone I know is coming. The boat parade and the food trucks seem to be the big draw. Can't wait. I'm meeting friends for dinner tonight. It should be fun."

Jade leaned forward and lowered her voice. "No comments from the nasty trolls?"

A quizzical look crossed the teen's face. "Nope. It's a happy weekend. I didn't see any troll snark. But you know how people are. They feel obligated to comment on everything whether they should or not."

"Do you know of a band called Stay at Home?"

Tori made a face. "Nope. Who are they?"

Jade realized Tori must not have heard about the weird posters. She'd scoured her social media sites the night before but hadn't seen any references to them. *Maybe it was a meaningless prank.* "I have no idea. Just curious. I saw it on a flyer. I hope everyone has a good time. Let me know if you need anything."

Tori nodded.

A gruff "Thanks a lot, Jade" interrupted their conversation. Emory Jessup in a long peacock-print caftan blew in like a nor'easter up the coast. The gauzy material and her wild hair fluttered for a few seconds after she came to an abrupt halt in front of Tori.

No one said anything.

"You didn't have to set the police on me. It wasn't that big a deal. I don't have time for Nick and his bunch to be poking around in my business." A slight sneer crossed her face.

"Vivian called me about the voodoo doll and the note. They upset her. We thought the sheriff needed to know. It looked personal."

"It's nothing. I get weird comments and reviews all the time. I ignore most of them. It's usually a bunch of whiney ne'er-do-wells. Nick asked too many personal questions, like I knew he would. I'm sure my private life has nothing to do with that stupid doll. And then Nell stopped by the store. She pretended to look at books, but I know she was nosing around, too." Emory's lip curled and her brows formed almost a perfect "V" in the middle of her forehead.

"The doll…" Jade started.

"Looked nothing like me," Emory snapped. "It. Was. Nothing."

Heads turned as the bookseller stomped off down the sidewalk.

"Some people." Tori arranged silver and gold stars on the tree.

"She's probably tired. Patti and I will be making rounds to check on things. Lorelei will be here to relieve you at lunch."

"Easy peasy. I get to catch some rays while I get paid." Tori stood straighter as a pair of women approached the table.

Jade scooted around the corner and across the parking lot. A line of cars turning onto Neptune Road crept by the store in search of elusive parking spaces. She walked past the brick building that housed the Pirate Chest antique shop, Claude Simpkins's CPA office, and Bay Breeze Realty. All three had tents and tables out front. She waved at Kelly Jamison, owner of the antique store, who was busy chatting with a group of customers.

"Hey, Jade. Come on over and spin the wheel. See what prize you can win." Claude Simpkins, a portly man in a pine green golf shirt, waved her over to his table. "Come on, give it a whirl. Everybody wins something."

She spun the rainbow-colored wheel that clicked and clacked and finally landed on "candy."

"Aww. You didn't win the air fryer. But grab yourself a piece of hard candy. And fill out this card if you want a chance to win a vacuum in tonight's drawing."

Jade picked up a piece of butterscotch, which she always called church candy because that was what her grandmother had handed her when she was too fidgety during a service. "I hope y'all have a good turnout today."

Claude spun the wheel, trying to entice the women at Kelly's table to come his way. Jade ducked under the next tent, where three realtors chatted with visitors and tried to talk them into a game of cornhole and a tour of a new condo community in Seaport. She continued her stroll to the brick building next to the pier that housed Mermaid Books and the Busy Bean.

She browsed the books on the tables out front. Lately, all she'd had time to read were vendor catalogs touting their new holiday lines for next season. Maybe it was time for some fun reading. The dusty books on Emory's table didn't hold her attention for long.

The wooden door to the store slammed against the wall, and a man in a black golf shirt and wrinkled khakis backed down the three wooden stairs.

"And, for the last time, I do not schedule book signings for fantasy or new authors. See the sign, Mermaid Books, a Literary Bookstore." Emory pointed to the sign at the edge of the parking lot. "You should listen more. It would probably benefit your writing." Her gauzy caftan fluttered in the breeze.

"But your customers probably want to sample a variety of genres," the man stammered.

"They don't. They're looking for literary fiction." Her last sentence trilled off her tongue, and she spread her arms wide for emphasis. "Do not approach me again with any more pitches or stupid gimmicks. I'm not interested." She tossed something off the porch toward the man.

"You'll be sorry," the man muttered. "Genre fiction sells better than memoirs and poetry. I'll make sure to let you know when I make the bestseller list." He mimicked Emory's arm motions as he slunk down the sidewalk to his Kia Soul.

"Make sure you do!" Emory bellowed. "I won't hold my breath." She turned to face Jade.

Jade leaned over and picked up the business card that had fluttered and landed on the sidewalk. A green eye surrounded by drops of blood on a black background graced the front. She flipped it over and read out loud, "Pierce Andino, Fantasy, Western, and Science Fiction Author, Travel Blogger, and Podcaster."

Emory let out an exaggerated sigh and tapped her foot on the wooden porch. "This was your idea, wasn't it?" She pointed a boney finger in Jade's direction.

"Excuse me?" She shielded her eyes with her hands as she looked at the bookseller.

"This whole festival. And that brought the stupid pranks and that, that pest. And now my internet and phone are down. And, to top it all off, the phone company can't send someone out until tomorrow. I can live without the phone, but it's a pain in the butt to be limited to cash and check payments on a busy weekend. Sheeesh."

"Is there anything I can help with? You can do online payments on a phone if you have a wireless connection."

"I don't have time for all that mumbo jumbo. I'll have to suffer in silence and lose business until the phone company gets around to showing up."

"Did you try resetting your router?" Jade asked.

"Yes. I tried resetting my internet thingy and my computer and my cash register. None of that worked because someone cut the bleeping wire out back." Emory made a face like she had licked a lemon.

"Do you want to use my phone to call the sheriff's office?"

"I'm fine." She turned on her heels and stomped off.

Jade walked over to the Busy Bean. Inside the aqua and white coffee shop, all the brightly colored wooden chairs were filled, and the line was five deep. On a whim, she pulled out her phone and tapped a text to Nick about Emory's internet.

When it was Jade's turn to approach the counter, Sophie Fournier brushed a long, dark corkscrew curl from her forehead. "Morning, Jade. What can I get for you?"

"It's hopping in here. I'll have a small mochaccino."

"Whip and chocolate syrup?"

"Sure. Why not. It's Christmas in July."

Sophie smiled as Jade handed her the debit card.

"Everything going well? There was a long line of cars headed for Mermaid Bay this morning." Jade glanced over her shoulder at the plate glass window.

"Crazy busy, but that's the way we like it. James will have your drink in just a sec. Want your receipt?"

Jade shook her head and stepped to the end of the counter, where Sophie's brother, James, and a teen Jade didn't recognize buzzed around filling orders.

"Here ya go, Jade. Enjoy." James drew a flower in black marker on her plastic cup.

She waved and dropped a tip in the jar on the counter. *Interesting. James and Sophie, whose store shares the building with Emory, weren't having any internet issues.*

Later that evening, Jade and Chloe mixed in with the crowds on the beach.

Following the scents from the row of food trucks, the pair climbed the small dune and looked at the variety of food options.

She turned to find the sheriff standing behind her.

Nick Driscoll nodded and stroked Chloe's head. "Have you had dinner yet?"

She shook her head and glanced down the street at the line of brightly colored trucks.

"Can't go wrong with tacos." He stepped toward the line by the green-and-orange truck.

After a short wait, Jade and Nick, followed closely by Chloe, found a spot to eat near a split-rail fence that divided the space between the sidewalk and the dunes. Jade handed him a napkin when he squeezed his fish taco too hard.

"Have y'all found out any more on the bag of bones or the notes?" she asked as he sipped his iced tea. "Or the voodoo doll?"

He shook his head. "I think someone's trying to stir up drama."

"Did Emory report her internet problem?"

"Didn't hear anything from her." He slipped Chloe a bite of cheese from his wrapper.

"When I talked to her this morning, she was fussing at some author and complaining her internet was down. She said someone had cut the wire."

One eyebrow shot up. "I'll check on it." As if on cue, Emory Jessup stormed up, followed by the weaselly-looking author from earlier.

"Sheriff. I demand that you do something. This man is harassing me. I need you to take action. He has been following me all evening, and if you don't do something, I'm going to need bail money." Her nostrils flared and her eyes flashed.

"Ms. Jessup, please start at the beginning." Nick stood straighter and handed Jade his taco wrapper.

"This, this man." She pointed her boney finger inches from the man's nose. "He came to the store to pitch some author signing ideas. I refused, and he has been stalking me up and down the beach. I want to swear out a warrant."

"That is your right," Nick said softly. "But you'll have to go see the magistrate. He turned his attention to the author. Sir, your name is?"

"Pierce Andino," Emory sneered. "But that can't be his real name."

Nick shot her a look, and the bookstore owner clamped her mouth shut.

"It's Don Weatherly. I'm trying to get Ms. Jessup to hear me out, but she won't listen. I'm a published author, and I'm trying to find a location for my book launch. It has a beach theme, so her store would be perfect."

"And I've told you no. I'd appreciate it if you would no longer have any contact with me." Emory crossed her arms.

"But," he stammered.

"Mr. Weatherly, Ms. Jessup has made it clear she's not interested in any kind of business relationship. She's within her rights to take out a restraining order against you. Is that what you want?"

He looked at Emory, with her wild hair blowing in the ocean breeze. "No. I guess not. But she didn't even give me a chance."

"I'm sorry, Mr. Weatherly, but she's not interested. I suggest you find other ways to market your book." Nick used his serious sheriff look.

The author turned and stared at Emory. "You'll regret this one day. You'll be truly sorry you acted this way. It's your loss." He took several steps forward and disappeared into the crowd.

"I don't think he'll bother you again. If he does, let me or one of the deputies know immediately." His eyes narrowed. "Do you think this has anything to do with the voodoo doll or your internet?"

"Probably not. There's always something. What a nuisance." Emory made a harumphing sound and headed toward her store.

"Sorry you had to deal with all that. But it made for an interesting dinner," Jade said.

"All in a day's work. I've got to check on my guys. Call me if you need me."

Jade waved. *I guess no one would consider this a date.* They had been friends for so long. It was awkward at times, especially during moments like these when Jade longed for more than just being the gal pal.

Chapter Six

A gush of productivity dominated Jade's morning. She turned her attention to the neglected mound of laundry before the sun peaked over the horizon.

"There. That feels pretty good. I'm going to take these two bags of trash out, and then we'll head for the office."

Chloe, not interested in chores of any kind, returned to her snoozefest on the couch.

The summer breeze greeted Jade as she stepped out and deposited the trash in her large blue bin. The smell of the ocean lured her down the oyster shell path to the bay. The sound of the waves lapping lulled her into a peaceful place. This was home. Sometimes, she missed the hustle of city life, but Mermaid Bay had always been her place of solace. She had fond memories of summers here with her grandparents, and then that tragic winter when her parents were killed in a car accident, she moved into the cottage's back bedroom permanently.

She shook off the dark thoughts and wiped a tear that escaped.

The beach looked almost deserted this morning, if you don't count gulls and sandpipers picking at leftovers from last night's festivities. She walked through the soft sand, picking up cans and a few discarded wrappers. By the time she got to Hot Diggity Dogs, she had quite a collection of jetsam.

She stomped on the asphalt to dislodge some of the sand in her sneakers and headed down the alley toward the dumpster to discard the trash. A mob of seagulls hopped around the dumpster like groupies at the backstage door of a concert. The trash from last night must have spilled over and created a feast for the scavengers. She waved her arms and growled to get closer to the container. Most of the gulls retreated to the smaller cans near the snack bar's back door.

Jade launched the handful of garbage into the dumpster like she was going for a penalty shot in basketball. "Score!" she said to the gulls.

The birds glared at her, unimpressed.

When she turned, a black shoe with a pointed toe jutted out from around the corner. Jade jumped.

Taking a deep breath to calm her jitters, she stuck her head around the dumpster. A woman in black leggings and a navy-blue stocking cap pulled down over her face leaned against the trash receptacle. Her head rested in her lap like she was sleeping off a rough night.

"Hey, hey, are you okay?" Jade touched the woman's shoulder. "Can you hear me?" She shook the woman slightly, and her head fell backward.

A string of Christmas lights, wrapped tightly around her neck, dug into the greyish-colored flesh. Long silver curls poked out from under her hat in all directions.

Jade screamed and stumbled backward.

When her heart rate slowed enough for her to speak coherently, she pulled out her phone and dialed 911.

"Hi, um, this is Jade Hicks. I was dumping trash from my walk this morning in the dumpster behind Hot Diggity Dogs on Neptune Road. And, and there's a body next to the trash cans."

"Do you need an ambulance?"

"I don't think so. It's a woman. I tried to wake her, but when I tilted her head back, I found a strand of Christmas lights wrapped around her neck. She's not breathing."

"Okay. Stay where you are. Police and rescue are on their way. It should only be a few minutes. I'll remain on the line with you."

"Shoo. Shooo. Go away."

"Excuse me," the dispatcher said.

"Oh, sorry. The seagulls are getting braver and coming toward the body." Jade waved her arms and lunged toward the brazen birds, who squawked and retreated to the nearby sand.

"Officers are approaching Neptune Road. You should hear them soon," the dispatcher said.

A few minutes later, footsteps pounded on the asphalt as Sebastian and another deputy Jade didn't recognize rounded the corner.

"They're here. I'm going to hang up now. Thank you." Jade clicked the red button and slipped her phone in her back pocket. As the deputies approached, she pointed to the body.

The deputies surrounded the woman, and a few minutes later, two EMTs ran with what looked like large, orange tackle boxes. Sebastian stepped back as the EMTs swooped in and checked the body's nonexistent vitals.

"Why were you back here this morning?" Sebastian asked.

"I was out walking, and I picked up some trash. I threw it in the dumpster, and that's when I spotted her shoe." Jade pointed as the EMTs removed the knit cap. Wild silver curls sprang out. "Oh no! It can't be."

Sebastian's glance bounced back and forth between the body and Jade like he was watching a tennis match.

"Emory!" Jade leaned over and gulped in several deep breaths, trying to choke back sobs.

"Jade…" Sebastian stepped closer to her. "Are you okay?"

She stood up and closed her eyes for a second. "That's Emory Jessup, the owner of Mermaid Books. I talked to her last night." Jade tried to keep her voice from cracking.

"Okay. Start from when you walked over here," Sebastian said. "Walk, garbage, dumpster, seagulls."

"And dead body. That's pretty much it. I was surprised to see the shoe after I threw the trash away. I thought it was somebody sleeping back here after too much fun last night. What is Emory doing behind the hotdog stand?"

The other deputy wrapped the perimeter in yellow crime scene tape. The jagged ends flapped in the breeze, creating a snapping sound.

"Don't know. But we'll find out. The forensic unit will be here soon. Anything else you remember? What was she like when you talked to her last?"

"Grumpy. She's always annoyed by something. Nick, uh Sheriff Driscoll, and I were eating tacos last night, and she stormed up with a complaint."

Sebastian's eyebrows merged in a slight frown.

"There was some author bothering her about a book signing. She shot him down with her typical sharp retorts."

"What did the sheriff say?"

"The guy was following Emory when she approached us. Nick talked to him and warned him to leave her alone. The author and Emory left in different directions. I thought it was settled." *Could someone be that angry with a bookseller to kill her in such a horrible way?*

"Anything else you can think of?" Sebastian asked.

"No."

More emergency personnel made their way through a small crowd gathering at the entrance to the alley.

"You can head out now. I'll stop by later to get your signed statement," Sebastian said.

"I'm going to the store. I should be there the rest of the day." Jade glanced down the alley and decided to trek home by way of the beach. She didn't feel like chatting with anyone at the moment.

Jade's key in the lock triggered a string of yips from Chloe. The pudgy dog rolled out when Jade pulled open the door. Scooping up the bulldog, she hugged her close. The dog snuggled in under Jade's chin.

"Oh, puppy. How did this happen? We didn't pay attention to the warnings."

Lost in thought, Jade moved around her bungalow like a robot, gathering her things and shutting off lights. "Let's go to the store. If I stay here, I'm only going to think about Emory and this morning." Jade shook off thoughts of the disheveled woman with the string of lights around her neck.

Unlocking the door to 'Tis the Season, she stepped inside and inhaled the cinnamon and evergreen tree smells. The store had always been her happy place. But today, the magic was dulled. How could Emory be dead? Jade looked around when she flipped the switch to illuminate all the trees. She managed a half-smile. Her thoughts flashed to the string of lights wrapped like barbed wire around the bookseller's neck. She shivered and hurried to her office.

Shaking her head like an Etch-a-Sketch, she hoped she'd be able to erase the last images she had of the bookseller. Jade booted up her laptop and launched into filling the overnight orders. Staying busy and away from social media would definitely help.

After packing all the orders for shipping, paying the bills, and doing payroll, she took a deep breath and flopped back in her seat.

The bells sent Chloe into high-alert mode. Jade poked her head through the doorway when she heard stamping on the wooden floor.

"Hey, Jade. I stopped by to get your formal statement." Sebastian took off his hat.

"Can I get you something to drink?"

The deputy, who had the stocky look of a wrestler, shook his head. "Can I get you to write down what you saw and did this morning?"

She nodded. "Come on back." She pointed to the wooden captain's chair across from her desk. Settling in behind her desk, she pulled out a yellow legal pad and scribbled a paragraph about this morning's events.

Chloe sniffed his boots and jumped in his lap.

"Oh, Chloe," Jade said.

"She's fine." The deputy patted the small dog, who curled up next to his gun belt.

Jade finished jotting down the morning's events. Funny how it started off as a peaceful day. Her phone chimed constantly with emails and text alerts. Ignoring her phone, Jade looked at her ramblings and added a few more sentences. Making sure she'd listed all key details, she signed and dated the paper. "Here you go. Let me know if I can do anything else."

Sebastian put Chloe on the floor and took the paper she offered. "Do you have any contacts for her family or staff?"

"No. She said she was from Boston, but I don't think I ever met any of her relatives. Lisa Jackson works for her part-time. She may know." Jade picked up her phone and found her entry. She jotted her number and email on a sticky note and handed it to him.

He nodded and turned to go out the door as Patti barreled in and almost ran into him. "Oh, so sorry, Deputy Sanchez." She leaned over to catch her breath. "Jade, I just heard the news, and I ran all the way to the bookstore to see for myself. It was dark and sad looking."

Sebastian nodded and let himself out.

Patti plopped down in the guest chair the deputy had vacated and blew the blond curls off her forehead. "What happened?"

"I went for a walk this morning. When I went to dump some trash behind Todd's place, I saw a foot, and it belonged to…"

"Emory. Oh, my stars. The warnings came true! I saw the police activity, and someone in the crowd said it was the bookstore owner. I ran down to the store to see if it were true, and the door was locked. I can't believe it." Swiping at the corners of her eyes with the backs of her hands, she wiped the tears that rolled down her cheeks.

"What is going on around here?" echoed through the store. Lorelei breezed in the back and stared at Patti and her niece.

Jade and Patti retold the morning's events in tandem, and Lorelei looked like all the air had been let out of her.

She leaned on the other desk with her mouth open. "This kind of stuff doesn't happen in Mermaid Bay. I mean, Emory was grouchy and all, but she was a good person down deep. You had to get to know her…" Lorelei's voice trailed off like she was lost in thought.

Jade glanced at her phone and scrolled through what felt like hundreds of emails and texts from neighbors and friends. "Vivian's scheduled an emergency meeting at five. She said it's for the business council, but I have a feeling there will be lots of folks there."

The three puttered around the office the rest of the afternoon like they were in a daze.

"It's four-ten," Jade said louder than she meant.

Patti and Lorelei stared at her.

"Let's pack it in and get ready for the meeting." Jade coasted through the store, checking the rooms.

After feeding Neville, she set the alarm and held the door for the others.

"See you all there."

The breeze had picked up and the cloudy afternoon added to the pall that dominated Jade's mood. She and Chloe trudged home. Jade rummaged through her closet for something that looked more somber than her red and green Christmas T-shirt and jeans.

Pulling out a black pencil skirt, she paired it with a white camisole and a gray shrug. She slipped on a pair of black sandals and grabbed her purse.

"Be good. I'll be back as soon as I can." Jade drove slowly through the neighborhood to the library.

Parking was at a premium at the government center. The name sounded larger than the actual three-building facility. She put the Jeep in gear and made a new row in the grass behind a black Mercedes. Large raindrops splatted on her windshield. She grabbed her umbrella and purse and hustled to the library.

Following voices down the aisles of bookcases, she navigated through the crowd that blocked the hallway and the doorway to the conference room.

Ruby Ellis, who sat on the end of one row of folding chairs, whoo hooed and got Jade's attention. "Scoot. Scoot," Ruby told Todd Brickman as she waved Jade over.

He slid down one seat as Vivian Turner approached the lectern.

Jade slid in the empty seat as Vivian adjusted the microphone. She tapped on it, and a squeal reverberated throughout the room, eliciting a series of groans from the audience.

"Good afternoon, residents and business owners. In case anyone doesn't know me, I'm Vivian Turner, president of the Mermaid Bay Business Council. I'm sorry we have to meet under these circumstances. One of our members, Emory Jessup, owner of Mermaid Books, was murdered today."

Whispers rippled through the crowd.

"I know. It's terrible. The board and I want to brief you on what we know so far. But before we get started, let's pause for a moment of silence as we reflect on Emory's life and work. And the countless hours she volunteered for our community." Vivian bowed her head.

The moment seemed to last an eternity. Large raindrops pelted the roof and windows, and the audience rustled in their seats.

"Thank you," Vivian finally said, and pent-up whispers spread across the room.

"I asked the sheriff to speak, but he's tied up with the investigation. He said they're bringing in state resources. He won't have a statement until the forensic investigation is completed. If you have any information on this or any crime, please call the sheriff's office or Crime Stoppers." She paused and looked around at the faces staring at her.

"The police are still contacting her next of kin. I don't have any information on services or where to send condolences. And according to Sheriff Driscoll, forensics is investigating her store and the area where she was found."

Todd's head dipped, and he ran his fingers through his long hair.

Loud sobbing echoed through the room. Lisa Jackson, who had worked part-time at the bookstore, covered her mouth with a tissue and ran out the door. Vivian looked around and motioned for Patti to check on the distraught woman.

After Patti hurried after her, Vivian continued, "The board and I crafted a public statement about this tragic situation. The town manager and his counsel are reviewing it now. That will go out this evening or first thing tomorrow. We want everyone to be vigilant and report anything unusual, no matter how small."

Whispers rippled through the room again.

"But we don't want to cause panic either," Vivian added. "We need to let the investigators do their job and get to the bottom of this. Who knows if her death is even related to us?"

Whispers turned into a dull roar of chatter.

Vivian banged on the lectern with her wooden gavel. "At this time, we don't know the reason, and I don't think we should speculate. We want to encourage folks to go about their normal routines but to report anything suspicious."

When she paused, Claude Simpkins yelled, "So we should act like nothing happened? What if someone is targeting Mermaid Bay?"

Vivian pursed her lips. "That's not what I said. We will certainly mourn our loss and support each other, but we shouldn't hide in our closets either. This is the middle of our summer season. We have an obligation to our visitors..."

"Yes, and we all know what happens to our bottom line for the rest of the year when our summers aren't profitable," Claude muttered loud enough for the room to hear.

"So, to recap, there will be a formal statement, and we'll send out the information on the funeral arrangements when we know something. Any other business or items for discussion?" Dark half-moons under Vivian's eyes made her look ten years older than the last time Jade had seen her.

"Yes," Ruby Ellis cleared her throat and stood. "Since the weather isn't cooperating tonight, I'm going to host a candlelight vigil tomorrow in front of her store at eight-thirty. Bring your candles."

Vivian pursed her lips. "Thank you, Ruby. Glowsticks would probably be safer. Anyone else?"

When no one spoke up, Vivian continued, "Then, our next council meeting is July twenty-eighth, and we plan to put together the fall calendar of events. See you then. Bring your ideas."

Not in the mood to chat, Jade waved to friends and filed out of the conference room. The rain had stopped, and she dodged puddles on her way to the Jeep.

As she opened the Wrangler's door, Ruby, in her bright yellow rain jacket and red boots, chased after her. "Jaaaaaaaaa-de. Hey. I'm so glad I caught you. Are you coming to the vigil tomorrow?"

Jade nodded. "That was nice of you to arrange. Emory would have appreciated it."

"Not really. She wouldn't have wanted a fuss, but it's the right thing to do." She paused and looked over her shoulder. "I heard what Vivian said, but I'm still concerned. We all got warnings. I mean, what if we've ticked off this person and he's not done. We could all be in danger," she whispered. "I hate to constantly check doors to make sure they're locked. I feel like I'm always looking over my shoulder. And I have guests at the B and B to worry about."

"I think we should let the police investigate and don't let worry take over.

But we should be alert and careful. You want a ride home?"

"Uh, sure." Ruby walked around to the passenger side as Jade clicked the button to unlock the door.

Ruby grabbed the bar and hoisted herself inside. She fastened her seatbelt and got situated. "I'm booked at the Pearl through September. I can't afford to lose business, but I'm not sure I want to hang around town if there's a killer running around loose." Ruby wrung her hands.

"I trust Nick. He'd tell us if there was reason to shelter in place. I'm going to go on with my normal schedule, but I'm going to be vigilant." Jade put the Jeep in drive and bumped over the grass to the main road.

Ruby winked. "Nick wouldn't steer us astray. You two have been close forever. He likes you."

After a quick ride, she pulled in front of the Pearl, a pale blue Victorian home with white gingerbread trim. Surrounded by an English garden and a wrap-around porch, the newly renovated bed and breakfast reminded Jade of a dollhouse. Ruby and her daughter, Josie, had given new life to the home, originally built in 1870 by a wealthy businessman as a summer retreat.

Jade pulled up to the brick and wrought iron driveway columns next to the Virginia historic marker about the property.

Ruby hopped out. "Thanks for the ride."

"It's going to be okay. They'll find out who did this."

Ruby nodded. "I hope so. But I'm still going to lock all the doors and carry my phone with me wherever I go. Maybe it wouldn't hurt to get some pepper spray, too."

Jade waited until Ruby let herself in the side door before she headed home to see what she could throw together for dinner.

Not finding anything that interested her in her pantry, she put a bag of popcorn in the microwave.

How long would it take the police to figure this out? And if they didn't, would everyone in town always be on edge, casting sideways glances at anyone who looked suspicious?

Chapter Seven

Jade switched Chloe's leash to her other hand, so she could sip her coffee as the pair wandered down the beach to watch the start of the Hollidazzle Fun Run. The runners outdid themselves with their colorful costumes. Her favorites were six guys in tutus and nutcracker outfits and a Santa who stood behind eight friends dressed as reindeer. She hoped the diversion would keep her mind off Emory's tragic death, even if for a little while.

Bernie's voice echoed from the speakers on the pier and seemed to bounce off the water. "Attention. Attention. Runners, take your mark."

Jade scooped up Chloe and stepped out of the fray. Hundreds of costumed runners in all shapes and sizes lined up behind the red and white crepe ribbon that stretched from a telephone pole to a volleyball pole near the water's edge.

Nell, with a camera around her neck and notebook in hand, stood next to Vivian, who brandished a starter pistol. She waved her hand around, and Bernie's voice boomed through the speakers again. "Runners, get ready. Get set."

A shot rang out, and the runners galloped across the sand, and the walkers brought up the rear. Jade waved at Vivian and Nell and then hurried to the shop to get ready for today's visitors. Yesterday's tallies were impressive. If the rest of the weekend followed suit, Jade would be way ahead of last year's numbers.

Chloe scampered up the steps to the store and did a happy dance to greet the visitor in the rocking chair.

"Hey, there. Aren't you cute?" A man in a casual grey shirt and jeans leaned over to scratch Chloe behind the ears.

"Good morning. How can I help you?" Jade asked.

"Hi. I'm Troy Novak, and I was hoping to catch you this morning before you got busy." Before Jade could reply, he stood and continued, "I want to talk to you about what washed up on shore this week. I'm a freelance reporter and podcaster. Do you have a few minutes to talk to me?"

"A few. I need to make sure we're ready to go when the vendors arrive. A podcaster?"

"I do true crime and travel segments," he said. "Bernie over at the pier mentioned that you were on the beach when the suitcase washed up."

Is he here for the crime or the sun and surf part? Jade gave him the once-over as she moved toward the door.

"This is a busy, little place. I'm going to have to come back for a visit later. But right now, I'm looking into where the bones came from. Stuff washing up on beaches keeps my podcast in business. Just a year or so ago, a woman and her lover murdered her husband and hid him in several suitcases that washed up on different beaches. There have been several mob hits that the tide brought in, too. But the prank angle here seems new to me. Any ideas you'd like to share?" He pulled out his phone. "Mind if I record this?"

"No, but I don't have that much I can add. I was as surprised as everyone else when the jogger tripped over the suitcase in the sand. And it was a relief to learn later that they weren't human bones," Jade said.

Troy's brow furrowed. "No reason to suspect anyone? No crazy pranksters in the hood?"

Jade counted to three before she answered. *What was he getting at?* "Not that I know of. Everyone was shocked by it. We're a beach town. Our population doubles or triples every summer. We have lots of visitors, and our year-round population is growing because folks realize how nice it is. It's a close-knit community."

The podcaster shrugged. "It's definitely quaint. The cottages all look liketime capsules from the 1950s. No crazy tourist problems or skyscraper hotels."

"That's part of our charm. The town council works really hard to preserve the nostalgia and the historic cottages that most other areas have bulldozed for condos and mega-mansions. So far, Mermaid Bay has been successful. And people bring their kids and grandkids here to show them what it was like when they were younger."

"You sure the bones weren't something one of your locals was responsible for? Know any disgruntled people?"

Why does he keep harping on this? "No, not really. Like I said. It's a peaceful kind of place." She neglected to mention Emory's murder.

"Any butcher shops around? Meat packing plants nearby?"

She furrowed her brow. "None that I can think of." Her voice trailed off. "I need to get my day started. Anything else I can help you with?"

"Nice store. You can make a living with a Christmas store?" he asked.

"Yes." Jade hoped her smile didn't look fake and that she didn't roll her eyes. "The holidays are always popular, and people love to decorate."

"Interesting. Thanks for your time. Here's my card if you think of anything else or if you hear anything related to the suitcase," the podcaster said.

"You may want to check with the sheriff's office. They have more details on the whole incident," she said.

"Will do. You never know when something weird turns into something nefarious. Make sure you check out my podcast, The Highway to Crime." The slender man made his way down the steps and disappeared around the corner.

Jade shook off the pall of doom and gloom and turned on all the holiday lights in the store. "That's better, Chloe. Let's see if we can find Neville."

At the mention of her nemesis, the dog's ears shot up, and she sniffed around the empty table that usually housed holiday snacks.

With no tuxedo cat sightings, Jade settled in at her desk and printed out the order list. "Yes, Mr. Nosy Podcaster, one can make a living from a Christmas shop. See." She pointed at the printouts, but Chloe didn't need convincing. She circled her puffy bed and settled in for a morning nap.

A little before eight, Patti bustled in. "Whooo hoooo. Who's ready for a fabulous day?"

"How are you?"

"Spec-tac-ular. Well, as good as I can be with a crazed murderer running around." The bells interrupted her.

Jade stepped into the front of the store and pulled the door shut behind her. Tori bounced in the front door. "Morning, all. I wanted to get a jump on things today. It was hopping yesterday. Lorelei and I have a bet going to see who has the most sales." The teen headed to the back to get the plastic bins.

"Who's winning?" Patti yelled after her.

"Lorelei has had the most customers, but I have the highest sales. We'll see what the rest of the weekend brings."

Patti put the iPad on top of the bin. "Need any help?"

"Just the door. I got this," the teen said.

Patti held the wooden door for Tori, and then she turned to Jade. "I made candy last night. Any news on the you-know-what?" She wrinkled her nose and grimaced.

"Nope. Just great sales. Let's see what we can do today," Jade said.

"I definitely got my steps in yesterday. I wore my Chucks today. I am ready for another busy one." She pulled up her pants leg to show off her red sequin-covered Converse Chuck Taylor high tops.

"Where did you find those?"

"Mr. Google," she giggled and straightened the papers on the front counter.

Neville sauntered through and jumped up on the Dutch door. He was greeted by a low growl on the other side. Ignoring Chloe's welcome, he licked his front paws and waited for Patti to scratch him behind the ears.

Jade immersed herself in updating the store's website. When she finished, she checked all the social media feeds and posted photos from yesterday. Her stomach grumbled and reminded her that she missed lunch. Jade pulled out a granola bar from her desk drawer, and Chloe sprang into action when she heard the crinkle of a wrapper.

"Sorry, this has chocolate in it." The dog pawed the air. "You've been good today. Let's go check on things. All the races should be over by now, but hopefully, some of the folks stuck around to visit the vendors."

Patti breezed in the back with the empty bin. "Simon was early today."

Jade turned her head slightly like Chloe did when she heard words like "dinner," "walk," and "treat."

"Simon," Patti continued. "The delivery driver."

"Ooooooh. That Simon. I'm headed out to check on things. I'll be back before closing."

"We have things covered here," Patti said.

Jade clicked Chloe's leash in place. It took a while to make the circuit of vendor tables because the Frenchie had to greet everyone she met.

When they approached the 'Tis the Season tent, Lorelei stood, fanning herself with a glossy Bay Breeze real estate brochure. "It's warm today. I am so glad you have the shade. That sweet James brought over iced drinks for Tori and me." Jade's aunt continued to fan herself as she took a swig from her Busy Bean cup.

"Do either of you want to go inside? I can stay out here." Jade offered as Chloe jumped in Lorelei's lap.

"Hey, sugar. You checking out the people?" Lorelei rubbed the white dog's head. "No. I'm good. I've seen everyone and his brother today. I think I'm almost caught up on all the happenings around here. Even Tish and her hunky new friend stopped by to chat up the people. She's hyping their new condo project near Yorktown." Lorelei waved the glossy brochure.

Jade raised one eyebrow and scanned the crowds that ebbed and flowed through the front parking lot. "You thinking about moving? I thought you liked your condo at Turtle Cay."

"I do. I'm not moving. I've got everything I need there. She foisted brochures on everyone who looked old enough to come up with a down payment."

"You going to the boat parade tonight?" Jade asked.

"Steve and I are having dinner. If we finish in time, we might swing by," Lorelei said.

Before Jade could comment about her aunt's latest beau, Tori piped up. "I'm going. My friends and I want to check out the food trucks and the band on the patio of Hot Diggity Dogs. It should be fun."

"Bernie said he has his boat all decked out. I'm hoping to get some good pictures tonight. I'll have to check out the band." Jade winked at the teen.

"It's an 80s cover band. I love old timey music," Tori cooed.

Lorelei gave the teen a sideways glance and rolled her eyes.

"Y'all need anything?" Jade asked.

"Nope, we're good." Lorelei returned to using Tish's brochure as a fan.

Jade picked up Chloe, who let out a little whine. "Come on, puppy. Let's see what's shaking down the block, and then we'll be back to spell Patti."

"That little dynamo? Patti's like that pink bunny with the bass drum. She never needs a nap." Lorelei pulled out a nail file and touched up her nails.

Jade wiggled a finger and followed Chloe through the crowd to the sidewalk.

She passed Claude Simpkins and his CPA prize wheel. He had both hands on his chin, slumped down on his plastic table. The realtor's booth was empty except for two kids playing cornhole. The foot traffic had slowed to a trickle on this end of the street.

Further down the block, a closed sign dangled from the metal doorknob of Mermaid Books. Jade focused on the beach to keep her thoughts of Emory at bay.

Chloe and Jade walked past the pier where the parking lots and the beach overflowed with families and sun soakers. People and beach towels lined the sand for as far as the eye could see. Jade spied a catamaran and a fishing trawler in the distance. She took a deep breath and let the sea breeze with a hint of sunscreen wash over her. There was nothing like the sounds and smells of the ocean. She didn't realize how much she had missed them until she moved to Richmond for her first job after college. The river was nice, but it wasn't the ocean.

Chloe interrupted her thoughts when she tugged on her leash and waddled after a butterfly. "Come on, girl. As beautiful is it out here, we need to head back and check on Patti."

At the mention of her friend's name, Chloe's head turned, and her little stubby tail wiggled. She trotted off in the direction of the store.

When Jade opened the front door, the arctic blast from the air conditioning caused her to shiver. Patti handed a pair of women their purchases. "Y'all come back and see us."

"We will," the taller woman in red capris said. "And I signed up for your mailing list." She pointed to the list on the clipboard. "I want to see what's new for the holiday season." Her shorter friend nodded vigorously and reached for her bag.

"You need a break?" Jade asked when the door shut behind the pair of shoppers.

"I'm good. It's been steady all day, but I think it's slowing down," Patti said, plunking down on the stool behind the counter.

A little before four, Jade checked on the vendors outside. The majority had started packing up. Tori had only a few ornaments to return to the store. "I beat Lorelei in customers and sales," she whispered.

Jade gave her a high five. "Good job."

"She gave me twenty dollars for the food trucks tonight," Tori said. "I was just in it for the bragging rights, but free food is cool, too. After I put these inside, I'm going to head out."

"I've got them. Go ahead. Thanks again for working the festival."

"Bye, Jade. See you at the boat parade." The teen danced off to her car.

After returning the bins and the iPad to Patti, Jade folded up the table and chairs and put them in the shed. She dusted off her hands.

Patti breezed in the back. "I'm about ready to pack up. Do you need me to help you with tents?"

"Bernie will be by tomorrow to take them down. I think we're all done here," Jade said.

"I inventoried what they sold outside, and it's all in the computer system. The books are balanced. I left the spreadsheet on your desk to check."

"You're the best," Jade said.

Patti, who looked today like a cross between a cheerleader and a tall elf in her green and red Christmas garb, blushed. "I'm going to go pick up my sister, and we'll be back for tonight's festivities. See you then." Patti waved, patted Chloe, and cha-chaed out the door.

All her staff had plans for the evening, and Nick was always working. Jade had been so busy with the festival that she didn't think to call anyone to see what they were doing on a Saturday night. "I guess it's you and me, kiddo." Chloe's ears perked up, and she wiggled her way to the back door.

"Let me check on all the rooms. I think I'll put the holiday lights on the timer tonight. Neville...." She heard a mew in the toy room. "What are you up to, kitty cat?"

After making her rounds and checking Neville's bowls, Jade locked the doors and put the deposit bag in the safe for Monday. She set the alarm and held the door for Chloe.

Determined to use her free time before tonight's events wisely, Jade unloaded and reloaded the dishwasher and dusted the living room while Chloe supervised from the couch. Jade plopped down next to her dog. "Okay. That's enough of that. I'm going to get ready."

Chloe opened one eye and returned to her nap when no snacks materialized.

Jade pulled out a cream camisole and green tunic made from light material to go with her skinny jeans and sandals. She added her snow globe earrings and a light-up Christmas necklace for the celebration.

Digging through her bag of outfits for Chloe, she found her lighted Christmas collar. "Now, we're ready." Chloe gave her a noncommittal glance and hopped off the couch.

She snapped Chloe's leash into place. "Let's go see the festivities."

The pair headed down the cut-through to the beach. A flotilla of multicolored boats in all sizes and a Coast Guard cutter sat anchored offshore near the pier.

Eighties music drifted from the deck of the hotdog shack while hundreds of people staked out spots with blankets and folding chairs in the sand. The line for Hot Diggity Dogs's walk-up window snaked around the side of the building and out onto the beach.

Jade scooped up Chloe and traveled through the throngs of people trudging through the sand. She looped around the restaurant and cut through the parking lot to Neptune Road. Deputy Sebastian Sanchez leaned on a wooden sawhorse that blocked traffic on the main road.

"What a crowd," she said as she got closer to the deputy. "And they're still coming. Big night in Mermaid Bay. Can I get you anything?"

He reached over and patted Chloe. "I'm good. The auxiliary guys will be here to take over the traffic detail, and I'll grab something to eat then. But thanks."

She and Chloe searched for a quiet spot to view the parade. The warm sand and the gentle breeze made it the perfect evening to be outside. It was nice to soak up the celebratory feeling, but foreboding thoughts kept ticking at her brain. She hoped the night brought only excitement of the lighted boat parade.

Chapter Eight

Two days had crawled past since Ruby's candlelight vigil for Emory where friends gathered in front of the bookstore to share memories. It was a somber evening, exactly the opposite of the more public Christmas in July festivities that drew people from all over.

Jade tried to stay busy with tasks at the store and planning the next quarter's marketing calendar, but it was hard to keep her mind focused on her work. Thoughts of Emory and the investigation kept popping into her head, and Nick, swamped with work and no time to talk, had been tight-lipped about any findings. The void of information fed the town's gossip mill that had ratcheted into overdrive. Jade had heard speculation about Emory's murder that ranged from a deranged lover to an underground network of antique book thieves. Most of the tales sounded like plots of true crime shows from faraway places. Stuff like that didn't happen in Mermaid Bay.

Trying to shake things up, she texted Nick to see if he wanted to come over for dinner. *Maybe a homecooked meal would loosen his tongue enough to talk about any progress they'd made in their investigation.*

Her phone binged with, **Sounds good. What time?**

Tonight at 6?

See you then.

That was fast. Either he was overworked and craving food that didn't come from a drive-thru, or they had solved the case. If so, he'd be back to the jaywalking and stolen bike calls.

Alone at the store and with no walk-ins since lunch, Jade packed up, checked on Neville, and hustled home. Chloe dawdled, and Jade used the time to plan the night's menu. Tuna steaks with a summer salad and au gratin potatoes would be a good light meal after a long, hot day.

When Chloe got bored with sniffing every blade of grass, Jade had enough time to give the house a quick once over and start dinner.

She rummaged in her closet to find an outfit that looked a little dressier than her jeans and green store T-shirt. Not sure if it was a date, even though their conversations are often flirty, she tried to quell the butterflies that bounced around her stomach every time she thought of Nick lately. He was smart and funny, and so far, he hadn't dated anyone since he had taken over as sheriff. She and Nick had a long history of being friends since elementary school summers. They hung out in middle school and high school until they drifted apart during the college years. It might be fun to have a permanent plus one to hang out with. But what if it didn't work out? She didn't want to ruin a friendship.

Shaking off all the what-if thoughts, Jade settled on a pale pink sweater and white capris. She scrunched her curls and did a couple of swipes of mascara and lipstick.

With just enough time to put the finishing touches on dinner, she streamed some soft jazz and set the table with her grandmother's white china.

Right on time, the doorbell chimed, and Chloe jumped into attack dog mode until Jade opened the door, and the pudgy dog greeted Nick with yips.

"Something smells good." He stepped into the foyer and handed her a cheesecake. "Dessert."

"Yum. I'll put it in the fridge for later."

"Can I help with anything?"

"Nope. Almost ready. I just have to put stuff on the table," she replied.

He followed her to the kitchen, and they filled plates and headed to the small table next to the bay window. Jade always joked that if you stood in the chair, she had a beach view through the neighbor's trees.

"What would you like to drink? I have Coke, water, wine, and iced tea."

"Iced tea is fine," he said, sitting in the chair with his back to the wall.

She poured two glasses from a white hobnail milk glass pitcher and sat in the chair next to him. "It's unsweetened. I have sugar if you want it." She pointed to the bowl on the lazy Susan in the center of the table.

He shook his head and dug into his meal.

"How are things going?" Would he share anything about Emory? Jade stared, waiting for a response.

"Fine. We had one missing child on the beach this morning. One of the lifeguards found him about a block away from where his family's chairs were. Other than that, today included a couple of stolen bikes, a shoplifting call at the Circle K on the highway, and a trespassing raccoon in the social hall of the Baptist church."

"Sounds like things are back to normal."

"Except for the raccoon. He annoyed the church secretary when she caught him gnawing on a hymnal. How was your day?" he asked.

Jade shrugged. "It was quiet after all the traffic last weekend. I get bored when it's slow. The online orders have been steady, and that's awesome. They're a huge chunk of my revenue lately. So about normal for me."

"Nothing to sneeze at. Be thankful it's thriving. A lot of shops have closed because they didn't develop online sales." Helping himself to seconds of the potatoes, he continued, "I'm glad our calls were back to normal for the middle of summer. It gives us more time to run down leads on Emory's case. I'm expecting the autopsy report later this week from Richmond, and there's a state police investigator helping us out."

"You think they'll be any surprises with the autopsy?" Jade took a bite of her tuna.

"You never can tell. We know she was strangled, but it didn't appear to be that she was killed where she was found. The forensic guys emptied the dumpster. All that time and effort yielded nothing." He took another bite and chewed slowly. "We did manage to track down her niece in Massachusetts. It looks like she's the only heir."

"I was wondering what was going to happen to the bookstore. It's been a part of the community for a long time. I hope someone is interested in keeping it open."

"Not sure. But the property's valuable." Nick polished off his tuna.

"With Mermaid Bay's strict zoning regulations, it wouldn't be that appealing to developers if they can't bulldoze and build big things. As the years pass, it seems like the giant condos are moving closer and closer to us. I'm glad for now that there's still an interest here to preserve a little bit of the past."

He nodded. "A lot of little beach communities have been squeezed out of existence by the developers and big corporations." He slipped Chloe a small piece of tuna and pushed his plate toward the center of the table. "That was good. I haven't had a meal that I didn't eat at my desk or in my car in forever. I can't remember the last sit-down meal I had. Thanks."

Jade rose and picked up the plates and her glass. "Wanna refill on tea?"

"I'm good for now." He brought over the remaining plates and helped her stack the dishwasher and straighten the kitchen.

They worked in silence until the last pan returned to its home in the cabinet.

"There. Back to normal," she said. "Thanks for helping."

"My pleasure. You up for a walk? I need some exercise after a big meal. You know, to settle things before dessert."

At the magic "W" word, Chloe danced at the back door, waiting for someone with thumbs to turn the knob. Jade snapped the leash in place, and Nick followed them outside. She wiggled the handle to ensure it was locked, and a smile crept across his face. Always the cop.

They took the cut-through and walked down the sand toward the pier. The evening breeze ruffled their hair. More sandpipers and gulls populated the beach than people. The sun sank lower and lower behind the pine trees across the street. Jade closed her eyes for a moment and breathed in the salty air. The smells and the sounds from the waves rolling in had a calming effect. The horror of Emory's death vanished for a few moments.

At the pier, they turned to retrace their steps. Jade paused and glanced at the back of Mermaid Books. The dark windows gave the store a lonely look, while the Busy Bean had laughing and chatting guests lounging on the deck under strings of white lights. She let out a sigh. The two shops that shared the same building couldn't be more different.

Nick draped his arm across her shoulders, and the melancholic feeling washed away. "We'll find who did this. It may take some time, but we'll catch him."

"It all seems surreal. And everyone's on edge."

"I know. My guys have fielded hundreds of calls. We have some good leads. It takes a lot of resources and time to validate hypotheses and to eliminate others."

Jade and Nick walked the rest of the way to the oyster shell path in silence. As she unlocked the door, a shrill chime pierced the quiet evening.

"Sorry." Nick pulled out his phone from the back pocket of his jeans. "Driscoll here. Uh huh. Got it. Be right there."

"They found Emory's car near the North Carolina border. I gotta go. Thanks for dinner."

"Do you want to take your cheesecake with you?"

"Keep it. I'll come by later this week or take it to the store for your gals."

"Be safe. And I hope this is a break y'all been looking for."

Nick waved over his shoulder and jogged down the path to his truck.

"Come on, Chloe. It looks like it's you and me and the TV tonight."

Chapter Nine

After a busy morning, Jade left Chloe and the standoffish Neville in Patti's capable hands while she made an afternoon coffee run. The ocean breeze tamped down the sultry temperatures from the hottest part of the day. She enjoyed her walk down the busy street where people with all kinds of gear made their way to and from the beach.

Finding a break in traffic, she jogged across the street. Loud music drifted from the open door of Mermaid Books. Curiosity got the better of her. Jade climbed the wooden steps and poked her head in the store.

A large gray Persian with piercing green eyes sat on the counter. It mewed as Jade walked in. "Hello," Jade yelled over the music.

"Oh, hi," a petite gal with jet-black hair with purple tips said, adjusting the volume on a boombox that had its heyday when Duran Duran and Culture Club dominated the radio airwaves. The woman moved a stack of books closer to the cat and wiped her hands on her jeans. "Can I help you?"

"Oh, sorry to barge in. I'm Jade Hicks. I own the Christmas shop down the street. I heard the music and wanted to check on things." Emory would have had a major meltdown at the mention of any changes to her beloved store.

"It's nice to meet you. I'm Amy Pemberton, Emory's niece. I got in town yesterday, and I'm poking around to see what's in the store."

"I'm so sorry for your family's loss. It was a shock to all of us." Jade looked at the stacks and stacks of books Amy had rearranged.

"Our family wasn't that close, but I do have memories of Aunt Em when I was little. She had a sassy streak that used to drive my mother and grandmother crazy. I liked her feistiness."

"Well, hello. Who are you?" The cat hopped off the counter and did figure eights around Jade's ankles.

"That's Mr. Darcy. He's still not too happy with me about having to ride in his case all the way down from Waterton, Massachusetts. But we're glad we're here. I'm liking the small-town vibe. And the beach is fabulous. The lawyer gave me the keys to this place and Aunt Em's apartment upstairs."

"The bookstore's been a fixture next to the bay for years. This street wouldn't be the same without it." Jade glanced around the room. Amy had emptied several of the heavy bookcases near the front of the store.

"I'm taking all of this as a sign. I got laid off recently, and it seemed like the right time to move south and try my hand at the store. If I never have to shovel snow again, it'll be worth it," she said with a big smile. "Aunt Em has a really good inventory of nonfiction and biography. I'm thinking about changing things up a bit. This is a beach community. I'm going to paint some of these dark shelves and set up a kids' area in the back." Amy zipped to the front of the store and opened her arms wide. "These two big windows are fabulous, and she hasn't done anything with them. I think they'd be perfect to showcase fun beach bag reads. I spent almost all night wandering through the store, looking at things. If nothing else, I have ideas."

"The improvements will be a nice change. We get a lot of foot traffic here in the summer. And everyone needs a beach read or two," Jade said.

"It's going to be a lot of work, but I'm up for a challenge. So, what do you all do for fun here? Not that I'm going to have much free time in the near future." Amy giggled and picked up Mr. Darcy, who let out a long purr that sounded like a motorboat.

"I totally get it. I run a small business that lives and dies by the tourist dollar. When I'm not at the shop, my dog Chloe and I like to walk on the beach. The Busy Bean and Hot Diggity Dogs often have bands on their decks, and Mermaid Bay has an active business council. They're always planning events to lure tourists to our little corner of the world." Jade rummaged through her purse and pulled out her business card, and jotted an email address on the back. "Here, this is Vivian Turner's contact. She's head of the council and will add you to the mailing list. She'll be over to visit as soon as she realizes you're here."

"Thanks. I talked to Tish, Jared, and the realtors in the parking lot this morning. And I met the Fourniers when the lawyer showed me around."

"It's a really nice community. Let me know if I can help with anything. Here's my contact information. 'Tis the Season is diagonally across the street. You can't miss all the twinkle lights. And I live further down at the end of the block." Jade pointed out the window.

Amy pointed upstairs. "I'm staying in Aunt Em's apartment for now. The back windows have a perfect view of the bay. I'm sorry she passed away, but I keep pinching myself to make sure this opportunity is real."

"Welcome to the neighborhood. Let me know if I can help with anything." Jade fingered the smooth surface of the pendant she always wore.

"Pretty necklace," Amy said. "Is that jade?"

Jade nodded. "I was my mother's. Green was her favorite color. It's how I ended up with my name."

"I love cool stories and the history of things," Amy replied. "And I will call you with a million questions. So be prepared. I may need someone to translate for me, too." Amy giggled again.

Jade squinted and stared at the woman.

"The realtors and the Fourniers didn't know what a radiator was, and no one could tell me any wicked restaurants."

Jade smiled. "Oh, just wait until you hear some of our Southern drawls. I'm sure it's a lot slower than what you're used to. But the food is great. You haven't lived until you've had biscuits, grits, or peach cobbler. And the people have big hearts."

"I'm excited for the change," Amy set Mr. Darcy on the counter. "I have to figure out how to order inventory and update Em's website. And I'm going to make sure I reach out to Vivian about the business council."

"They've been a big help to me through the years. It's nice to know that you're not alone. When you have time for lunch or coffee, give me a call."

"Sounds like fun. Hopefully, this place will look a lot different the next time you're here," Amy said.

"Can't wait to see all of your changes." Jade waved and trotted over to the Busy Bean.

"Hey, Christmas Lady," James yelled when she closed the wooden door with glass panes behind her.

"How's everybody?" she asked, sidling up the counter.

Sophie waved with her free hand and disappeared in the back with a large cardboard box.

"What can I get for you today?" James asked.

"How about a small iced white mocha and a mocha frappuccino for Patti. I met your new neighbor this morning. She's making all kinds of improvements over there." Jade pointed toward the wall they shared with the bookstore.

"Our new landlord. She seems nice." James added whipped cream and sprinkles to the drinks.

"Emory owned the building?" Jade stared across the counter at him.

James nodded. "Emory bought the building when she took over the bookstore. Sophie and I are kind of relieved Amy wants to keep the store going. Emory was adamant about not being interested in offers on the property, so we never worried until this week. We had no idea what was going to happen. Our lease renews in January."

"The zoning is strict around here. If it were sold, the new owners couldn't build condos or bring in big box stores."

"That's good. But she could still sell the property, and that would affect us when our lease is up. We've grown to like it here." He handed her two cups. "Your drinks, ma'am. Can I get you anything else?"

"Thanks so much. I'm glad things worked out with Emory's niece." Jade balanced the drinks and managed to get the door open. Outside, she dodged tourists on the sidewalk and street. All part of the summer invasion.

"Patti," Jade called when she stepped into the cool interior of her store.

"Back here," came from somewhere in one of the rooms.

Patti bustled in and dropped an empty box on the cabinet. "A box of Mark Roberts's Christmas Fairies arrived this morning. I put two on display in the glass cabinet in the collectibles room and locked the others in the storeroom."

"Cool. They are really popular lately. And very cute." Jade handed her the coffee.

"What a great afternoon treat. Thanks!" Patti pulled off the paper cover on her straw.

"Did you know Emory had a niece?"

Patti shook her head and continued to swig her coffee. "Ow. Brain freeze. That's what I get for slurping. I knew Emory was from Massachusetts, but she didn't really share much about her family or her past."

"Her niece Amy is moving into the apartment above the store."

"Interesting. That didn't take long."

"She decided to come down and take over the store." Jade pulled out her phone and tapped a text with the news to Vivian.

"Whew! That's good. I hadn't thought about it after, you know, what happened. I don't like to see stores close. It would be sad not to have a local bookstore."

Jade's phone dinged with a reply from Vivian. **I'm on it**. Jade smiled. Vivian would have Amy signed up for planning and project committees before she knew what hit her.

"I updated the inventory files and put the mail on your desk. I'm going to scoot out in a bit if you don't mind. I need to swing by the post office before it closes," Patti said, straightening the flyers on the counter.

"Not a problem. Chloe and I are gonna call it a day soon, too."

After walking through the store and setting the alarm, Jade took the long way home. She and Chloe jogged across the street and down the path by Hot Diggity Dogs.

Todd Brickman leaned over his deck railing. He balled up a piece of paper and slammed his fist on the wooden railing.

"Everything okay?" Jade looked up and shielded her eyes with her hand from the late afternoon sun.

"Just another one of those stupid notes. I have enough to worry about around here without this." Her friend with the longish hair and three silver rings in his ear let out a heavy sigh.

"What's going on?" Jade picked up Chloe and carried her up the chipped wooden steps to the deck. The dog looked longingly at the sand where she was trying to find a crab that disappeared in a small hole.

Todd tossed her the crumpled paper.

Unfolding the cream-colored stationery, Jade recognized the ransom note look with the cut-out letters. This one read, "Just give up. You know you need the money."

"Give up what?" she asked.

"The store, I guess. It feels like someone is trying to put me out of business. I've been bombarded with bad news lately." Todd looked way older and more tired than someone in his thirties should.

She stared at Todd. "Did you call the police?"

"Not yet. It's been a rough week with Emory, this, and a slew of crappy online reviews. Oh, and I got a notice from the health inspector that he's coming for a not-so-friendly visit."

"I'm sorry. Is there anything I can do?"

"Not really. Not sure if anybody can do anything." He stretched both arms above his head, and his tribal design tattoos peaked out from under his T-shirt sleeves.

When Jade didn't say anything, he continued, "I'm really trying to make a go of this, and it's way harder than I thought. Summer is our make-it-or-break-it season for the rest of the year. I've never had problems like this in the past." He paused and watched a freighter cross the horizon in the distance. "Maybe I should sell. But this property has been in my family since my grandfather was young. But it seems to be jinxed lately. My grandfather started this place as a pub that was the neighborhood hangout in the days of Kennedy and Johnson. It did okay until it burned down. Then he decided to rebuild as a seafood shack. That lasted a few years. My dad took over when he inherited the property and built the hot dog stand. It flourished until recently. I thought I was getting back on my feet. Maybe I do need a change."

"Are you really interested in selling?" Jade asked.

"I don't want to, but on days like this, it would be easier." Todd sighed and rested his elbows on the deck railing.

"I think you need to call the sheriff's office. Maybe these threats and the other bad luck are related?" She snapped a picture of the note with her phone. "A bunch of us got these earlier in the week, including Emory," Jade's voice trailed off.

Todd nodded. "I'll call Nick as soon as I finish my pity party here. I love running Hot Diggity Dogs and hanging out at the beach all day. I think I'm having an 'I don't know what I want to be when I grow up' moment. Thirty is way in my rearview mirror. I guess I should figure it out, but I have no idea what else I would do."

She patted his arm. "Let me know if I can help."

He smiled, and she and Chloe climbed down to finish their walk across the warm sand.

The thought of someone targeting Emory and Todd caused Jade to shiver, despite the warm evening. There was too much weirdness to chalk up to random events.

Chapter Ten

Jade added photos from Christmas in July to the shop's newsletter. Her phone binged with a text from Amy at the bookstore. **Hey, wanna grab lunch this week? Love to chat.**

Today good?

Perfect. 12 at the Busy Bean?

See you then, Jade tapped into her phone.

She had enough time to get a few tasks like adding photos and blurbs about the new items in her inventory and researching a holiday cookie recipe for eggnog snickerdoodles before she had to meet Amy.

A few minutes before noon, Jade popped her head in the store, and Patti jumped. "Sorry to startle you. I'm headed over to the Busy Bean for lunch. Do you want anything?"

"Nope. I'm good. Did you see the Holly Jolly distributor's catalog I left on the counter? They had some really cute animal ornaments. I dog-eared some pages for you to check out."

"Thanks. I'll look at them this afternoon. Pet items are always hot sellers. Be back in a bit."

Jade crossed the street and walked up behind Tish St. James, who stood at the bottom of the steps talking to Amy.

Tish planted one fist on her hips. "Amy, you really should think about joining us at Jared's condo tomorrow night. The food and drinks are always to die for, and everyone who is anyone will be there. You'll need connections if you want to survive here."

A slight frown crossed Amy's brow. "I'll think about it. Not sure if I brought anything to wear."

"It's beachy casual, but I'd wear pearls." Tish turned on her strappy Christian Louboutin sandals, a perfect match for her pale blue linen suit and its coordinating silk blouse. The blouse reminded Jade of an Impressionist painting. "Oh, hi, Jade. I was telling Amy about some of the cocktail soirees that Jared and his crew throw. Great for making business contacts. It couldn't hurt for you either. Ciao." The slender woman who always looked the fashion plate wiggled her fingers and sauntered to her black Mercedes.

Amy pulled the door shut behind her and jiggled the knob. "If I tried to pull off a look with a linen suit like that, it would be covered in wrinkles in under ten minutes. Is she always like that?"

Jade scrunched her nose. "I've never, ever seen her in sweatpants or shorts, if that's what you mean."

"She probably wears one of those 1960s peignoir sets to bed. Too hoity-toity for me," Amy chuckled. "I'm starving. Thanks for meeting me for lunch."

"How are things going?" Jade asked as they walked to the shop next door.

"Good. I'm painting inside the store, so it's a total mess. When I'm done, I'm going to have a grand reopening and schedule a bunch of events."

When it was their turn at the counter, the pair ordered salads and iced teas and waited by the cash register.

"Here you go," James said, handing each a brown bag and a paper cup.

The pair found a seat on the deck under a teal umbrella.

"It's crowded today," Amy said, glancing up and down the sand. "I'm thinking of having a poetry slam at the store on the weekends and lots more author signings. I was doing some research last night, and there are quite a few local writers. Aunt Em wasn't big on events. I'm hoping my ideas will make the bookstore a fun place. I'd love for it to be somewhere people want to hang out. Plus, I'm going to do some bookstagram posts to build interest in our inventory. Hey, I might even try a TikTok."

"Sounds good. I know the authors will be thrilled. They've been hounding Emory for years, but she stuck to her guns about her book signing policy. She wanted her store to be more literary."

Amy made a pickle face and stabbed a stray slice of cucumber with her plastic fork. "I'm all about *lit-raah-ture*, but popular fiction sells. And that pays the bills. I hope Aunt Em's highbrow clients don't get offended by my changes. From her recent sales numbers, it probably won't matter. Anything would be an improvement."

"Hmmm. I thought the store was doing well."

Amy raised one eyebrow. "From what I can tell, most of her money came from the rent on the Fournier's place. I'm going to try to make a go of it. We'll see. I met Lisa today. I explained my plans, and she said she needed a day to two to decide if this is the path she wants to continue on."

It was Jade's turn to raise an eyebrow. Lisa had worked for Emory for several years. "Well, if she's not interested, I'm sure you won't have any trouble finding a replacement," Jade said.

"What are you doing tomorrow night? Wanna go to that cocktail party Tish mentioned?" Amy's smile showed off her dimples.

Jade grunted and rolled her eyes. "I'm not sure what I'd wear."

"Who cares. Wear whatever you want as long as you have pearls. It sounded like a real who's who in beach society shindig. We should pop in and make some connections. Come on. And if it's a big waste of time, we'll make sure to eat and drink enough to make it worthwhile."

Jade attempted her best half-smile. "Sure. Why not. Let's go hobnob with Tish's crowd."

"You're a peach. We'll have fun regardless. Thanks for going with me. I'll text Tish later and send you the deets."

"I haven't been to a cocktail party in years. I'll have to put on my sociable face." She grinned with all her teeth showing.

Amy laughed. "That's the spirit! This was fun. Thanks for meeting me. I needed a break. This remodel is more than I imagined. Aunt Em had this thing for big, heavy books. I'm definitely getting my workout. Swing by next week. I want you to see my new kids' corner. I'm painting a mural on the wall and adding all kinds of fun touches."

"What kinds of book signings are you thinking about?" Jade asked, reaching for her iced tea.

"I reached out to some of my connections, and they're spreading the word that I have openings. I think I'm going to come up with some catchy titles. I'm going to do a Mysterypalooza once a month with some suspense writers. And maybe a Love is in the Air for the romance one. And I can't forget the fantasy and sci-fi fans."

"I think your changes will go over well. I never understood why Emory didn't shelve fun beach reads. That's what people want when they're on vacation," Jade said, watching two toddlers chase the tide in and out.

"And I'm going to build one of those free little libraries and put it in the parking lot near the shore for folks who forgot a book."

"You're going to do great here. Send me your calendar when it's finalized, and I'll put it in my newsletter."

"I need to work on building my mailing list. I found one Em had on her computer, but it had only about fifty names on it. I get that she felt quality was better than quantity, but she didn't embrace social media or any kind of progress. I'm broadening the store's reach. I've got to drum up some new business fast."

"You're doing the right thing. The business council can help with ideas and projects. And everyone is always willing to help and share. They're planning for Labor Day now. Vivian said she was going to reach out to you."

"Oh, I've met Vivian. She's been by the store twice. I'm on the social media team now for the council." Amy's sheepish grin made Jade laugh.

Jade laughed. "She's an excellent organizer. You'll like the council members. They're a good bunch." She picked up their trash and dropped it in the bin by the back door.

"I've got to get back. The paint should be dry by now, and hopefully, Mr. Darcy didn't trek over my new white shelves. And if he did, I may have cat tracks art," Amy said.

Jade and Amy parted at the street corner. On the short walk back to the store, Jade wracked her brain about what to wear to Jared Carswell's party. She didn't want to be overdressed or too casual. She liked to fly under the radar. Maybe Lorelei would have a bead on Tish's social scene.

As Jade began her store closing routine, her phone dinged.

It's definitely a pretentious affair. I'd wear summer slacks and a blouse.

And pearls, her aunt added.

Thanks, Jade responded. **Probably won't stay long. What's up with pearls?**

Always in fashion. Jared's place is good for people-watching, her aunt responded. **He's boorish, and the crowd's stuck up.**

R U Going? Jade asked.

Wouldn't miss it. Her aunt ended the text with a string of heart emojis.

On the walk home, Jade did a mental inventory of her closet, trying to think of what to wear to the shindig, while Chloe sniffed every blade of grass between the store and the cottage.

Not finding anything in the fridge that was dinner-worthy, Jade threw together a ham sandwich and scooped what was left of the cottage cheese on her plate. She and Chloe cuddled on the couch and binge-watched the latest season of "Father Brown."

After Chloe's evening walk, Jade hung up the leash and locked the side door. "Puppy, 'bout ready for bed?"

The little, roly-poly dog ran for the bedroom and plopped in her fuzzy bed. Within minutes, the dog snored loud enough to wake the dead. Sleep didn't come as easily for Jade, and she read several chapters in a Lee Child novel that had been sitting on her nightstand for months.

A loud thunk jarred Jade awake. She rolled over on her book. The light on the nightstand was still on. She checked the time on her phone: one-thirty. Another series of thunks. Jade's heart raced, and this time, Chloe sat up and yipped in her bed.

"Shhh. Stay here," she whispered to the dog. Chloe, not wanting to be left alone, chased after Jade as she slipped into the living room.

Pulling the sheer curtains back slightly, she looked out the front window. No movement under the streetlight. She tiptoed to the kitchen and peeked through the plantation shutters. No movement on the cut-through path. She stood still, holding her breath. No more thunks.

Chiding herself for being too jumpy, she picked up Chloe and went back to bed. She and the dog snuggled under the blanket, but she left the light on, just in case.

74

Chapter Eleven

The next morning, Jade juggled her to-go cup, messenger bag, and Chloe's leash as she pulled her cottage's front door locked behind her. She tripped and caught herself before tumbling down the three cement steps. Looking back, she spotted the culprit, a thick envelope on her doormat. Picking it up, she stuffed it in her bag and muttered under her breath as she and Chloe moseyed to the store.

It took longer than usual to do her opening rounds. Jade hadn't slept well, and her normal dose of caffeine wasn't doing the trick. She rummaged through the coffee pods for a dark blend and started the machine brewing on her second cup.

Remembering the package, she fished it out of her bag and slit the flap open. A familiar cream-colored piece of paper fell out with a bubble-wrapped wad. She cut the tape, avoiding the urge to pop some of the wrapping. Jade removed the plastic and gasped, dropping two voodoo dolls on her desk. The one with silver curls had a nail stuck through the chest and a green ribbon tied around the neck. The eyes were two large, black Xs. The second doll had long brown hair and pins sticking out of it. Someone had drawn a tribal tattoo on both arms in black marker.

Why would someone leave these for her? Grabbing the note, she lifted the fold. "You need to help him understand before it's too late." The message, in the all too familiar cut-out letters, sent a chill down her spine.

Leaning on her desk, she took several deep breaths and closed her eyes to fight back the wave of bile rising from her stomach. Biting her lip, she fished out her phone from her purse and dialed Nick.

After several rings, she almost clicked off until she heard, "Hey, what's up?"

"Sorry to bother you this morning. Can you stop by the store?"

"I'm leaving the gym now. You okay?"

"I'm a little shaken, but okay. Just wanted to show you something. Something weird was left on my porch last night."

"Be there as quick as I can," Nick said.

Jade whispered, "Thank you," but he had already disconnected. She snapped several pictures of the note and the creepy dolls. *Why would someone send this to me at home?*

After what seemed like an eternity, Jade heard heavy shoes on the porch. "Jade?" Nick called through the empty store.

"Back here in the office." Chloe yipped and skittered to the door.

He slipped inside her office and pulled the bottom half of the door shut behind him and Chloe. After a pause to pat the dancing dog, he stepped toward Jade. "What's going on? You sure you're okay? You're kinda pale, even for you."

"I found this package this morning. It's another one of those notes." She tried to keep her voice from cracking. "And these dolls."

"Neither of them looks like you," he said, poking the dolls with a pen.

"No. But the note's for me." She took another deep breath to calm the bats bouncing around in her stomach. "I thought it was a prank until we found Emory," she whispered.

"Who's this one supposed to be?" Nick asked, flipping the doll over with his pen. "It is a guy, right? It's not wearing a dress thing like the other one."

"I think it's Todd from Hot Diggity Dogs."

"You have any run-ins with anyone lately?" he asked.

She shook her head slowly. "None. Not sure what it has to do with me, except our only connection is having businesses on the same street. And we attend business council meetings." Jade shrugged her shoulder.

"I'm going to take these and go talk to Todd. If anyone makes contact about this or you see anything suspicious, call me immediately. Do you have cameras?"

She shook her head again. "I spent a boatload on the website. I chose expanding sales over inventory security. I can't tell you the last time I had a shoplifting issue here. Plus, only the first note was delivered here. This package was on my porch at home." She shuddered at the thought of this creep watching her business and home.

"I'm going to step up patrols. We'll see if there are any interesting prints on this. You have a large envelope?"

Jade rummaged around in the closet and handed him an oversized mailing envelope.

"Thanks. Let me know if you find anything else."

She nodded slightly. *I really need to talk to Todd, but I guess it can wait until lunch.* Jade filled her morning with all kinds of restocking and cleaning tasks.

"What has gotten into you?" Patti asked as Jade blew through the front room for the third time.

"Just trying to stay busy."

Patti furrowed her eyebrows. "I know you better than that. What's on your mind?"

"Don't tell anyone." Jade leaned over the counter. "There was a threatening package on my porch this morning."

Patti gasped, and both hands flew to her face, Macaulay Culkin style. "Oh, my stars. Did you get your own voodoo doll?"

"Not me. Emory and Todd," Jade whispered.

"Why are we whispering? And what is going on around here?"

Jade shook her head. "I have no idea. But I'm headed over for a hotdog for lunch. Can I bring you anything back?"

"Just the details of what you find. And don't worry. My lips are sealed." She mimed zipping her lips and tossing the key over her shoulder.

Jade grabbed her purse and scooted out the back door. Trying to ignore the butterflies and bats at war in her stomach, she jogged across the street and found a place in line at the busy hotdog stand.

The line inched to the counter. After placing her order and getting her number, Jade asked the teen with the green hair, "Is Todd working?"

"He's in the back. Todd, hey Todd," she bellowed.

He stuck his head out of a doorway in the small kitchen area. "What's up?"

"Someone out front asking for you," she said, pointing at Jade.

"Oh, hey, Jade. I'll be out in a few. You going to be around for a while?"

Jade nodded and pointed toward the deck.

Finding an empty table outside, Jade brushed the sand off a wooden bench and plunked down, facing the beach. Kids, blankets, and beach umbrellas covered every bit of real estate to the water's edge. She pulled her sunglasses out of her purse and gazed out across the bay. Only one fishing trawler, surrounded by a flock of seagulls, bobbed offshore. The crew must have dumped remnants of the catch overboard.

"Hey, Jade. What's up on this beautiful day?" Todd put her hotdog with mustard and an iced tea on the table.

"Thanks for bringing that out for me. Anything weird happen here lately?"

He grinned. "Define weird. It's summer at the beach."

She laughed. "I received an anonymous package this morning. It had two more voodoo dolls." She showed him the picture on her phone.

Todd plopped down across from her. "You think that's me?"

Jade shrugged her shoulders. "The ink looks like yours."

"But not the hair. Mine's classier." His grin showed his dimples. "The sheriff came by earlier. I think it's kinda funny. I told him to save me the doll when he's done with it. I'm going to hang it up inside."

Jade felt a flush cross her cheeks. "I'm worried about you, especially after, uh…."

"Emory. I know." The grin faded from his face. "There's a kook out there with a weird sense of humor. I'll be fine."

"But that kook murdered someone we know. I want you to be careful," she said.

"Don't worry. I sell hotdogs for a living to beachgoers. How threatening can that be to anyone?" Todd rose and stretched. "Speaking of which. I need to get back to the lunch rush. See ya."

Why was someone so interested in Todd? Was there something hidden in his personal life? This didn't make sense from what she knew about him.

Jade took a couple of bites of her hotdog and wiped the stray mustard off her lips. She drained her tea and dumped her trash. Who was targeting her Mermaid Bay friends?

She tried to shake the pall of the eerie warnings. Her phone dinged, and she laughed loudly when she saw Amy's photo of a woman in a red velvet ballgown with a train and tiara. **Too much for tonight?**

Just a little. I'm wearing slacks and bolero jacket.

Don't know yet, texted Amy. **I may need to make an entrance.** She followed her last text with a string of laughing emojis. **I wish I had a pink boa.**

Go for it, Jade responded. **Pick you up at 5:30.**

Chapter Twelve

Jade pulled up in front of the bookstore and tapped her horn. Amy came flying out the front door in black slacks and a beaded midnight-blue jacket with a pair of black stilettos in her hand.

She hopped in the lime-green Jeep and slammed the door. "Thanks for driving. I haven't figured my way around here yet. It's not like Boston."

"No problem. Mermaid Bay proper stretches about two miles north of the pier. Then it bumps into the little community of Seaport. If you head further north, you'll be in Yorktown. Then it stretches about fifteen miles west of the bay. Unlike Boston, if you blink, you may miss it."

"I came down here once when I was in middle school for a band festival. We saw Williamsburg and Yorktown before we drove up to Washington, D. C. I need to take a weekend and drive around to see the area." She leaned over and slipped on her shoes.

"I'm glad you settled on slacks. The red number probably wouldn't have fit in the vehicle." Jade winked.

Amy laughed. "I figured velvet was too much for the middle of July. And I didn't want to show up the host."

"That'll be hard to do. Tish and Jared always look like they stepped out of a New York fashion shoot. I don't think I've ever seen either one in what normal people call casual clothes."

"That does it. Instead of snooping through his medicine cabinet, I'm going to check out his closet. He must have a pair of shorts and a ratty T-shirt stashed away somewhere."

The pair giggled the rest of the way to Jared's condo, one of the many units in the gleaming white high-rise in Seaport. Jade turned at the white and gold Atlantic Shores sign.

"Looks like the Taj Mahal," Amy remarked as Jade found a visitor spot next to the building. The towering monstrosity dominated this end of Seaport Beach, and construction on another high-rise next door blocked the view of the water.

"Seaport used to be a sleepy little community when I was growing up. They got a new town council a few years back and decided progress meant development. The area's now loaded with expensive condos and McMansions on tiny lots where the amusement park and arcade used to be."

"I'm glad Mermaid Bay took steps to preserve its heritage," Amy said, climbing out of the Wrangler. "I found a thick folder in Em's office of her research for town council. Lots of notes about preservation efforts and anti-development causes."

Jade nodded and locked the driver's door. "They were rabid about keeping big development out. There was a major fight when one of the big box stores wanted to buy up a block for a twenty-four-hour store. That's the closest thing I've seen to protests here. Most of the town was fired up and ready to chain themselves to nearby trees or block the roads. There were a few who sided with the growth and progress side. There were some hard feelings between the factions for a while."

The pair made their way to the gold and white marble atrium. Looking up made Jade dizzy. The front doors of all the condos opened onto the lobby, which housed a security desk, coffee shop, and bar.

"Fancy," Amy said, pushing the button next to the line of brass elevators.

They stepped inside, and the doors swooshed closed. The elevator zoomed skyward like the pneumatic tubes at the bank's drive-thru.

When they stepped out, a crowd milled around in the hallway. Some vaping, and others trying to hide that they were smoking indoors. Amy and Jade followed two men in golf shirts and white pants to the condo's foyer. "I guess they're not too worried about the fire marshal stopping by," Jade whispered as they made their way through the crowd to the living room with its floor-to-ceiling windows overlooking the bay.

Amy shrugged and made a beeline toward a server with the tray of sparkling flutes. She snagged two. A crowd of smartly dressed people schmoozed on the condo's wrap-around balcony as smooth jazz streamed from speakers in every corner of the room.

Jade scanned the living room. The furnishings looked like something from an HGTV makeover show. White and pale yellow were the signature colors, and some designer had added pops of aqua to tie in an island theme with the palm and sea turtle designs. Large palms with fairy lights stood sentry in the corners. She followed Amy to the buffet, where they stacked little square plates with appetizers and dessert samples.

"Here, hold this," Amy said, handing Jade her plate. "I'll be right back."

Jade found a spot near one of the palms. It didn't take long before she was absorbed into a nearby conversation. "Hi, there. I haven't seen you at one of Jared's shindigs before. What do you do?" asked A woman with a pointy nose and chin. Her steely glare made Jade want to fidget.

"I own 'Tis the Season in Mermaid Bay. I'm Jade Hicks."

"Nice to meet you," the woman replied. "I'm Margot. What a cute little job. I bet your store is adorable. I'll have to try to swing by sometime."

Jade bit her lip to keep a sharp retort from slipping out.

"You live here?" The man in a gray suit asked, downing the dregs in his martini glass.

Jade nodded. "Well, in Mermaid Bay."

"Oh," he replied. "I thought maybe you had bought one of the empty units Jared had here. "I was going to welcome you to the neighborhood. It's always a party with this fun bunch." After an awkward pause, he turned to the woman next to him.

"So, what's your connection to Jared? Everyone has a story." Margot looked down at her blood-red manicure and twisted the emerald-cut diamond on her right hand.

"I see him from time to time at our business council meetings. He's friends with Tish St. James."

"Everyone's friends with Tish," the man with the lavender bowtie next to Margot added. "I'm Leroy, by the way. It's nice to meet you. And I do mean everyone." He wiggled his fuzzy eyebrows. His frizzy white hair on the fringes of his head, paired with his bowtie and plaid pants, gave him a clown-like look. Jade glanced down to see if he had on oversized red shoes. *Nope. Brown loafers with no socks.*

When a waiter passed with a tray of drinks, Leroy hustled off to chase him down in the sea of well-dressed bodies.

"I guess that's the last we'll see of him for a while." Margot pulled an e-cigarette from her tiny purse and disappeared toward the patio.

Jade's phone dinged. She glanced down at a photo of a closet. **No sloppy clothes**.

Another picture of a medicine cabinet appeared. **Nothing interesting here either**, Amy texted.

Jade laughed and pocketed her phone.

"What's so funny?" A tall man in a linen suit asked, sidling up next to her. If he had had a fedora and a gold pocket watch, he would have looked like Jay Gatsby from another era.

"Sorry. My friend sent me a joke."

"You're over here all by yourself. If you like people-watching, this is the place to be. You'll see everything, including over the top and humorous. I'm Kyle, by the way." He extended his hand.

When she reached out, he took her hand and kissed it. "Uh, it's nice to meet you," she said. Was she at some crazy cosplay party?

"It's very nice to meet you, too. I don't think I've seen you around before." The man who towered over her stepped closer. *So much for personal space.*

"My first time."

The man raised one eyebrow. "What brings you here? Shopping for real estate deals or trying to meet new friends? Jared's got quite a few condo deals in the works."

"No, I live in Mermaid Bay."

"I'm sure it's quaint," he said. "But we're more fun here. They've got some archaic rules down your way. Jared rails about it ad nauseam, but he's trying to make some changes on your town council."

Jade turned her head. Fishing for more information, she asked. "What kind of changes?"

"It's kinda hush hush." The man lowered his voice. "But you look trustworthy. Jared and some others are pooling their resources to get some more people with, let's say, more modern views elected or appointed to decision-making bodies. If he can't change what's there, then he'll do his best to blow it up. Knowing him, he'll stop at nothing to get his way."

"That's interesting. Some of the folks on the town council have been there a while. Who's he backing to replace them?"

"Oh, no. I don't kiss and tell. You'll just have to wait and see." The man's Cheshire cat grin looked more like a leer to Jade. "How about we go find a dark corner somewhere to swap secrets, and maybe I'll drop some names. It might curl your toenails."

Not wanting curly toenails, Jade searched for an excuse that didn't sound too lame. "I'm here with a friend." Jade glanced around the room. "Not sure where she is. I probably need to go and find her. She's been gone for a bit."

"If she looks anything like you, she's probably met some new friends if Jared hasn't found her first. He's quite the collector of fine things." The man swung his arm with his drink out wide, jostling ice and dribbling liquid on the white furry area rug.

Jade pasted on what she hoped looked like a sincere smile. "Excuse me. I need to check on her." She hurried off before he could comment further. **Where are you?** she texted Amy. Glancing over her shoulder to make sure Kyle didn't follow her, she ducked into an alcove off the foyer.

In the hallway. Meet me in the kitchen.

Jade dodged elbows as she made her way through the crowd that thinned out near an eat-in nook. The room opened up to an all-white professional-grade kitchen that looked like a set from the Food Network. Waiters zinged in and out to swap trays off the gigantic island while a pair of caterers in black and red removed empties and reloaded food in a choreographed dance.

Amy's head peeked around the corner. She picked up a stuffed mushroom from a tray on the counter and skidded to a stop next to Jade. "This is fun. We've got to go to more of these parties. I've heard all kinds of gossip and wild stories."

"I've met quite a few characters, too. Not sure I want to bump into them again." Jade wrinkled her nose.

Amy laughed. "Tish, who looks like a Jared groupie, is hanging on his every word on the patio. She laughs like a hyena at whatever he says," Amy whispered. "And there's a blond in a bikini sleeping across the king-size bed in the main bedroom. She didn't move except to snore loudly when I walked in, so I tiptoed out. The conversations are boring, but the food's pretty good." Amy popped another mushroom in her mouth and licked her fingers.

"Everyone I've met talks about Jared's condos." Jade rolled her eyes.

"Nobody I bumped into knew my aunt or that there was even a bookstore in the area. Anybody you want to chat with? Have you done the patio? Jared's holding court out there by the fire pit," Amy said.

Jade shook her head. "I'm about done peopling for the evening, but maybe we should say goodbye to Tish and Jared."

"Go ahead. I'll wait here. I've experienced enough Jared for one evening. Watch out. He's quite friendly." She gave Jade a quick jazz-hands wave.

Jade set down her plates and glass on a tray piled high with half-eaten food and dirty dishes. She dusted her hands and made her way through the crowd to the glass door at the back.

Men and women stood around the railing with drinks as Jared sat on a padded, white wicker chair next to an outdoor kitchen and metal fire pit. His chair had a high, rounded back that resembled a throne. Tish, his court jester, stood at his right, nodding vigorously at whatever he said.

Jade tried several times to make eye contact with Tish to thank her for the invitation, but she frowned and turned her attention back to Jared. Turning on her heels, Jade gave up and moved on to find Amy.

After a quick ride back to Mermaid Bay as twilight descended, Jade pulled her Wrangler to a stop in front of Amy's bookstore.

"Thanks so much for driving. I had fun. Not sure if I made any business contacts. There didn't seem to be too many readers there. But we looked fabulous and rubbed elbows with the beach's finest. And don't forget the free food. I ate enough crab cakes and lobster to make it worthwhile." Amy winked and hopped out of the Jeep.

"Let's do lunch this week if you get a break from all your renovations," Jade said.

"Sounds good. I should have the store pretty much the way I want it by midweek. Can you do a walk-thru and tell me what you think?"

"Be glad to. Text me." Jade put the Jeep in gear. But in the meantime, she wanted to see what she could find about the town council to see if she could corroborate any of what Kyle had said.

Chapter Thirteen

Jade kicked off her heels and changed into her pajamas and fuzzy slippers. She picked up her laptop and an iced tea and plopped on the couch beside Chloe. Kyle's comments about Jared and his interest in Mermaid Bay made her curious. She searched for any information she could find about members of the town council and Jared Carswell.

After hours of perusing websites, she created a spreadsheet with what she'd learned. There were five members on the council. Four were elected, and the fifth was the town manager, a paid employee of the municipality. Right now, in addition to the town manager Charles Winters, Tom Hawkins, Ruby Ellis, Vivian Turner, and the late Emory Jessup made up the board. Claude Simpkins, Tish St. James, Kelly Jamison, and Todd Brickman served on the zoning committee, and several of the folks also served on the business council.

She grabbed a notebook and listed all the players' names, and drew arrows to the connections. Most everyone on the list had received a warning note. As far as she knew, only two others besides herself received the dolls. She circled and starred all those names.

No other connections jumped out, so she pulled up minutes and decisions from meetings from the past two years. She slogged through page after page, occasionally jotting down a note. It felt like rereading *War and Peace*.

The next morning, Jade opened one eye. Light streamed in through the front window. A bird's shrill chirp caught Chloe's attention, and she jumped on the side chair to see out. Jade rolled over on her laptop and felt a jab in her ribcage. Seven-thirty. She needed to get a move on.

After a quick shower, she packed her laptop and notes, picked up a yogurt and coffee, and hightailed it with Chloe out the door. Not that there was a line waiting to get in the store, but she liked to be consistent with opening and closing times.

The quick walk down the street helped work out some of the kinks from sleeping on the couch on top of her laptop.

She buzzed through the store, checking inventory and turning on the twinkles. Lorelei wouldn't be in until lunchtime, so she'd have to entertain herself this morning. To liven up the empty store, she selected her rock 'n roll Christmas playlist, and seconds later, Band Aid belted out its Eighties classic from all the speakers. Jade answered email and filled online orders all morning while Chloe snoozed on her back.

Lorelei blew in a little before noon like a storm coming up the coast. "Hey, y'all. How's it going?" she called from the lobby.

"We're back here," Jade yelled, taping the last box for the afternoon pickup. "Just finishing up the orders."

"The weather's beautiful. I think folks are all outside having fun."

"We've been busy with our web business." Jade waved her hand at the fifty-three orders she'd filled since last night's report.

"Wow! Your grandma would be so proud. You've opened up new markets that she never had access to. Business is booming."

"I like to have options and to be able to flex as shopping preferences changes." Jade yawned.

"Did you howl all night?" her aunt asked, sorting through the coffee pods.

"Not hardly. I was doing some research after I got back from a party with Amy. Have you met Emory's niece yet?"

"Nope. I haven't been over to the bookstore since, well, you know." Her aunt waited for the coffee maker to come to life.

"She and I went to Jared Carswell's party last night. I didn't see you there."

"Nah. I didn't have the energy to mingle. Did you make any, uh, contacts?" her aunt asked, settling in at the other desk.

"I couldn't bring myself to deal with all the drama. It was more like a carnival sideshow. The fashions were interesting, but the convos were boring. Hey, what do you know about our town council?"

"Same as everybody else. It's pretty much the same folks year after year. I guess they'll have to have a special election this quarter to fill Emory's spot. Why the sudden interest in local politics? You thinking about running?"

"Not hardly. One of the guys at the party was talking about how arcane our zoning ordinances were and that change was in the air. I'm curious. Heard anything along those lines?"

"I haven't heard any complaints. Change happens slowly around here. It's like turning an aircraft carrier in the middle of the ocean. Nope. This town prides itself on not being like the other beaches that dot the coastline. Hadn't heard any chatter about changing the guard. This town likes things the way they've always been," Lorelei said.

"Keep your antennae up. It was a weird conversation. Well, actually, most of the evening at Jared's was strange."

"Jared's been around here a long time. He and his brother came down from New York in the nineties. He likes to talk a lot and collect people who owe him favors, but he bulldozes those who don't agree with him."

"His condo was nice. And the food was good." Jade wrinkled her nose.

"It's always over the top. Those events are usually for him to get new buyers, fodder for his real estate friends. I'm surprised no one tried to talk you out of selling your cottage."

Jade shook her head. "I guess it's not that close to the ocean."

The doorbell rang, and Lorelei jumped into action. "I've got this."

As Jade heard, "Welcome to 'Tis the Season, where it's always Christmas," she booted her computer to put in an order to restock some of the summer's popular items.

Kyle, the Jay Gatsby wannabe, and the town council kept popping into her thoughts. Could there be something from one of their recent meetings that started all of this?

Sifting through pages and pages of meeting minutes wasn't how she wanted to spend her afternoon, but if there was something there, she needed to find it. Pulling out her notebook, she looked for any major discussion items, especially things that appeared multiple times. Sadly, there were a lot of repeat topics without any decisions.

After hours of reading with not many notes, Jade stood and stretched. The only thing mildly controversial over the past quarter was that the council debated at length about whether committee members needed to live in Mermaid Bay. After what looked like much discussion, the group voted not to amend the charter. All council and committee members must live or own property in Mermaid Bay proper. If one chose to move or no longer own property in the town, he or she could finish the existing term, but the position had to be vacated. *Sounds fair.*

Disappointed that her hours of research turned up nothing earth-shattering, Jade stood and stretched. She straightened her desk and moseyed into the lobby.

"How goes it?"

Lorelei stifled a yawn. "Business was pretty steady for a while, but I think folks are heading home for dinner. I haven't even seen Neville today. I miss seeing his furry, little face."

"It's about quitting time. You have big plans for the evening?"

"Steve and I are supposed to try a new sushi place in Seaport. What about you?"

Jade wrinkled her nose. "Enjoy. Not sure what's in my fridge for dinner. But it'll probably be a quiet night at home."

"You should get out more. There's got to be a band playing somewhere around here," her aunt said.

Jade's thoughts flashed to Jared's party scene. She hoped she didn't roll her eyes. "Maybe you're right, but I'm tired tonight."

She moved through the store, checking on the display trees. At last count, she had three hundred and twenty trees in all shapes and sizes in the store. Pausing in the toy room, the colorful twinkle lights on the bear tree caught her eye. Then something moved under the nutcracker tree next to it. Tiny soldiers on several branches looked like they were marching.

Stifling a squeal, she moved in for a closer look. Neville, curled around one of the branches, batted the colorful soldiers. "What are you doing in there? You gave me a fright."

He purred and continued his work.

"I'll leave you to it. Just don't destroy anything. Remember our agreement." Jade winked at the tuxedo cat.

After one last check of the store, she filled Neville's bowls, and the black and white cat made a dramatic entrance to antagonize Chloe. To ease cat and dog tensions, she picked up the French bulldog and her bags. "Come on, puppy. Let's go find some dinner."

As she climbed the cement steps to her cottage, her phone rang. "Hey. Whatcha doing?" Amy asked.

"Just made it home."

"I'm tired of moving furniture and lugging books. Wanna come by and help me with a mural? I'll order dinner," Amy said.

"Sounds fun."

"Wear old clothes. It's probably going to get messy."

What had she signed up for? "Be there in a half hour or so." Jade disconnected and moved inside to get Chloe settled.

Twenty minutes later, Jade pulled into the lot in front of the bookstore. She stuck her head in the open door. "Whooo hooo, Amy."

"Back here. I'm getting ready to order Chinese. What do you want?"

Jade followed her voice through the store around tables and bookshelves. "Wow. It looks so different. You've been busy." She took the menu Amy handed her.

"Write down what you want here. I have water, wine, and tea."

"Tea's fine." Jade scribbled down a small order of honey chicken with fried rice.

After Amy placed the order, she dusted off her hands on her jeans. "Let me show you what I'm doing back here."

In the back, in what had been a dark corner, Amy had painted the walls a pale robin's egg blue. She had a projector aimed at one wall with a picture of a huge tree with lots of branches. "I'm going to put the reading tree on this wall and my cool book dragon on that one. Once we trace the picture, we can start painting."

Jade watched as Amy traced the projected outline on the wall.

"There. That's good." Amy climbed down the stepladder and shut off the projector. She handed Jade a picture of the tree surrounded by a squirrel, rabbit, raccoon, and several birds. "The paints and brushes are down there. Thanks so much for helping me with this. It would take me weeks by myself."

"This will be fun. Be careful. I could get ideas, and I may call you to paint Christmas murals at my place." Jade winked and leaned over to pry the lid off the dark brown can. She found a small roller and started painting the tree's thick trunk. The pair concentrated on their work, stopping only to eat dinner and refill their drinks.

Mr. Darcy strode through the back room and hopped on a low bookcase. "Whaddya think, kitty cat?" Amy asked. "I think it's coming along nicely. We'll let that dry overnight. I'll work on this some more tomorrow and my grand opening plans."

"Send me the information when you have it, and I'll add it to my promo stuff."

"You're the best. This is all kinda overwhelming, but I know it's all going to be worth it." Amy tapped the lids on all the paint cans with a small hammer. "It has to be. I left Massachusetts to do this."

"You can do it. You have to be able to pivot and market, but it's possible. This is a great location. Most everybody loves books."

"Tish and her realtor friend have stopped by to try to talk me into selling. She keeps making comments like don't work too hard if it's a sinking ship. I've had more than a couple of visits and a fruit basket from her."

"Stick to your guns and go with it. You've worked hard. And I think you should give it a go."

"Tonight was fun." Amy pushed her long bangs out of her eyes.

"It was. Thanks for the invitation and dinner. And call me if you ever need to talk. I've been there. I took over the shop when my grandmother died, and I'd never run a store before, either. I did a lot of on-the-job training."

Amy hugged her. "It's nice to know I'm not in this by myself."

"Call anytime. And I was serious about the Christmas murals." Jade winked.

They laughed and chatted out the door and in the parking lot for another half hour.

Jade started the Jeep and let out a breath. Why would Tish plant seeds of doubt for Amy? And what's with the bum's rush to sell the property? Did James and Sophie know?

Chapter Fourteen

s Jade closed the store the next afternoon, her phone rang, and Amy's name popped up on the screen.

"Hey there. What's up? Got more murals to paint?"

Amy laughed. "No, but I need another favor. Sorry for the short notice. Tish called and asked me to meet her for a girls' night and drinks. I tried to bow out, but she's pretty persuasive. Wanna go with me? Please. Please. She said her realtor buddy Farrah would be there, too."

Jade hoped she didn't sigh out loud. "Sure, I guess. When and where?"

"Five-ish at somewhere called McCavities."

"It's in Seaport. What are you wearing?"

"A blousy tunic and some capris and my flipflops. Are you telling me it's going to be a fashion show? I knew I should have said I needed to bathe the cat," Amy whined.

"Tish and her crew always look like they've stepped off a runway somewhere. And not the airport kind," Jade said.

"I bet they were the popular girls, huh." Amy sighed. "I'll call and tell her I have a migraine."

"If you do, she'll keep hounding you. I'm super casual today, too, skinny jeans and a summer sweater. Let's see what she wants. Lemme take Chloe home, and I'll pick you up in twenty minutes."

"Love it. We should be fashionably late and act like we're too cool to care about anything." Amy giggled. "Thanks for being my partner in crime. See ya."

"Come on, Chloe, we need to get a move on." The Frenchie gave her an over-the-shoulder I don't care look. "That's the spirit."

Ten minutes after picking up Amy, Jade pulled her Jeep in front of the Harbor View condos in Seaport. The flamingo decorations started in the traffic loop and carried inside to the lobby and bar. Pink was definitely the signature color.

Amy looked around at all the pink marble. "Fancy place. I'm hungry. I hope they have food here."

"Pub food."

"Yum. But I bet Tish and Farrrr-ahhh don't eat either." She rolled her eyes and headed toward the bar.

Jade snickered and followed her friend.

Not seeing Tish or her crew in the semi-crowded bar, the pair found a high-top table with a clear view of the front door.

A rail-thin waiter approached with two pink menus. "Welcome, ladies. What can I get you?"

"I'm starving. Let's start with the pretzel bites and pub cheese, and I'll have one of those big, pink drinks." Amy pointed to the tall glass on the bar with fruit and a flamingo swizzle stick.

"Let's do one of your sampler platters," Jade said. "We can all share, and I'll have an iced tea."

"Be right back." The waiter moved on to another table.

"The crowd so far doesn't look super ritzy. A bunch of them are wearing golf shirts and shorts," Amy whispered.

"The guys," Jade said as a shadow passed over the table.

Tish St. James rested her hand on the tall wooden chair. "Hi, all. Glad you could meet us, Amy. Hi, Jade. This is Farrah Rogers, one of my favorite colleagues."

The two women, dressed head-to-toe in designer duds and shoes, claimed the remaining chairs.

Setting her phone next to her place setting, Tish glanced down as alerts popped on her screen at regular intervals. The constant beeping was annoying.

The waiter dropped off the platters of appetizers and the drinks. "Hi, there.

What can I get you ladies?"

"I'll have a Gibson," Tish said, tapping a response into her phone.

"I'll have a Flamingo Margarita like hers," Farrah said, adjusting her skin-tight skirt.

"My pleasure. Be right back with your drinks." The waiter disappeared into the growing after-work crowd.

"I see someone's hungry." Tish looked down her sculpted nose at the steaming platters.

"Here, help yourself. We ordered enough for everyone." Amy offered an appetizer plate to the two women. Neither of them moved toward it.

"I'll save my calories for the drinks," Farrah said, searching through her purse for her phone that was playing "Money, Money, Money." "Sorry. I thought I put that on vibrate. I'm always working."

Amy ignored the slight and piled appetizers on her plate. "Thanks for inviting us here. I'm still learning the area, so it's interesting to try new places. How was your day?" She stared at Tish.

When the extended pause continued, Tish looked up and put her phone down. "It's a nice place for drinks and to get away from the busy work day. I was on the phone all day today."

"Me, too," Farrah squeaked. "Everyone's in the mood to move, and I have some fab listings. What about you two?"

"I just moved in," Amy said. "Give me a year or so."

Tish raised one manicured eyebrow and took the drink the waiter offered. "What about you?" she asked Jade.

"Oh, I love my bungalow."

"It's adorable, and I could sell it in a heartbeat. Maybe you should think about some beachfront property."

"Tish, you're at the top of my contact list the minute I decide to move." Jade popped a cheesy bite in her mouth.

"Amy, I know that you're new to the area. Are you still planning to make a go of Emory's place? She was so instrumental on town council and a bunch of committees. You've got big shoes to fill."

Amy wiped her hands after finishing a crab-filled stuffed mushroom. "I know. Aunt Em was really plugged into the community. Give me a few months to get situated, and I'll be ready to volunteer."

"When you do, call me. Emory and I worked closely on several projects for Mermaid Bay. I can give you the lay of the land and all the dirt."

"Or sand." Farrah giggled.

The three women looked at her.

"The lay of the sand. Get it? Oh, look. There's Bruce and Terry. Excuse me. I have to go talk to them about Jared's new condo. They're both looking for something exciting." She hopped off her chair and zeroed in on the men.

"We're always working." Tish glanced down at her phone again. The alerts moved up her screen like a stock ticker. "Amy, if the book business doesn't pan out, let me know if you're interested in becoming a realtor. There are so many opportunities." Her voice went up an octave.

"Thanks for the offer. It's always good to have options. But I'm really excited about inheriting Aunt Em's property and making a go of the store. I'm loving this place already. Everybody has been so warm and helpful. And I could live here forever."

"You have to watch that southern passive-aggressive hospitality. They're sweet to your face, and when you're not looking, they'll cut you off at the knees. Not everything is what it seems. Be careful," Tish added, raising an eyebrow.

Jade opened her mouth, but Tish continued, "That's why town council is so important. There is a faction of crazies that are trying to take over everything and force their arcane ways on everyone. We've got to make sure Emory's replacement isn't one of those."

"Who do you have in mind?" Jade leaned forward and whispered as Tish signaled the waiter for another drink.

"It's got to be someone who's rooted in the business world, not one of these, uh, retired tree and turtle huggers."

Jade's eyebrows shot up behind her bangs. "Trees and turtles are good things."

"Without them, the beach environment would suffer." Amy took a bit of her loaded potato skins.

"I know that," Tish snapped. "But having business sense and the courage to challenge things are important, too. Heard anything about anyone vying for Emory's seat?" Tish's stare felt like it bored into Jade's skull.

"I haven't heard anyone say anything. I think it's too early. Maybe as we get closer to the next meeting," Jade said.

"You're not planning to throw your hat in, are you?" Tish continued to stare.

Jade paused. *And what if I was?* "No. The store keeps me plenty busy right now. I'll continue to help on the publicity and social media teams."

"And what about you? Everyone will think you're a natural fit to replace Emory."

"I just got here," Amy said. "I need some time to get acclimated. But don't you worry, you'll know when I get involved." Amy paused and looked at her watch. "One of these pink fruity drinks is enough for me. Thanks, Tish, for inviting us to join you. Jade, I need to head out soon to check on my main man, Mr. Darcy. How about a ride home?"

Jade opened her purse. Amy put her hand on the top of it. "No, don't worry about that. Tish was so kind to invite us out tonight. Thanks again, Tish." She picked up her own purse and headed for the front door.

"Thanks, Tish," Jade said, following her friend.

The realtor's mouth hung slightly ajar.

Amy giggled as she climbed into the Jeep. "Did you see her face? It looked like she licked a persimmon or something worse. And don't you feel any guilt about sticking her with the check? She invited us, and I didn't appreciate the way she was looking down her nose at us."

"I hope we haven't made her mortal enemy list. She's a force to be reckoned with."

"Who cares," Amy said. "And maybe I will get involved with the council. I didn't like her tone."

The two women dissolved into giggles and headed to Mermaid Bay.

Chapter Fifteen

Jade looked up from the vendor catalog when she heard the bells. "Hi, Todd. What brings you by this afternoon?"

"Hey, I need some advice." He strode up to the front counter and leaned forward. "Are you having any issues with reviews?" His tattoos peeked out from under the sleeve of his Hot Diggity Dogs golf shirt.

"I always get a few whackadoos who complain about things I can't control. But for the most part, the customer reviews are good. Most people like Christmas. A majority of my business is online now. What's up?"

"It's been weird lately. It's like I'm under attack. Maybe I'm paranoid, but it feels out of control."

"Can I get you something to drink? Do you want to come in the back and sit down?" she asked.

Todd shook his head. "I can't stay long. I need to get back. I know you're big on social media, so I wanted to get your take on this. I've had two complaints filed with the Health Department in the last few weeks. One resulted in an inspection. Okay, that happens, but not that often. It hasn't happened to me in the last three years." He stared at Jade. "In the height of the summer, I usually get thirty or forty comments on all my social media posts and five or ten check-ins or reviews each day." He took a deep breath and paused. "This summer started out like normal."

Todd ran his hand through his longish hair. "I monitor my traffic throughout the day to make sure I'm responsive. About a week ago, I started getting hundreds of comments and links every day. My reviews are now in the hundreds per day, and I'd say eighty percent of them are bad." He took a deep breath. "You know, stuff like your food is terrible, and your staff is super rude. We serve a lot of people, but some days, the reviews are more than the customers for that day. Something's not right. And most of them are from these generic accounts that don't even look like real people." He let out another heavy sigh. "First, they find Emory murdered behind my place, and now this."

"Do you have anyone who helps you with your marketing?"

Todd shook his head sluggishly. "My promo is usually on social media or in partnership with my food vendors."

"Who do we know who's good at computers? Know any super gamers or hackers?" Jade asked.

Todd paused. "Good idea. I may know someone from school." He whipped out his phone and fired off a series of texts.

"Maybe he could poke around and see what's going on in the dark web, and then you could call the authorities. It's worth a shot."

"She," Todd said. "Her name is Delia. She's a programmer who spends all her free time gaming." His phone dinged and distracted him. "Thanks, Jade. She wants to talk. I'll see what she can do. You're the best."

"Let me know how it goes," she yelled at his back as he disappeared out the front door.

Jade wandered back to her desk and checked the store's social media sites. No sign of anything fishy. Her comments and reviews looked normal. She pulled up her files of all the things going on since Emory's murder and added a row about Todd's reviews. Lots of facts. Lots of dead-ends.

She scanned through her phone contacts and sent a text to Nick.

Dinner sometime soon?

Off at 6. Whatcha making?

Spaghetti?? she replied.

See ya tonight.

Jade's phone dinged again with an email from Vivian, reminding members of next week's business council agenda and tomorrow night's town council meeting to replace Emory Jessup. Jade normally didn't attend the government meetings, but it might be a good idea to keep up with what's going on.

The door creaked, and Jade returned to the front.

"Oh, hey. I was expecting to see Patti," the delivery driver said.

"She's off today." Jade handed him the plastic carton full of packages.

"Tell her Simon said hey." He winked and picked up the container.

"Will do. She'll be back tomorrow."

He nodded and hustled out as quickly as he arrived. *Patti will be over the moon when she finds out Simon asked about her.*

"Come on, Chloe. We need to start closing up. Nick's coming over tonight for dinner." The little dog's tail wiggled in excitement. Jade wasn't sure if it was caused by the mention of Nick or dinner.

After prepping baked spaghetti and making a salad, Jade chased Chloe through the house with the vacuum and picked up the clutter in the living room. She rummaged through the sideboard and pulled out her red and white check placemats and white plates. She found an antique white vase and filled it with red, artificial flowers for the centerpiece.

With enough time to change outfits twice and floof her hair, Jade was ready for Nick's arrival. The butterflies bounced around inside. *We're just friends hanging out. This isn't a date.* Her affirmations didn't quell the butterflies or her thoughts.

The doorbell chimed, and Chloe jumped into bark mode. When she saw Nick, she danced on her hind legs until he picked her up.

"Thanks for the invitation." Nick stepped inside, sporting a romance novel model look with jeans and a red shirt. His fresh-from-the-shower smell and slightly damp hair sent her butterflies into overdrive.

"No problem. I hadn't heard from you in a while. I thought we could hang out."

"Need any help?" he asked.

"Everything's ready. You could pour the drinks. I have Coke, tea, water, wine, and maybe OJ."

He picked up the glasses from the table and followed her to the kitchen. "What do you want?"

"Tea's fine." Jade added the salad to the table next to the large pan of baked spaghetti and a basket of breadsticks.

The pair sat down, and Chloe looked up at them with the saddest eyes she could muster.

"You know the rules, kiddo. Go get in your bed." Jade pointed toward the living room.

The dog made a noise and walked to her bed like she was going to the gallows.

"Did she just mutter?" Nick laughed.

"She does that. It's the Frenchie way. She's always got some kind of sassy commentary."

Nick laughed and picked up a breadstick. "So, what's been going on in your world?"

"Business has been steady, which is good. I think the Mermaid Bay folks are still on edge. Any new information about Emory? I haven't heard anything in the last few days," Jade said, trying her version of puppy-dog eyes.

"Still waiting on the full autopsy and forensic reports. We don't think she was killed behind the hot dog stand, though. Not sure why someone would move her there unless it was the most convenient place."

"Todd Brickman came by today. He said someone's sicced the health department on him twice, and he's getting a ton of bad reviews on social media. He asked me if I was having any problems."

"Are you?"

"No, everything's fine at the store. I'm not sure who Todd's had a run-in with, but he's had a lot of issues lately. Speaking of new, have you met Amy yet? She's Emory's niece."

"We talked briefly on the phone. I haven't seen her in person," Nick replied.

"She moved into Emory's apartment and is running the store. She's done some nice improvements. We're going to partner on some marketing efforts."

Nick nodded. "That's good. I hate to see businesses close. Spaghetti's good." He shoveled in another forkful.

"Anybody else get weird messages or any more voodoo dolls?" she asked.

He shook his head. "Just you, Todd, and Emory."

"Notes, posters, threatening dolls, a murder, and then nothing," Jade mused.

"We're still investigating. It's a process. There are tons of leads we have to sift through. Hopefully, the autopsy and other reports will provide us with more details."

"I'm going to the town council meeting tomorrow night. I'm curious who will replace Emory." Jade put her utensils on her plate as Nick reached for seconds.

"We'll be there, too. For a long time, the politics were basically the same around here, and the goal was to keep unchecked development out of Mermaid Bay. There are rumblings of factions trying to change that. Other localities have had an influx of growth, and the revenue that it spawns is appealing to a lot of folks. We'll see how the wind blows tomorrow and who gets nominated. My guys will be there to keep the peace."

"I like that we still have the old beach town feel, but as a business owner, I don't want the world to pass us by if we don't adapt. It's going to be interesting. I hope we can compete with surrounding areas that have glittery timeshares and big oceanfront hotels," Jade mused.

"Right now, it's a place where people forget to lock doors. They know everyone. We need to be vigilant."

"Whatcha want to do tonight?"

Nick shrugged.

Jade rose to clear the table. "You done? I have apple pie for dessert."

"Sounds good. How about a walk on the beach? My pal down here has some energy to burn."

"Chloe, when did you sneak back in here?" Jade cleared the table and loaded the dishwasher.

"What can I help with?" Nick asked, slipping Chloe part of a meatball.

"Nothing. All done here. I'm going to let the pan soak. Let me go change my shoes, and I'll be back in a flash. Her leash is over there."

By the time she returned, Nick and Chloe were waiting. Jade locked the door and trailed them down the steps to the oyster shell path beside her house. Nick led the way to the pier. A few people fished from the shore, and a pickup volleyball game dominated the real estate in front of Hot Diggity

Dogs. They watched for a little while until Chloe got bored and chased a sandpiper. Nick and Jade walked under the pier and headed back as twilight pushed the last bit of sun behind the trees. The hordes of beachgoers were replaced with a few locals who walked dogs or jogged in the still-warm sand.

A jarring noise echoed across the alley as the pair, led by the French bulldog, made their way to Jade's bungalow.

"Sorry," Nick said, fishing his phone out of his pocket. "Driscoll here. Yes. Got it. Be there in ten minutes." He ended the call. "Jade, thanks for dinner. I have to respond to this call. The next dinner's on me. Gotta run."

"Bye." *Maybe we'll make it to dessert next time.* Jade waved as he jogged down the path to his truck. "I guess duty calls, Chloe." The little dog turned her head. "Maybe I need to get a police scanner."

Jade plopped down on her couch to scroll through Facebook, and pictures of a bad car accident near the main road caught her attention. Her phone rang, and Amy's picture popped up on her screen.

"Hey, girl. What's up?"

"I need a favor," a subdued Amy said. "Someone t-boned me at the four-way stop near the mini-mart."

"Are you okay?" Jade's thoughts flitted to the mangled Mini Cooper pictures. "Oh, my stars, someone posted pictures of the accident online."

"Already? Sheesh! I'm fine, but my beautiful car isn't. It did its job and protected me, but it didn't survive the accident. I'm at the Riverside Hospital. Can you pick me up? I'm in the lobby next to the emergency exit."

"Sure. I'll be right there. Maybe in fifteen or twenty minutes?"

Jade broke the sound barrier on her trip to the hospital. She rushed in through the glass doors and let out a deep breath when she spotted Amy in a chair near the TV.

"Are you sure you're okay?" Jade rushed to her friend's side. "What happened?"

"I just want to go home and mourn the loss of my little car. I dislocated my shoulder, and my nose is bruised. I'm going to look lovely tomorrow. And this blue sling is such a cool accessory. Don't be jealous. All the hip kids are going to want one."

"Come on. Let's get out of here. Do you need to check out?"

"Nope. I have all my paperwork. Let's roll," Amy said.

"Do you need me to stop at a drug store or to get you dinner?"

"I'm good. I ate before the accident. I really want to go to bed. Thanks so much for coming to get me," Amy said, almost above a whisper.

"Do you want to stay in my guest room?" Jade led her to the doors that swooshed open.

"Awww. I appreciate it. I'll take a rain check. I need sleep. We'll do it later when I'm more fun. I have a feeling that I'll be even crankier tomorrow."

"Be right back. I'll go get the Jeep."

A few minutes later, Jade pulled up to the curb. Jumping out, she ran around to the passenger side to help her friend with the step up. After she belted herself in, Jade drove slower than normal back to Mermaid Bay.

"What happened?" Jade asked.

"I was coming back from a run for office supplies and dinner. I stopped at the four-way stop. There was no one there, and then out of nowhere, this big black truck barreled through, sent me into a spin, and drove off. And I'm sure my little car is totaled."

"I'm so sorry. Maybe the police can find witnesses or camera feeds. You don't hit someone that hard and not know it. Someone has pictures. I saw them on the Mermaid Bay Residents' page on Facebook."

"Exactly. And now I have to deal with the insurance and getting a loaner and a new car. The timing stinks."

"Let me know what I can help you with," Jade said.

"I got most of the remodels in the store done, but I may take you up on your offer. Lisa decided to stay on, so she'll help me with inventory stuff. She can do the lifting for a while."

Jade pulled up to the bookstore's porch. "Here, let me get the door for you."

"I appreciate all your help." Amy looked small, hunkered down in the passenger seat with her sling and icepack.

Jade locked the Jeep and followed Amy inside and upstairs, where she got her settled on the couch in her apartment.

"Thanks again. I've got to make some phone calls, and then I'm hitting the hay. I'll text you tomorrow."

"No problem. Don't hesitate to call if you need me. I can let myself out."

"The door in the kitchen is a back exit from the deck," Amy said.

"Take care. See you tomorrow." Jade locked the door behind her and trekked down the wooden stairs. The ocean breeze fluttered her bangs. She took a deep breath, and some of the stress seeped out. What else is going to happen around here?

Chapter Sixteen

Jade pulled into the high school parking lot with fifteen minutes to spare before the town council meeting started. She found a parking spot in the back and wished she hadn't worn heels for the hike to the auditorium. She followed the crowd through the blue doors and down the hallway. An institutional smell gave her a flashback to the ninth grade and the first time she walked through this entrance. At least she felt more confident than she did at fifteen.

A few open seats remained in the middle rows. She scooted past a crowd chatting in the aisle and stood next to an empty end seat by Sophie and James Fournier. "Are you saving this?" She pointed at the scarred wooden seat with names, hearts, and other sentiments carved into it.

James shook his head. "It's yours. How're you doing?"

"Good. I didn't expect such a crowd here." Jade scanned the room and waved to friends. *Definitely a packed house.*

"Council's gotten so partisan over the years. And the factions are here to make sure their side vies for the empty seat. I think some want to make sure the old guard doesn't completely dominate, and the others want to be the majority," James said.

"I'm curious to see who gets it," Sophie added, leaning forward. "This could be an interesting special election. We should have brought popcorn." She raised one stylized eyebrow. "Who knows what's gonna happen?"

"Either of you throwing your hat in the ring?" Jade asked.

The brother-sister team shook their heads.

Sophie laughed. "The Busy Bean keeps us both fully allocated and then some. Plus, I don't have time for all the council drama."

"And I don't have the patience for all the discussions and rehashing of the same old topics. No, thank you. What about you?" James asked.

"Not right now. I'm good with volunteering for business council events, but I don't have a lot of free time either." Jade wedged her purse next to her and shifted in hopes of finding comfort on the flip-down, plywood seat.

The noise level died down as Vivian Turner and Charles Winters approached the lectern.

Charles, a balding man with Clark Kent glasses, thunked the microphone with his index finger, and the dull thuds echoed through the auditorium. When the microphone squealed, everyone groaned.

"Hello, all. If you'll take your seats, we'll get started here in a few minutes. Thank you all for making the time to come out here. The board decided not to appoint a temporary backfill for Emory and to open it up to a vote. Thank you for doing your civic duty."

Vivian and the other council members filed behind the long table with microphones. Each found a spot. A melancholic pall fell over Jade when she zeroed in on Emory's empty chair at the end of the table with the white flower arrangement in front of it.

"Good evening," Charles said again. "And welcome to the Mermaid Bay town council meeting." The agenda appeared on the screen behind him. "I call this meeting to order. I'd like for us all to observe a moment of silence for Emory Jessup, whose life ended too soon." A hush descended on the crowd. The only sound was the hum and an occasional crack of the speakers.

The solemn moment disappeared like the tide when Charles banged the gavel and launched into a review of the agenda. After almost an hour of reading and accepting the minutes from the last meeting and reviewing the treasurer's report, Charles finally announced the topic that interested everyone. "We are prepared to accept nominations for the empty seat on the council." Low murmurs traveled through the crowd. "Nominees need to live or own property within the boundaries of Mermaid Bay, and they have to be at least eighteen years old. If you would like to nominate someone, please come to the microphone at the edge of the stage."

People rustled, and a small group approached the front of the room. In a matter of minutes, there were ten names, including Tish St. James and Claude Simpkins. Then before Charles could gavel the nomination process closed, Amy, holding her slinged arm, hurried down the aisle. She took a deep breath and approached the microphone. "I would also like to nominate myself. I'm Amy Pemberton, Emory's niece. I'm new in town, but I have lots of ideas and energy."

Low murmurs and rustling rippled through the crowd.

"Anyone else?" Charles scanned the audience. "If not, the nominations are closed. Each of you, please meet at the edge of the stage at the end of this meeting to go over the requirements. We will collect the information needed and meet next week for each nominee to introduce him or herself, and then we'll vote. The last item on today's agenda is the business council announcements. The MBBC meets next week to plan the Labor Day celebration and our annual Octoberfest. If you're interested in helping, please contact Kelly Jamison."

The platinum blond in the middle of the table stood and waved. "We could use some more volunteers," Kelly yelled into her microphone. "Let me know if you can sign up."

"Okay, then that concludes today's agenda. All nominees for the open seat, please come forward." Charles banged the gavel. The noise level increased exponentially as people gathered their things and chatted with neighbors.

Jade remained in her seat until most of the audience filed out. She waited as Amy made her way up the aisle with her folder. "Hey, how are you? I didn't know you were coming."

"I wasn't, but I was lying in bed at four a.m. thinking. Emory would have wanted me to try to fill her seat. I found more of her files, and she was really determined to fight for her store and to preserve this community. I felt like I needed to get involved."

"Good for you. This is exciting. What's next?" Jade asked, following Amy up the center aisle.

"I didn't think it all the way through. I don't have a plan. I guess I'll be figuring it out this week. I don't have any history here, and nobody really knows me." Amy let out a breath that made her bangs flutter. "I hope it's not a lost cause."

"You have my vote. I think we should start campaigning." Jade winked at her friend as they exited the auditorium. "You look good. How are you feeling?"

"It hurts when I move too fast or when I sleep on my side, but things are getting back to normal. I'm tired a lot, but anxious to roll out my changes at the store. How about we get together and plot? Tonight? Have you eaten?" Amy asked.

"Sounds good. I'll bring a pizza. Your place?"

"That's a plan. I'll bring the wine. Let's make it happen. What have I gotten myself into?" Amy asked.

After getting Chloe settled on the couch, Jade picked up a pizza in Seaport. She juggled the box and her purse as she locked the Jeep's door and made her way into the bookstore.

Amy rang up purchases for two senior women in bright shorts sets. When she was done, she wiped her hands. "Hey, thanks for bringing dinner. How about if we eat in one of my new reading nooks." She picked up her laptop and several folders with her good arm.

The pair settled in on eclectic chairs surrounding a low wooden coffee table.

"I like what you've done here. It's so warm and friendly. I could hang out here," Jade said.

"Be back in a flash," Amy said.

Jade looked around the room that used to be dark and full of large bookcases. The murals and bright paint, along with the new seating areas, made this a fun place. She snapped a few photos for her newsletter and social media posts.

Amy returned and handed a glass to Jade. "I've been working furiously on the launch of the 'under new management' campaign. I'm going to have events on Saturday and Sunday." Amy plopped down on an orange loveseat. "Then, I'm adding a poetry slam, a game night, and author events. And in a moment of weakness, I go and sign up to run for town council. I'm not sure what I was thinking." She took a bite of pizza and twirled the string of mozzarella on her index finger.

"Hey, busy people get stuff done."

"I know. But now I have to put together what I stand for, why I should be selected, and a bio. Not to mention a short speech and create a short video for the council's website." Amy sighed.

"You still want to do it?" Jade asked.

Amy nodded. "Yep. I want to give it a try. There are eleven candidates for one slot. Not sure about the odds. Who knows. But I want to give it a try."

"What can I help with?" Jade asked.

"I'll work on the information packet for the council, and I'm pretty good at social media. I haven't really had the opportunity to meet people. When they see me on election day, that is probably the first chance they'll have to put my face with my name. I need my speech to be spectacular."

"Maybe I could host a 'meet the candidate' event for you?"

"I am honored that you want to help me. And relieved. Would it be crass if we did it here during opening weekend? I need as much foot traffic as I can get to the store."

Jade shook her head. "Why not? What did you have in mind?"

"Like maybe at closing, we could have a wine and cheese thing?"

"I have an idea. What about if we do it the Friday before and tell them it's a sneak peek at the store and a chance to meet you?" Jade asked.

"I love it. What do you need me to do?" Amy asked, popping the last bit of crust in her mouth.

"Send me a list of folks you want me to include, and I'll set up an online sign-up for the event. How about we do it like an open house on that Friday from four to say six."

"You are the best. I've ordered a bunch of food trays for the weekend. I can use some of those. And I can pick up some wine. I'd hate for you to go to all that expense. You're already coordinating the invitations. This sounds like so much fun. I can put a long table in the back, and folks can wander around and chat. I like it."

"You sure about the food? You don't need me to bring anything?" Jade set her paper plate next to the pizza box.

"It's the least I can do. I appreciate you being the social butterfly," Amy said.

"I'll work on some graphics tomorrow. Do you have a headshot or some casual photos I can use?"

"I'll send you some and my bio. Wow, that sounds all official." Amy wiped her mouth and set her plate and napkin on the table.

Mr. Darcy tiptoed in and made an appearance. He rubbed against Jade's shoe and mewed loudly. "Hey, kitty. You're a lot like Neville the Devil cat. He always has to check things out." *Emory would have had a fit to find an animal in the bookstore. Times are changing around here.* "It's getting late. I need to head out and work on some things before I call it a night." Jade rose and picked up the trash.

"Don't worry about that. I've got it. Thanks for dinner and all your help. You've made me feel welcome. I wondered how a Bostonian would fit in a small Virginia town. I'm glad I made the trip." Amy followed Jade to the front door.

As excited as she was about planning the party and Amy's grand reopening, a weird feeling caused Jade to pause. She felt like she was being watched. After chiding herself for being paranoid, she looked over her shoulder and then hurried to her Jeep. After locking herself inside, she did one more glance around. She couldn't shake the creepy feeling.

Chapter Seventeen

Jade leaned back in her chair and let out a long breath as Chloe scampered over and jumped in her lap. "Hey, puppy. I know. It's been a long day. I've emailed and called just about everyone I know in town. I hope we get a turnout tonight for Amy's meet and greet. A lot of the folks have already made up their minds about their candidate to fill Emory's open seat."

As she stroked the soft fur between Chloe's ears, Lorelei breezed in. "That's probably true, but folks will come for the curiosity factor. They want to see what she's done to Emory's store. You'll get a crowd."

"I always second guess myself and worry about what happens if no one shows up."

"They'll be there. They're too nosey not to." Lorelei pulled her red Coach bag from the cubby. "I've got to take care of a couple of errands, but I'll stop by."

"Thanks. The store is really cute. Amy has some good ideas," Jade said.

"She'll do well. That place needed some fresh air. I hope she doesn't ger her hopes too high about the council. Ten other people are vying for that one seat. There are going to be a lot of disappointed people. See you later." Lorelei waved over her shoulder as she headed out.

Jade locked the door behind her aunt and began her closing routine. Neville shot out from under a tree decked out with a country Christmas theme, and the dog and cat race was on.

She hurried after them and found Neville on the front counter and Chloe at the base, daring him to jump down and continue the fun. "All right, guys.

I need to get ready for the open house. Neville, let's get you fed, and Chloe, we need to head home."

About a half hour later, Jade climbed the wood steps to the bookstore. Amy had propped the door with a wrought iron statue of a cat. A wave of AC greeted Jade as she crossed the threshold. Light jazz floated through the air, and Amy, in her navy and white striped sundress, buzzed around the store straightening new displays and the reading nooks.

"Looks good in here. Definitely brighter. Can I help you with anything?" Jade asked.

"Nope. Thanks for being here early. The food and drinks are ready. I'm going to go print out some signup sheets in case anyone wants to join my newsletter. Be back in a sec."

Jade wandered through the store. The murals and comfy seating areas changed the whole atmosphere of Emory's store. She snapped a picture of the finished book dragon. Maybe she should consider a mural or two for 'Tis the Season.

"Okay, that's it. Now we fidget and worry while we wait," Amy said from somewhere in the front.

"It'll be fine. And you're going to have a grand reopening this weekend," Jade replied.

"I'm excited and a bit nervous. I haven't run for anything since SCA secretary in the fourth grade. Back then, candy and construction paper 'vote for me' buttons were all that were needed." Amy drifted to the food table and straightened the platters and plates. All corners aligned horizontally and vertically.

Before Jade could comment on her plate precision, footsteps echoed on the porch as a small gaggle of locals made their way inside.

"Welcome to the Mermaid Books. I'm Amy Pemberton. Help yourself to the snacks, and feel free to wander around."

"Hey, Amy. I'm Kelly Jamison from the Pirate Chest across the street. And I love what you've done here in such a short amount of time. This store is beautiful."

Vivian nodded and made a beeline toward the snacks. Patti breezed in and handed Amy a vase of sunflowers.

"Thank you so much. They're beautiful." Amy set the vase on the counter.

All evening, small groups of folks, including Lorelei, stopped by to welcome Amy or to get a gander at what she had done to Emory's store. Lorelei was right about the lookie-loos.

When Tish Taylor and two of her realtor friends stepped through the doorway, conversations paused as all eyes were on the fashion plates. Jade chided herself for having thoughts of the arrival of a Disney villain and her posse as the three strode in and looked around.

Claude Simpkins almost tripped over an ottoman trying to get near Tish. "Hey. It's good to see you. How are things?" he asked as he recovered from his stumble.

Ignoring him, Tish said, louder than necessary, "Hi, Amy. We stopped in to check out the competition for council and wish you the best." Her two friends, who looked like Tish's backup singers, glanced around the store and grinned.

"It's so nice of you to come," Amy said. "Make yourself at home."

"We can't stay long. We have to head over to meet some clients for some big-time negotiations. I wanted to pop in and check out your reno." Tish scanned the room. "It's definitely less cluttered in here. If you have any old books that you're getting rid of, let me know. I can always use them when I stage a home."

Amy hesitated and smiled. "Well, welcome. And yes, I wish you luck, too, for the election."

Tish paused and stared daggers. Then a cat that ate the canary smile crossed her lips. "Yes, there's that. Are you sure you really want to run? What if you can't keep the business open? Aren't you worried that you might not be able to finish your term? And it would be tragic if your business suffered because of all the time you'll have to devote to council."

Amy's eyes flashed. "Nope. I've got a plan. I can run my business and still serve the community. What about you? I thought all your time was tied up with your high-rolling deals and fancy condos. I would have thought someone as plugged in as you wouldn't have time for non-money-making tasks."

Tish continued to smile. "I can always make time for public service. I'm established in this community with thousands of contacts. And I have a strong support team. Don't you worry about me."

The two realtors behind her nodded in unison like bobbleheads. Tish pursed her lips and then continued, "Well, good luck. And may the best woman win." She turned on her heels and exited.

"Hey, there are other candidates like me," Claude yelled out the door as Tish and her entourage exited.

The muscles in Amy's jaw and neck tightened. "Claude, can I get you a refill?"

"I'm good. I need to take off, too. Bye." He adjusted his tie and hurried after Tish and her gals.

Amy smiled and mingled with the guests, who started moving toward the door. They said their goodbyes and trickled out in groups of ones and twos.

Jade picked up discarded plates and cups that seemed to be on every flat surface.

"Don't worry about that. I've got this. Thank you for all of your help. We had a good turnout. I'm hoping that my weekend events go as well."

"You got to meet a lot of folks. I hope it helps your campaign." Jade picked up her purse.

"And I got to see my true competition." Amy sighed loudly. "I'm going to still give it my all, but it may be an uphill battle. You know, new Yankee girl in town. Plus, there are a lot of candidates." She shrugged her shoulders. "We'll see what happens."

Jade hugged her friend. "Don't let Tish get to you."

"Nah. I know how to deal with mean girls. I've been snapping back at her type for years."

Jade laughed. "Southern girls snark and they can be passive-aggressive. You have to deal with them like any other bully."

"I just love the sweet lilt in the voices, especially when they say, 'bless your heart," Amy said.

"It's our way of saying, oh, he's as dumb as a bag of rocks." Jade wrinkled her nose.

Amy dissolved into a fit of giggles. "Really, they sound so sweet when they say it. I needed that. That's going to be my new favorite phrase. Stop by if you have time this weekend. Mermaid Books is under new management."

Amy followed Jade out to the porch. The sun, sinking fast behind the pine trees across the street, gave the woods an orangey glow.

"Here. This was on your porch," Jade said, handing her a padded manila envelope.

Amy tore it open and pulled out one of the infamous ransom notes. "Get out while you can. You'll be sorry." She chuckled and turned it over. When she tipped the envelope over, the voodoo doll hit the wooden decking of the porch.

Jade picked it up. It had black and purple hair and a sling wrapped around one arm.

"I guess that's supposed to be me." Amy rolled her eyes. "Not a very good likeness. Maybe, I'll set it next to the register."

Jade felt the stress returning to her shoulders. "You need to call Sheriff Driscoll. Several people around here have received them recently."

"Great. Creepy dolls, too. Just what I need. I'll call him later. See you this weekend." Amy wiggled her fingers and retreated inside the store with the doll.

Jade texted Nick the latest as she walked to the Jeep. Someone was trying to spook the locals.

Chapter Eighteen

Jade hopped out and slammed the door to her Jeep. Not wanting to be late for the special election, Jade picked up her pace. When she walked by a gray Honda, movement inside the parked car caught her eye. Amy sat in the driver's seat, talking and waving her arms around.

Jade tapped on the driver's window.

Amy jumped and squealed. Rolling down the window, she said, "I was rehearsing my speech. I didn't see you there. How are you?"

"Good. You ready?"

"Probably as ready as I'll ever be. It's show time." Amy stepped out of the rental car and grabbed her oversized black purse. She took a deep breath and held it for a few seconds. "Let's see what happens. This started out as a lark, but the more I got into it, the more I want to win. Is that bad? Plus, I'd really like to say nanny, nanny boo boo to Tish." Amy cut her eyes and then cracked a smile.

"No. You'd be a great addition to the council. And you'll be fine tonight. When I have to speak to a large group, I look at the top of their heads. It's not as scary as watching all those eyes stare back at you."

Amy smiled. "Thanks for all of your help. I got so busy this weekend with the grand reopening I didn't have time to text you and thank you for all the social media tags."

"It looked like you had a good crowd," Jade said as the pair walked toward the high school's main entrance.

"I'm pleased. I saw you pop in on Saturday. I'm sorry that I was swamped at the time and couldn't talk."

"No worries. You had your hands full. I understand the retail life. Anything unusual happen?" Jade asked.

Amy shook her head as they entered the auditorium. "Nope. No warnings, kooks, or more crazy voodoo dolls. Maybe he or she got tired or found something else to do." Amy paused and looked around. "Vivian said I needed to sit in the front row. Wish me luck."

"Break a leg." Jade waved over her shoulder and found a seat several rows behind the reserved section for the candidates.

By the time she had checked her emails and waved to friends, Vivian, Charles, and a couple of other council members had started to find seats on the stage. Charles made the introductions, and Vivian droned on too long about the rules for the speeches and the expected behavior from the audience.

Jade stifled a yawn. The first of eleven candidates approached the lectern and tried to convince the audience why she was the best fit to fill Emory's seat. Amy was the fourth to go. Her voice cracked at times, and she lost her place when she dropped her notes. Jade thought she made some good points about continuing her aunt's legacy on the town council.

Tish St. James followed Amy and approached the microphone to roaring applause. Her peach dress and matching stilettos created a look way more chic than everyone else's beachy casual.

Tish spent her allotted time talking about the community, the need for growth, and her plans for bringing Mermaid Bay into this century. Thunderous applause droned out her last few sentences. She bowed her head slightly and mouthed. "Thank you. Thank you very much," as she exited the stage with a royal wave to the crowd.

After several more candidates with similar speeches, Claude Simpkins bounded up the steps to the stage and nattered on and on about the same things Tish had emphasized. His face turned red at times, and he pounded his fist on the wooden lectern. "It is time for our community to be viable and a center of excellence. We should be a shining example to the communities around us. And just so you know, this shouldn't be a popularity contest. We need a person of substance in this role. I've lived and worked in this community for over ten years. I'm a professional." Polite applause followed him as he trotted down the steps and returned to his seat.

"Thank you, candidates," Vivian said, smiling at the audience. "Town members, please approach the four tables placed strategically throughout the room. Show your ID with your Mermaid Bay address and complete your ballot. You may vote for only one candidate. The results will be tallied this evening." She waved her arms and pointed like a flight attendant highlighting the nearby exits.

The crowd shuffled to the nearest spot and queued up to vote. Jade looked around for Amy, but she didn't see her. **Did you go home?** she texted.

Almost an hour later and no response from Amy, Vivian's voice echoed through the speakers. "Last call for voting. If you want to cast your ballot, get in line now. The counting will begin, and we'll send out an email with the results in case you don't want to stay."

Jade stayed in her seat as her neighbors trickled out the door. By nine o'clock, only a handful of people remained in the audience, including Nell. Charles and Vivian brought all of the ballot boxes to the stage and began the count.

After what felt like an eternity, Charles stood. "We have a clear winner."

Jade scooted to the edge of her seat during the uncomfortable pause.

"We'd like to congratulate Tish St. James as our newest council member," Charles said.

The handful of people left in the auditorium clapped.

"What were the totals?" Claude yelled from the edge of the stage. The remaining audience froze in place.

"We'll post all the counts in the email. But the top three were Tish St. James with 187 votes, Marco Azura with 119, and you with 84 votes."

"I want a recount," Claude bellowed. "That's too close to go with one count. I'm a CPA. I want to audit it."

"Sit down, Claude. You're one of the candidates," Vivian said.

"I don't think that will be necessary. We have a clear winner," Charles said.

"Well, I think it is necessary," Claude stomped on the stage and charged toward the town manager and Vivian. "I want to see the totals. It's within my rights. This is town government business, not some beauty pageant."

"Mr. Simpkins, I need to ask you to leave the stage," Vivian said in her best librarian voice. Her over-the-glasses glare matched the tone in her voice.

"Not until I see the numbers." Claude edged closer to the table.

Vivian planted both hands on her hips. "Claude, I'm not going to tell you again. Get off this stage now. You can make an appointment with Charles's office to review the ballots and the tallies."

Deputy Sanchez climbed the steps in two strides and stood next to the beet-red-faced Claude, who waved his arms around. "This is not fair. I'm going to talk to my lawyer."

"Mr. Simpkins, you are well within your rights to do that, and you can make an appointment with the town manager later. But you can't disrupt the meeting tonight. I suggest you go home," Deputy Sanchez said.

"I know my rights. Something is fishy here, and I want it exposed. Nell, are you getting all this?"

The reporter stood at the edge of the stage, recording the drama. "Gotcha, Claude. I'm on it."

"Mr. Simpkins." Deputy Sanchez pointed to the exit. "It's late."

"I don't agree with what transpired here. You will all hear more about this. And I won't go quietly." The vein on his neck bulged as he raised his fist in the air. "I will take any chance I can find to denounce what went on here tonight."

As the deputy took several steps toward him, he turned and scurried down the stairs and huddled with Nell. When the deputy approached them, the pair strode toward the exit.

Jade checked her phone. Still no response from Amy. **I stayed until the end. Lots of drama**. Jade texted.

I'm drowning my sorrows in ice cream with Mr. Darcy. See ya tomorrow, Amy replied.

Chapter Nineteen

Jade hit the main switch and flooded the store with thousands of twinkle lights. She smiled as she looked at her trees and decorations. The store reminded her of happy childhood memories and the magic of the holiday season. She picked up a stack of catalogs from the front counter and made her way to her office for coffee and a quick check of her social media sites. She had been watching her reviews and comments since Todd's visit. Not noticing anything out of the ordinary, she settled in with her mug to look at what was new in the ornament world for next season in the stack of catalogs. Jade tagged pages with glass ornaments in every design from ballerinas to baby animals. Then she moved on to flamingo and beach ornaments. Christmas ornaments were like potato chips to her. A few were never enough.

Neville jumped on the ledge of the Dutch door, and Chloe greeted him with several growls.

"You hungry, baby?"

Neville purred and licked his front paw.

Jade filled his food and water bowls and slipped Chloe a treat. "You already ate at home. Let Neville enjoy his breakfast in peace." She scooped up the little dog, who was still licking her lips after her peanut butter-flavored morsel.

Her phone binged with a text from Amy. **Can you do lunch today? My treat.**

12:30?

Perfect. I'll get boxed lunches. Ham? Chicken Salad?

Ham's great. Thanks! Jade tapped into her phone.

Can we meet at my place? Don't have staff today, Amy replied.

Jade responded with a few smiley faces, and a pig emoji as Patti breezed in a few minutes later, bringing her infectious laugh with her. "Morning, all. What a glorious day."

"How are you doing? I love your pink and white Christmas sweater." Patti must have a closet full of holiday outfits. Today's sweater, pale pink covered in white snowflakes, reminded Jade of Cindy Loo Who.

"Thanks. I try to buy some in colors other than red and green when I can find them. Gotta mix it up." Patti headed for the coffee maker. "Anything exciting going on?"

"Nope. Just the town council election."

"Oh, dear. I left after I voted, but I heard there was a little dustup." Patti pulled out a mug and waited for her tea. "It was all over Facebook this morning. I heard that hunky deputy had to calm Claude down."

Jade nodded. "Claude was definitely upset. Hopefully, he had time to think things over."

Patti raised one eyebrow. "He carries a grudge. We'll see what happens. I'm sure Emory's turning over in her grave knowing that Tish replaced her."

"She won't like that all of her preservation work isn't taken seriously," Jade added.

"I'm all for change, especially if it's an improvement. But I hope Mermaid Bay doesn't shift to massive condos and hotels that block the view. That's not who we are." She blew out a long breath that fluttered her blond bangs. "We'll have to see how things go. Sorry that Amy didn't win. Emory would have liked that."

"I'm going to meet her for lunch. I'll see how she's doing. I'm sure she has her hands full with the store."

"Totally amazing. It's my new favorite spot, besides 'Tis the Season, of course. She's going to do well. I'm trying to set up something with my book club there." The bells on the front door interrupted their conversation, and Patti hustled to the lobby.

Jade placed several ornament orders to refresh the inventory and filled the requests that had come in since yesterday.

"Here," she said, putting two plastic bins of packages behind the counter. "For Simon." Jade dusted her hands on her jeans and winked.

Patti's face turned a rosy pink. Her grin showed her dimples. "I do look forward to his visits."

"I'm going to head over to the bookstore. Do you want me to bring lunch back for you?" Jade asked.

"I'm good. I brought a salad."

"Be back in a flash." Jade picked up her purse and headed out the door. She wandered down the sidewalk and soaked up the summer sun and the ocean breeze that had a slightly salty taste. Another perfect beach day.

A blast of AC greeted Jade at the bookstore's front door. Inside, families and beachgoers browsed the shelves and filled the reading nooks.

"Looks like you've got quite a crowd." Jade stepped closer to the counter.

"It's been hopping all day. If this keeps up, I may have to add another part-timer, or I'm going to be exhausted. Pull up a stool. I hope you don't mind eating here, but it's way busier than I expected." Amy disappeared in the back.

She returned a few seconds later with box lunches and two bottles of water.

Jade dug into her box that had a ham sandwich, pasta salad, cheese crackers, and a gourmet white chocolate cookie. "Yum. Thanks for lunch. How are things going? All work?"

Amy nodded and took a bite of her chicken salad on a croissant. After a swig of water, Amy said, "Mostly. I've had some time to go through Emory's stuff at night. I decided not to sulk about town council. I'll use my time to build relationships. I called the sheriff. He didn't have any updates on Emory's murder, and he let me keep the voodoo doll, a weird little souvenir." Her voice trailed off as she looked around to see if any customers were nearby.

"No updates on the autopsy?" Jade wiped her mouth with the Busy Bean napkin.

"Nope. Not that he mentioned. It's still an open case. It feels like it's going nowhere. I'll keep following up. This is frustrating, and I'm constantly looking over my shoulder. I hate being paranoid. So that's why I've been combing through her stuff to see if there is anything that might have led to her death."

"Any luck?" Jade asked.

Amy shook her head and took another swig of her water. "I've been over and over her business files. She was in the red with sales. Her business was on the brink. I'm hoping to turn that around. I've launched social media sites for the store. If you get a minute, follow me. I followed all your sites and used them to get ideas for posts. I hope you don't mind me copycatting."

"Not at all. It's called inspiration. Maybe we can work on some ideas to cross-pollinate our customer base. I'm sure it overlaps some of the demographics."

"I appreciate all of your help. I want to feature you in an upcoming newsletter. Could you do a little piece on bookish Christmas ornaments or decorations?"

"I'd be glad to," Jade said. "I've got some cute ones in the store. I'll put something together for you."

"I'm thinking it should go out either end of summer or fall in time for those early bird holiday shoppers. Can you have it done by August?"

"I'll get you something by next week." Jade balled up her napkins and put her trash in the box.

"I have another favor. If it's not too much. It's back to Emory. I found a bunch of folders of stuff related to other business owners. Nothing jumped out at me. Do you think you could take a look and let me know if any of it looks hinky to you? If it's weird, I can take it to the sheriff."

"Sure. That's no problem."

"You say that now." Amy disappeared in the back again and returned with a plastic crate full of manila files.

"If you don't have time, I understand. I have this nagging feeling that there has got to be something in one of these folders. Some encounter. Some deal. Some relationship gone bad that caused her death. It's kind of my quest lately. I need to know what she'd gotten herself into. Maybe if it's bad, I need to follow Tish's advice and get out while I can still sell this place." Amy closed her eyes for a moment.

"You're really thinking of selling?" Jade asked.

"No. I want to make a go of this. I love it here. But I keep hearing Tish's nagging voice in the back of my head, telling me not to put too much effort into something that's going to fail. She said I should be practical."

"Don't let her get to you. She always does a hard sales job on folks. I guess that's why she's so successful with her deals. Lately, she's been selling luxury condos in nearby communities."

"I've seen her smiling face on a lot of signs. I did an online search, and she's got a bunch of little cottages for sale. They don't stay on the market long. I was thinking that I might want to move out of the apartment someday. I could either rent it out or turn it into more retail space. Anyway, she and her team have beaucoup listings. Maybe she could help me even if she did beat me out for the council spot."

"She has a spidery network of contacts. Tish has always been involved in everything for as long as I've known her. But don't let her get to you. I'll be glad to take a look at these and see what I can find." Jade picked up the box and her water bottle.

"You're the best." Amy hugged her friend. "I'll recycle those. Just leave 'em here."

A woman with two small children hiding behind her dropped a stack of books on the counter. "We went a little crazy, but I'm not going to discourage them if they want to read." She pulled out her credit card and offered it to Amy, who scanned the stack of picture books.

"Thanks so much. Here you go." Amy handed the woman her card and a shopping bag full of her purchases. "And if you have a few minutes, you may want to check out 'Tis the Season across the street. The Christmas displays are magical."

"Thanks. Sounds like an adventure. We'll be back next week." The woman turned, and her two children followed her like ducklings out the door.

"I've got to be getting back, too. Patti will need a break. I'll let you know what I find in these." Jade hoisted the crate up.

"Thank you. Thank you. Thank you," Amy yelled behind her. "I know you'll spot something I missed."

Jade schlepped the crate back to the store. It was heavier than it appeared, and her arms started to cramp as she got to the back door of her store. Balancing the crate on one hip, she punched in the code and turned the knob.

Chloe danced on the other side of the door. "Hey, puppy. I'm back. Miss me?"

Jade slid the crate under her desk and picked up the little French bulldog. "I wasn't gone that long." Chloe's pink tongue licked Jade's nose. "And thanks for the greeting."

She picked up several of Amy's files and popped her head through the doorway. "Everything going okay?"

Patti smiled. "Lots of customers. And Neville entertained a family of kids. We're low on some popular ornaments. I made a list. Everybody's buying pet ornaments and beach ones. Oh, I sold five or six of the college-themed ones, too."

"Thanks. Do you want a break for lunch?"

"I ate my salad earlier. Neville tried to scam part of it, but he wasn't interested when he saw what it was. I may take a few minutes and walk up and down the block."

"Enjoy. It's beautiful out there." Jade plopped down on the stool behind the counter and flipped through the first file.

She had skimmed the items in three folders by the time Patti reclaimed the front counter. Jade read the current file as she walked to her desk to pour over the rest of the folders. Jotting anything interesting in a notebook, she tagged the original with a paperclip. Most of what she had thumbed through were business council events or old calendars for the bookstore. Emory had dedicated many hours over the years to council projects.

Patti bustled in with the bank bag and a folder a little after four. "Here are the receipts and everything from the register. Do you need me to do anything else before I head to the gym?"

"No. Thanks for closing out. I'll lock everything up. See you on Thursday."

Chloe followed Jade through the store as she set the alarm and turned off the lights. She double-checked all the doors and Neville's bowls. "Come on, puppy. Let's head out. Neville, we're going home." The cat had trotted off to one of the display rooms.

She juggled her purse, Chloe's leash, and Amy's bin of files. Maybe she'd uncover something besides event planning if she kept poking through the folders. Was Emory's death random, or did it really have something to do with Mermaid Bay?

Chapter Twenty

fter dinner, Jade changed into her jammies and settled in to binge watch *Sherlock* and peruse the contents of Amy's files. Maybe channeling one of the greatest detectives would provide some luck, but it would be helpful if she had known what needle she was looking for in this file stack.

Two episodes and ten folders later, Jade hadn't made any progress. She padded to the kitchen for a glass of water and some grapes.

When she plopped down on the couch, Chloe curled up beside her. "Hey girl. I'm beginning to think this is a useless effort. I'm not finding anything. Maybe it's why Nick's team is having a hard time, too. Could it have just been a random killing?"

Chloe opened one eye and turned her head.

"Who knows. We'll keep going. I've invested a bunch of time already. What's a few more folders and one more episode with Benedict Cumberbatch?" Jade settled back on the couch and started looking through a set of folders full of book distributor information.

She didn't glean anything from Emory's inventory except one overdue payment that caused a distributor to require her to make a reserve payment in advance to continue to get shipments, and there were no accounting issues she could find. Jade didn't see anything else that was glaringly out of order.

Just as she was wrapping up for the evening, she spotted a green folder stuck between two manila ones. She pulled it out. Copies of emails were stuffed randomly inside. It took about twenty minutes to lay all the pages out and order them according to the conversations. Jade read through each.

They were chains between Emory and Claude, the CPA, and Tish, the realtor. The gist was Tish and Jared, the developer, were trying hard to get her to sell the building that housed the bookstore and the coffee shop. In the early conversations, Emory was adamant about not selling. About midway through the stack, her tone changed. Not sure what caused her to do a one-eighty-degree switch, but there were copies of a conversation with Claude about the possibility of selling. He was adamant that it would be a quick process. The CPA bloviated about how she should think of retiring because of her age. He egged Emory on about selling the property while she could still get a good price, and he hinted that something big was coming.

A tingly feeling of curiosity spurred her to read on to see what this big thing was.

An hour later, Jade yawned and stretched. No hint at what the impending thing was. But by the end of the stack, it looked like Emory and Claude had reached some kind of agreement that either he or his investors would buy her property. Claude wanted to keep it a secret for as long as possible, and he didn't want Tish to know. *That was definitely a switch.*

As she adjusted the folders in the bin, a scrunched piece of paper caught her eye. Another partial email chain. Jade flattened it out on her coffee table. This time Tish presented her case to Emory to represent the property. The realtor listed a bunch of scary examples of people who tried to cut deals without professional help. She stuffed it in the front of the green folder and would let Amy know about it in the morning after a good dose of caffeine.

Jade drove the Jeep to work. She didn't have the energy to lug Amy's files back after a restless night of tossing and turning. Emory's emails kept popping in her head. Did this have something to do with her death?

Leaving the crate in the back, Jade helped Chloe out. The French bulldog trotted to the back door and waited on the top step.

Neville greeted them, and the cat and dog chase around the workroom rivaled any on-track action of NASCAR. Jade busied herself with opening the store and checking food and water bowls. Needing additional caffeine to fortify her for the morning, she rummaged through the drawer for a pod.

While the coffee maker chugged to life, she printed the order inventory from last evening. Four pages. A new record.

Doing some chair yoga after filling orders and packing the shipping envelopes, she looked up as Lorelei waltzed in the front door.

"Wow. Is all of that outgoing? That is amazing." Her aunt put her yellow Kate Spade clutch under the front counter.

"A new record. When you get settled, I'm going to run over to the bookstore to drop off some files, and I was going to Hot Diggity Dogs. Want me to bring you anything?" Jade asked.

"As much as I would love it, Steve and I are going out for seafood tonight, so I'll be good and eat my cottage cheese for lunch."

Chloe's ears perked up at the mention of food.

Lorelei scratched the dog's head. "Of course, I'll save you a bite. Anything I should know about?"

"Traffic's been slow today. Maybe it'll pick up after lunch." Jade fiddled with a button on her blouse. "Did you and Emory talk often?"

"Not really. We had coffee every couple of months. Why?"

"Did she ever indicate that she wanted to retire or sell her property?" Jade asked.

A frown crossed Lorelei's face. "No. She was always on the warpath about keeping Mermaid Bay the way it was. She had some strong opinions about developers and shopping malls. I thought she'd be a fixture here forever. Why?"

"Just curious. I thought I heard someone mention that she was planning to sell the store."

"Nope. She never said anything like that to me."

"Interesting. I'm going to head out. I'll be back," Jade said.

"Okay, Terminator. Neville, Chloe, and I will hang out."

Jade drove a few yards down Neptune Road and found a spot in Amy's empty lot. Hauling the crate out of the back, she trudged up the stairs and did a balancing act to get the heavy door open.

"Hey, Amy. You here?" Jade yelled through the empty store.

Mr. Darcy meowed his greeting from the front counter.

Setting the crate beside the cat, Jade said, "Hey, kitty cat. Where's the boss?"

"He's the boss, or at least he thinks he is," Amy said, drifting in from the back hallway.

"I brought back your files. Most of it's what you said. I did find a file of emails crammed in the back. Did you go through these?" Jade waved the green folder.

"I don't think so. I was skimming files. I got through about the first twenty or so. What did you find?"

"It looks like Emory printed out a chain of email conversations about retiring and selling her property. She had one convo with Claude and another with Tish."

"Interesting. Wait. I found her day planner in the bottom of her desk the other day. I wonder if anything jives with the emails. Be right back."

Jade spread the papers on the front counter.

Amy rushed back. "What's the earliest date?"

"The ones with Claude started almost two years ago in August."

Amy flipped through the book. "It's a three-year planner. So maybe we're in luck. Let's see. She had lunch with Claude a couple of times that August. And then there was coffee with Lorelei. That's it for the whole month."

"Anything with Tish?" Jade asked.

Amy shook her head. "Oh, wait. I flipped ahead to October. Right around last Halloween, Tish is penciled in once for drinks and once for dinner. As I flip forward, most of the things involved Tish through the spring months. I don't see anything else with Claude."

"Hmm. The dates seem to jive. I think Nick needs to see these," Jade said.

"It'll give me a reason to stop by and talk to him. I call him every week, and he never has much of an update. Maybe this will help with the investigation. Lisa's working the evening shift, so I'll see if I can swing by when she's covering the store. It's been dead here all day. I was hoping that the excitement from my weekend events would carry over, but it seemed to fizzle."

"Foot traffic was quiet at my place today, too. Have you eaten yet?"

Amy nodded. "A power bar and a salad. Thanks for going through the folders. This was the last place to search Emory's store stuff. I'm running out of ideas."

"Let me know what Nick says." Jade headed out the door. Driving another two hundred yards to the hot dog stand seemed silly, so she walked over and soaked up some of the early afternoon sun.

With no line, she zipped in the door of the red and yellow building. Todd and two teens worked the front counter and the walk-up window.

"Hey, Jade. What can I do for you?"

"Where's everybody?" Jade looked over her shoulder at the empty restaurant.

He smiled a half-smile. "Too quiet. Not sure what's going on. What can I get you?"

"Let's have the number four special with just mustard and an iced tea."

"Sounds good. I'll have it up in a minute. Grab a bag of chips, and I'll bring it out to you."

Jade handed him a ten-dollar bill and dropped the change in the empty tip cup by the register. "Thanks. I think I'm going to soak up some rays on your deck."

Wandering outside, she claimed a table in the corner of the empty deck. Small waves rolled toward the sand. A nice breeze rustled her hair and kept the summer temperatures at bay. She shielded her eyes with her hand and glanced up and down the beach. There wasn't an inch of unoccupied sand as far as she could see.

She hoped today was a fluke with customer traffic. Definitely something to keep an eye on.

The wooden screen door creaked. Todd hustled out with her lunch. "Want some company?" He plopped down in the seat across from her with a drink.

"How are the reviews going?" she asked, taking a sip of her iced tea. "Any better?"

His grin faded. "The blast of bad reviews has slowed down to a trickle. My friend has been monitoring it from the weird corners of the dark web. If she finds anything, I'll report it. But I'm concerned that the damage is already done. It's all taking a toll on my business."

"Have you thought about doing some counter posts? Maybe testimonials or quick videos. Not sure it will help, but if you get a positive response, maybe it'll push the other stuff down in the search results. And people don't usually spend a lot of time on pages three and four of the results." Jade took a bite of her hot dog.

"It may be worth a shot. I'm toying with the idea of posting about being under attack. Maybe there's a sympathy vote out there? Not sure if it will make things better or worse. From what I've read online, the experts recommend addressing the issue publicly from a customer service standpoint and not engaging in social media wars. I'm willing to try anything. I just can't spring for a publicist right now."

"Hmmm. Maybe a good news campaign would work. I'll be glad to share and post comments. Anything to help. Any other ominous warnings?"

"The bad reviews are enough." Todd let out a long sigh. "Not sure who I ticked off. And that doesn't even cover the bad publicity of having a dead body found by my dumpster. Now the customers who do show up want to see the crime scene."

Jade patted his arm. "I know it doesn't feel like it. But you will get through this." Jade pulled out her phone and did a quick review of her lunch for Todd.

"And the timing during the middle of tourist season couldn't be worse. That's where I'm supposed to have a surplus of funds to carry me through the rest of the year." Todd slurped his drink. "The last two years were break-even. I was hoping this would be an outstanding year." He rested his elbows on the scarred picnic table. "Maybe I should look at selling. Just not sure what to do. I've worked here all my life."

"If you can, finish out the season before you make any big decisions. Labor Day weekend might be a boon with all the activities planned."

"I don't get it. This is a little hot dog shack on the beach. I make enough to live the life I want. It's not like this is a multi-million-dollar operation that's threatening other businesses."

"If I were you, I'd focus on flooding your social media sites with your story.

And get friends and employees to help spread the buzz. At least there will be counter-programming out there, and you don't specifically have to admit to being targeted." Jade finished her hotdog and folded the edge of the chip bag down.

"Maybe you're right. I'm going to talk to my friend Delia later to see if she has any ideas about pushing the bad reviews down in the search results. Thanks, Jade. You're always helpful." Todd rose and picked up her trash.

Jade waved goodbye and hiked around the building. Her lime-green Jeep sat alone in Amy's parking lot.

Chapter Twenty-One

After her conversation with Todd dampened her mood, Jade headed back to the office and dabbled with her own social media posts. Thankfully, 'Tis the Season didn't have any negative comments. She posted a five-star review of her lunch at Todd's on several more sites. On a whim, she picked up her phone and texted Nick. **Wanna have dinner sometime this week?**

A few minutes later, he responded, **Tonight? How bout the new pub in Seaport? You cooked last time.**

Knowing she'd have to eat more hotdogs than she wanted to in one week, Jade replied, **How about somewhere here in MB?**

Not a big selection, but ok. Pick you up around 6.

She replied with a string of hotdogs and thumbs up emojis. Todd needed all the support he could get, even if it meant she had to have hotdogs again.

"Uh, Jade, you might want to see this," Lorelei yelled from the front of the store.

Jade followed her aunt's voice to the window where a tour bus pulled up in the front lot. "Wow. Our afternoon got a little bit more exciting." She slid behind the counter, ready to welcome the new guests.

After an hour and a half of constant questions and ringing up purchases, Jade collapsed on the barstool behind the register as the tour guide shooed the rest of her charges out to the front porch.

"That was fun," Lorelei said. "I'm definitely ready for a quiet night tonight."

"Totally unexpected, but I'll take it. I'm going to do a walk-through the store to make sure everything's where it's supposed to be."

"I'll do the day's tally and leave it on your desk," her aunt said, pulling on her reading glasses.

As Jade packed her things, Lorelei breezed in the back and hovered near Jade's desk. She stood there for a bit without saying anything.

"Everything okay? Cat got your tongue?" Jade asked.

"Sort of. I have a favor to ask."

"Sure. What is it?" Jade watched her aunt, who was rarely at a loss for words.

"I'm by myself a lot. I was wondering if you would mind if I take Neville home at night and on weekends. I know he was your grandma's cat. I just thought he and I would enjoy each other's company."

"That sounds wonderful." She rose and hugged her aunt. "We tried it at our house for a few days, but he and Chloe decided they were mortal enemies. I brought him back here because Grandma had him as the store's mouser. I think it would be great for you to take him home."

"We've bonded lately, and he likes to snuggle."

Jade smiled. "He and I have an understanding. He's in charge as long as he doesn't trash the place. I tried to cuddle a couple of times, and he would have none of it. I'm glad you guys get along. His box is under the sink if you want to use it for travel. He's not very fond of it, and I need welders' gloves when I try to convince him to go in."

"Neville and I will be just fine. He and I are going to hang out." Her aunt beamed when she talked about Neville.

"He is a lucky cat. He has a job and a new home."

Lorelei drifted through the store in search of Neville. She whistled, and Chloe traipsed after her. "Neville. Neville, honey. Let's go home."

Jade was shocked when the cat popped out from under the teddy bear tree and waltzed over to Lorelei. *He did know how lucky he was.*

Lorelei scooped up Neville and her purse. "We're headed to the pet store to stock up. We'll see you tomorrow. Ciao."

"Come on, Chloe. Let's wrap things up here. We have to meet Nick in a bit."

After turning off all the lights and rechecking the doors, Jade and Chloe headed home.

Inside her bungalow, Chloe journeyed to the couch and Jade to her closet. She wanted to find something fun and casual. She and Nick had been friends forever, but lately, she had been getting butterflies. She liked hanging out with him, but she wanted to find out if she was just the gal pal or if there was a chance for more. Maybe tonight was a real date? If not, at least it was a chance to find out more about his investigation.

A knock at the door interrupted Jade's last-minute primping. Chloe beat her to the front door.

When she opened the door, Nick bent over to greet the little dog.

"Hey. You look nice," he said, straightening up.

"You, too. Hungry?" Jade picked up her purse.

"Yup. Ate lunch in my squad car today. Busy Bean or Hot Diggity Dogs?"

"Both have a deck, and it's a nice evening." Jade smiled and tucked a loose curl behind her ear.

"Let's go for hotdogs," he said, holding the door for her. "The portions are bigger and not as frou-frou."

They walked down the path to the beach. Gulls darted in and out of the surf. A freighter steamed by, and several catamarans bobbed in the waves.

"How's life in your world?" Jade asked, kicking off her sandals. She picked them up and walked in the warm sand.

"Busy. But I guess that's good. I always get suspicious when it's too quiet."

"Anything new about Emory?" Jade asked.

A slight frown crossed his face. "The autopsy was what we expected. They're doing some more toxicology tests. We'll do some kind of press release when those come back. We know she wasn't killed behind Todd's place."

"Did Amy reach out to you?" Jade asked.

"We've been playing phone tag. What's up?" Nick looked out at the bay.

"She brought over some of Emory's files. I don't want to steal her thunder."

Nick stopped and stared at her. "It's okay. She said she had some stuff she wanted me to take a look at. You saw them?"

Jade nodded. "She's still new and wanted me to see if anything looked out of place because I've lived here a while. I guess I'm a dinosaur."

He laughed. "And?" he asked, turning to face her.

"There were a lot of files on the bookstore and its finances. There were also some emails about selling and not selling her building." She paused to slip her shoes back on.

He raised one eyebrow as they climbed the sandy steps to the restaurant's deck. He held the door for her, and she ducked under his arm.

Jade stared at the chalkboard menu that hadn't changed that much in the last few years, and especially not since lunch. Nick stood behind her, and she got a whiff of his spicy cologne. More butterflies.

When it was their turn at the counter, Todd said, "Hey, guys. It's good to see you. It's been a while, Nick, but it's probably good that I haven't had to call you recently. And Jade, long time no see since lunch. What can I get y'all?"

Nick gave Jade a sideways glance. She tried to telepathically let him know with a slight frown that she'd explain her sudden fondness for hotdogs when Todd wasn't around.

Jade chewed on her top lip. Before they could reply, a crash echoed through the restaurant's small counter area, and the front window exploded into hundreds of shards all over the floor.

Jade stifled a squeal and covered her face. When Nick moved, she raced to the door behind him. He looked up and down the sidewalk and sprinted off.

On a whim, Jade ran down the sidewalk in the opposite direction. There were a few people strolling by. A thin man across the street let out a long whistle and pointed toward her store. He yelled, "A guy in jeans and a hoodie ran that way."

Jade nodded and jogged down the street, dodging tourists. She caught a glimpse of someone darting through the parking lot toward her store. Pouring on the speed, she dodged a car and a bicycle as she crossed the street. A stocky man in jeans and a gray hoodie jumped in a black SUV with racks on the front and top that made the vehicle look like it was ready for the outback. Jade snapped several pictures with her phone as he zoomed down a cross street.

She caught her breath as she scanned through the photos. She captured one side of his face and another of part of his license plate. She hoped Nick's guys could find out something from the partial plate.

Jade returned to the restaurant, where a small crowd had gathered on the sidewalk. A squad car approached with lights and sirens flashing. Sebastian hopped out, and she followed him inside.

Nick nodded at his deputy while Todd and his young employees stood behind the counter, shellshocked.

"Sorry to interrupt, but I got some photos of the guy," Jade said, waving her phone. Broken glass crunched under her feet.

Nick stifled a surprised look and took her phone. He handed it to Sebastian, who clicked his shoulder mic and updated dispatch. When he finished, he asked, "Which way?"

"His SUV was parked in my side lot. I saw him drive off down Tortuga Avenue," she replied.

"I'm going to send these to myself," Sebastian said, tapping on Jade's phone before she could reply.

"Did you get a good look at him?" Nick asked.

"Not really. The odd thing was that he was wearing a zipped-up gray hoodie in the heat of summer. Tallish and kind of muscular with brown hair. Or at least his bangs were brown. It was hard to tell because he had the hood up," Jade said.

Sebastian finished his update and pulled out his notebook. He moved toward the counter and talked to Todd and his crew in low tones.

"You okay? I didn't know where you went." Nick said, resting his hand on her shoulder.

"I'm fine. It startled me when the window came crashing down. Is everyone okay?" Jade asked.

Nick nodded. "It looks like our perp threw a weight through the window."

Jade looked at the round, silver thing lying in the pile of glass shards. "That could have killed someone if it had hit them. And to be crazy enough to do it in broad daylight with customers in the store."

"No one said that bad guys were always the smartest. Maybe he was trying to send a message," Sebastian said.

"We were lucky that no one was standing close to the window," Nick said.

Sebastian took photos of the window from all angles while Nick made call after call.

Jade gingerly stepped over the glass and leaned on the counter.

"Hey, you want a drink or something?" Todd asked. "You never did get your dinner."

"I'm good. Thanks. I'm sorry about your window. You recognize this guy?" Jade held up her phone for Todd to see. His workers peered over his shoulder.

The blond with long straight hair said, "That kinda looks like Vince. Vince Zimmers. He hangs out at some of the bars in Seaport."

"Yep, it might be him. If I could see his tats, I could identify him for sure," the brunette with the ponytail replied. "If he's not at the bars showing off his bike, then he's at the gym."

"Interesting." Jade did a quick search, and a bunch of photos of a muscle-bound guy posing with girls in bikinis or with his motorcycle popped up on her screen. "Him?" She held the phone up again.

Both girls nodded. "He doesn't hang around Mermaid Bay too much. It's too tame for him," the brunette replied. "Why would he break our window?"

Todd shook his head. "I have no idea. I don't think I've ever seen him in here before."

Nick sauntered over. "We're waiting on the forensic team to get here and do their thing. Do you have something to secure this with when they're done?"

"Not a problem," Todd said. "I always have plywood for hurricane season. Be back in a sec. Carlie, do you mind helping me?"

"Sure," the brunette said, following her boss out the back exit.

"I'm going to be here for some time. I hate to mess up your evening. Raincheck on dinner?"

"Not a problem. Anything I can do?" Jade asked.

"Nah. I'll swing by and get my truck when we're done here."

"Give me your keys. I'll go get it," Jade said.

"You don't have to," he said.

"I won't hurt your baby," she grinned. "Plus, it'll be late by the time you get out of here."

He tossed her the keys. "Thanks.

Jade picked her way over the glass and exited out the back. She made the roundtrip truck delivery in a flat fifteen minutes. His gigantic truck was fun to drive, and she resisted the urge to poke through his glove compartment and center console.

Chapter Twenty-Two

Jade fidgeted all morning and tried to busy herself with store tasks. When she couldn't concentrate, she returned to her social media search for Vince Zimmers. She thumbed through hundreds of pictures of him, his muscles, and his motorcycle. Not finding any with the black SUV, she made a list of his friends and the places in his pictures, mostly beach bars.

A little before ten, Patti flitted in, wearing her lime green Christmas sweater and black leggings. "Howdy! How's everyone on this gorgeous summer day?"

"Just dandy. I like the sweater." Jade shook off the ominous feelings about the recent happenings and tried to focus on the positive.

"I found this company on Facebook that has them in all colors. I figure I'll be set for all year. I have way too many in green and red in my closet." Patti pulled a mug from the cabinet and turned on the coffee maker. "All quiet here?"

"So far. But the last time I said that, a tour bus pulled up."

Patti's laughter made Chloe's ears perk up. When the dog didn't spot any snacks, she rolled over to return to her nap.

"I'm going to run out for an errand when you get settled. Will you be okay by yourself for about an hour?" Jade asked.

"No problemo. Chloe and Neville will keep me company. Maybe we'll have a team meeting."

"Oh, I forgot to mention, Lorelei asked if she could take Neville home. So don't panic if you don't see him around today. I'm sure he's lounging around her condo this afternoon."

"Awww. They make a great pair. I think that's a fantastic idea. As soon as this brews, I'm going to check the inventory for you. Some of the toy room items need to be restocked."

"Thanks. I filled the online orders. I pulled a lot of the bears and college-themed ones for this order. They're in the bins waiting for your Simon."

Patti's face flushed several shades of pink. "The highlight of my day. Keep those online orders coming."

Jade winked and picked up her Vince notes, and stuffed them in a folder. "Be back in a few."

She cruised toward the outskirts of Seaport in search of the Sweat Shop. After missing her turn, she looped back to a 1970s strip mall. The gym occupied the large space in the middle where a grocery store probably had been in a past life.

Jade waltzed in the front door. "Can I help you?" a buff doppelganger of Lou Ferrigno asked. Jade was definitely having 70s flashbacks today. Too many Nick at Night reruns.

"Good morning. I'm looking for a gym, and I was kinda hoping to look around and maybe get a tour?"

Most of the clientele were men on weight machines. A few women walked on treadmills or marched on ellipticals. At first glance, she didn't spot anyone who looked like Vince. She checked the photo on her phone for a refresher.

"I'm the only one here right now, so I can't give you a tour. But if you'd like to walk around, suit yourself. We have lots of classes and personal trainers for gals like you who want to lose a few pounds."

A real charmer. That's definitely the way to motivate me to buy a membership. "Thanks. I'll be back if I have any questions."

Jade walked through what looked like acres of exercise equipment. Besides a few treadmills and stationary bikes, most of it looked like medieval torture devices. Jade covered her nose to block out the sweaty smell that hung in the air. Moving toward the back, there were dozens of benches and shelves with all kinds of weights and barbells. Every flat spot on the wall seemed to sport a TV, most tuned to ESPN or some other sports channel. *I wonder if Nick's guys could link the weight that broke the window to this place?*

Two racquetball courts and an exercise room filled the back corner. Jade did a slow circuit of the facility, and then she retraced her steps and walked through in the opposite direction. She got a couple of winks and waves along her trek. No sign of anyone who looked like Vince.

"See anything you like? If you want to, I can give you a guest pass," the bodybuilder at the front desk said when she returned.

"It's really big. And there's a lot of equipment. I would definitely need someone to help me," Jade said, batting her eyelashes.

"We have personal trainers." He pushed several sheets of copy paper toward her. "Here are our packages."

"Sounds good. My friends and I were talking with this guy we met at the beach, and he mentioned how great this place was. So, I stopped in to check it out." Jade pretended to read the handouts.

"What's his name? We have a referral program. He'll get a discount if you join."

"Uh, we just met him. Vince, maybe."

"Big guy with brown hair and lots of tattoos?"

"Sounds like him. He was wearing a hoodie. He recommended this place. And he talks a lot about his motorcycle."

"He's here a lot. I haven't seen him today. He usually comes in late afternoons. Not a morning person." The phone rang, and the guy reached to answer it.

Jade used the distraction to slip out the door. Two rows from her vehicle, she passed a guy with a black gym bag slung over his shoulder. She stared for a moment, and when his return stare bore through her, bats awakened in her stomach. Without having to double-check the photo on her phone, she knew it was Vince.

His smile looked like a leer. She continued walking to her Jeep. Stalling to give him time to go inside, she meandered around the parking lot through several rows of cars.

By the time she looked back, Vince had disappeared through the glass doors into the gym. Relieved, she dashed toward her Jeep. In the spot in front of hers was a tricked-out SUV. She froze and let out a mew sound. *That's the vehicle.* Jagged gashes and red paint, and mud smears dotted the metal grill guard. Looking over her shoulder and not noticing anyone watching, she snapped a quick series of photos and then jumped into her Wrangler. She didn't exhale until the door locks clicked.

Did he recognize her? The whole encounter was scary. And why was he so interested in Mermaid Bay?

Too hyped up to eat lunch, she grabbed two iced coffees from a nearby drive-thru and headed back to the store. There had to be a connection between Vince and Todd.

Back at the store, Jade patted Chloe on the head and handed Patti an iced coffee. "I didn't do lunch, but caffeine and sugar seemed in order for the afternoon."

"Thanks for the great treat. I finished my salad, so I can splurge a little. I updated the inventory spreadsheet on what we're low on and restocked with what we had on hand. I also filled the online orders that popped in since this morning. It's been pretty quiet except the dance-off Chloe and I had back here."

Jade smiled as she settled in at her desk. She Googled Vince again, only to find more pictures of him posing for the camera. From his tags, he frequented the gym, several bars, and a Harley Davidson store. No indication that he had a job. When she searched for him on the online White Pages, his name was linked to a Margie and Jimmy Zimmers. Scribbling down the address, she plugged it into Google Maps.

The street view showed a brick rancher with a detached garage in Yorktown. She found a site for local property searches and typed in the address. "Bingo. There you are," she said. The address showed the owner as Marjory Hilman Zimmers. On the previous property owners' section, it showed a James and Marjory, but his name disappeared after 2010. "So, you live with your mother."

"Who lives with his mother?" Patti asked as she stuck her head in over the Dutch door.

"This guy that broke Todd's window last night."

"Oh, I heard about that. What is going on around here? We're having a regular crime spree. Oh, by the way, there are two buses in the parking lot."

"What?" Jade jumped up. "This is awesome. We could be in for a big day. I need to send these tour companies a big thank you."

"Let's get this party started," Patti said as they headed to the front room to greet their guests.

"Two buses of senior citizens from New Jersey," Patti said. "Wow! They kept us hoppin'."

"I'm exhausted. But it was fun." Jade plopped down on the stool.

"And profitable. Let me run the totals. We may need to expedite our restocking order from this morning," Patti said.

"Thanks. And if you want to hit the road after that, you deserve it. You are in your element with our customers."

Patti giggled. "It's the best job in the world. Who else besides Mr. and Mrs. Claus gets to have this much fun?" She collected the long receipt that spiraled from the register and handed it to Jade.

She whistled. "Not bad. I'm sending the tour company a thank you. Hopefully, they'll add us to all of their tour schedules. I'm going to close up and put in our order before I leave."

"I'll see you on Saturday." Patti disappeared out the front door.

"Come on, Chloe. We have a little bit more to do, and then we'll go for a ride." The little dog's ears perked up. Jade Googled security cameras and found a low-maintenance system. "It's also time to add some of these. I'll call Bernie to do his magic when they come in."

After placing all the orders to refresh the inventory and checking the doors and the alarm, Jade and Chloe headed outside. She drove slowly out of Mermaid Bay and stopped at the Circle K near the highway. Scooping up Chloe like a football, she trekked into the store for an iced tea and a disposable phone. She wanted to find out more about Vince Zimmers, but she needed a way that couldn't be traced to her, especially if he was as dangerous as he appeared. The look he'd given her in the parking lot of the gym gave her the creeps.

Jade paid cash for her purchase and hurried out of the store before she lost her nerve. After taking a couple of deep breaths to calm down, she did a drive-thru run for a salad and headed home.

Back at their kitchen table, Jade spread out her notes and pulled out the burner phone. She plugged it in to get a quick charge as she decided what she wanted to do. On a whim, she called Amy.

"Hey, you. What's up?" Amy asked.

"How are you feeling?"

"Back to normal," Amy said. "I'm getting ready to close up and head upstairs. You have big plans?"

"Nope. Just poking around to see what I can find out about all the craziness going on around here."

"Anything new?"

"Maybe. Wanna come over? I can catch you up," Jade said.

"I'll get a pizza and be there in an hour or so. Do you have any wine? Or dessert?" Amy asked.

"Uh. I have wine, beer, and soft drinks. Do Oreos count as dessert?"

"Yes. Yes, they do. See ya in a bit." Amy clicked off.

Jade wrapped up her salad for lunch tomorrow. "You could help me straighten up here, you know." The little dog raised one eyebrow and decided to stay in her bed.

When the doorbell rang, Chloe moved into full attack mode until she smelled the pizza. Then she was Amy's new best friend.

"Come on in. Let me get that." Jade took the pizza box and put it on the dining room table.

"I love your cottage." Amy took the seat facing the window.

"It belonged to my grandparents. They bought it and the one the store's in now. I moved in when my parents died, so Mermaid Bay has been home for a long time." Jade poured two glasses of chardonnay and sat across from her friend.

"It's definitely you. I love the bright colors."

Jade handed her a plate, and they dug into the pizza. Chloe stood on high alert in case anything landed on the floor.

CHAPTER TWENTY-TWO

"So, what have you uncovered, Nancy Drew?" Amy asked.

"You know about Emory's files. Did you get a chance to talk to Nick?"

"We played phone tag for about two days, and I finally left it for him at the front desk. He said he'd call me in a couple of days."

"He and I were supposed to have dinner last night."

"How did that turn out?" Amy wiggled her eyebrows.

"'Supposed' was the keyword. We were in line at Hot Diggity Dogs when someone threw a weight through the front window. It shook everyone up, and Nick stayed with his deputy to investigate."

Amy scrunched her face. "I saw it boarded up this morning. Lisa said that there was some vandalism, but she didn't know any details. You had front-row seats. Poor Todd. Now he has to replace that big window."

"It was a guy in a dark hoodie." Jade reached for her phone. "Does he look familiar?"

"It's hard to tell from just his profile," Amy said.

Jade tapped on her phone until she found his Facebook page.

"Nope, don't recognize him. Not my type. He likes to show off his guns. Bodybuilder?" Amy asked.

Jade nodded. "Gym rat. He drives a big honking black SUV."

Amy's eyes widened, and her smile disappeared. "Tell me more."

"It had red paint on that grill guard thingy on the front."

Amy's mouth formed a small "o." "I didn't really see the guy who hit me. It was a big SUV with all these racks and lights on it. He barreled into me, sent me flying, and zoomed off. And how did you get so close to his SUV?"

"I spotted him running away from Todd's after he broke the window. I took a couple of quick pictures, and one of the gals at Hot Diggity Dogs thought she recognized him. I did some internet research, and voila, he hangs out at the Sweat Shop in Seaport."

"That's the name of a gym?"

Jade cracked a slight smile. "He was going in as I was leaving. And as luck would have it, he parked right next to me. So when he wasn't looking, I checked out his ride." She waved her phone with the grill pictures.

"That careless so-and-so. I could have been killed, and he didn't even stop."

"And he hurled a metal weight thingy through Todd's front window," Jade said.

"Do you think he killed Emory, too?" Amy whispered.

"Why are you whispering?"

"I don't know. It felt like a secret."

"I want to know why he's after you and Todd. I bought a burner phone," Jade said.

"Now it's your turn to whisper, Secret Squirrel," Amy said with a laugh.

"I have his home number. I just lost my nerve to call." Jade rose and retrieved the pay-by-the-minute cell phone. "I've activated it."

"Holy cannoli. This is Spy Versus Spy. Yes, you have to do it. What are you going to say?" Amy's eyes sparkled like this was some kind of big adventure.

Jade shrugged her shoulders. "I want to know where he works and how he's linked to Mermaid Bay. I've seen him twice, and he's not someone I want to tangle with. I don't want him to know it's me calling."

"Maybe you could say you were trying to reach him for advice or that he won a contest?"

Jade pursed her lips. "It's now or never before I lose my nerve." She fished through her folder for Vince's number. She cleared her throat and punched in the numbers. Pushing the speaker phone button, she signaled for Amy to be quiet.

After three rings, they heard a high-pitched "Hello."

"Hello. This is Tabbi Davidson, and I'm trying to reach Vince Zimmers. My friend recommended that I give him a call. She said he'd know someone who maybe could help me. I, uh, wanted to talk to him about motorcycles."

"Vince's not here right now. I'm not sure when he'll be back. Let me give you his cell. It's 757-330-8179," the woman replied. "You'll have a better chance of catching him there. I have no idea when he'll be home."

"Thank you so much. I'm hoping he can help me. Do you know if he's at work?"

After a short coughing jag, the woman said, "Sorry. I've been sick. Can't shake this dang cough. I said that's doubtful. He does odd jobs to pay for his toys. He's a fixer for some of the real estate and rental companies in town.

Let's just say he doesn't keep regular hours like everybody else."

"He's a handyman?" Jade asked.

"More like odd jobs. He takes care of things. I don't know everything he's into," the woman replied. "Call him on his cell. If you buy him drinks, I'm sure he'll talk to you." The woman coughed again and disconnected.

Jade jotted down what she had learned. "So odd jobs pay for his bike and his gym membership?"

"Well," Amy said, staring at her friend. "Aren't you going to call him?"

"Maybe. I need to think through this cover story."

"Take a deep breath and do it. I'm dying to know. And you can take whatever you find to your Nick. Maybe this'll be the breakthrough he's been looking for." Amy's voice went up several octaves when she said Nick's name.

Jade closed her eyes and took a deep breath and a swig of her wine. "Here goes nothing." She punched in Vince's cell phone number and waited. A gruff, "This is Vince. You know what to do," was followed by a beep.

"Uh, hi. Vince. This is Tabbi Davidson. I'm a friend of Brittany's. We met over in Seaport a while back. Anyway, I want to buy a bike, and I was hoping I could talk to you first." Jade rattled off the number to the burner and disconnected, letting out a long breath that made her bangs flutter.

"You did great."

"Thanks. I hope it was good enough to get him to call me back," Jade said.

"Of course, with that sultry phone voice. Plus, any friend of Brittany's…"

"Now we wait," Jade topped off their wine.

Chapter Twenty-Three

"Special delivery from Simon," Patti sang as she put a large box on Jade's desk.

"My cameras. After all the craziness going on around here, I decided to add some outdoor security." Especially if Vince Z. comes back and hangs out in the parking lot. She texted Bernie to see if he could install them.

Her handyman responded, **Be there in a jiff. Fixin' some crab pots**.

Jade smiled. "Bernie will be by in a while to hang them for me." She opened the box and activated the app on her phone.

She skimmed through the user guide and filled some store orders by the time Bernie shuffled in with his toolbox. "Mornin', Jade."

"Good morning. Thanks so much for coming over so fast. I'd like to hang these under the eaves on the front and back porches. And then two are for the sides. They need to have a good view, but I know we're going to have to recharge the batteries in a few months, so I'll need to be able to reach them."

"Come on, let's take a walk and see what ya got." He picked up one of the camera mounts and turned it around in his hands.

Chloe heard the magic "W" word and sprang into her excited mode.

"Okay, puppy. You can go, too." Jade held the door for the dog and Bernie.

"Let's do one under that eave. I'd like it to pick up as much of the back as possible." She pointed toward the grassy area and the building next door that housed Tish's office.

"How about we point it closer to the sidewalk, so you'll make sure to catch anyone approaching the back door? You know, at face level."

"Sounds good. Now for the others."

The trio hiked around the building, stopping to find the best locations.

When they completed their circuit, Bernie said, "No problem. Shouldn't take too long. Let me get my ladder and drill, and I'll have these up in a flash. A lot of stuff's been going on in town. I helped Todd get his window replaced. And that doofus broke it when the store was open, and everybody could see him. Pretty stupid if you ask me."

"You never know about people." Jade paused. "Hey, do you know any handymen in Seaport?"

Bernie closed one eye and frowned. "Trying to get rid of me?"

"Never. I ran into this guy, and he called himself a fixer. I wanted to know if you've heard of him. You know a Vince Zimmers?"

Bernie tilted his head for a moment. "Nope. Fixer sounds like a mafia guy." He smiled and winked.

"He said he did work for realtors and property managers."

"You should check with Tish. She knows everything that goes on around here. I'll be done with this in a bit. You should be good to go with these cameras. Check the view on them and let me know if I need to make any adjustments."

Jade pulled out her phone and activated all the units. "Everything looks good so far. Thanks so much."

Jade and Chloe slipped inside the office.

A loud buzz jarred Jade from her thoughts. She looked around, not quite sure what it was. The noise increased as she approached her desk. The burner phone vibrated on a stack of folders.

Scrambling to get it before it went to a voicemail she didn't set up, she clicked the button. "Hello."

"Tara? Tina? Christy? Something like that. This is Vince. You called me."

"Oh, hey. It's Tabbi. I'm thinking about buying a bike, and I remember you talking about yours. I was hoping you could give some advice before I chicken out."

"Get a helmet." He laughed.

"Definitely. I don't know whether I should splurge and get a new bike or maybe a used one to try out. Any recommendations on brands."

"I've got some friends with bikes for sale. What's your price range? And how tall are you?"

"Huh? I've got about nine thousand in cash. My height?"

"I'm trying to figure out if you're sturdy enough for some bikes. If it falls over, you have to be able to pick it back up. Nine k is kinda low. You may have to start with a used one."

"Oh. I didn't think of that. I saw some really pretty bikes in Seaport. I want something pink or purple or maybe teal. And I'm five-three." She giggled for effect. "I like the motorcycles with sparkles."

"Sweetheart, real bikes don't have glitter and unicorns. I'll ask around to see if anybody has a chick bike."

"Oooh, thanks for all of your help. See ya around."

"I'll be at Beach Bodies tonight. Stop by and say hi." Vince disconnected before she could reply.

"Lovely sort. And I had my heart set on a pink one with handlebar streamers and glitter paint," Jade said out loud.

"Sounds like my Schwinn from back in the day," Patti said as she breezed in at about the same time as there was a knock on the back door. "It had a banana seat with sparkles and a tiny white basket with daisies on it."

Patti held the door for Bernie.

"Hey, gals. I'm all done. Jade, your cameras good?" Bernie stomped the sand off his shoes before climbing the three wooden stairs.

She reached for her phone and showed the clip of him approaching the back door. "Looking good. Thank you so much. How much do I owe you?"

"Let's call it an even thirty-five. Here's you go." Bernie handed her a folded invoice.

Jade pulled out her checkbook. "Thank you for always taking care of us." She signed her name with a flourish.

Bernie took the check she offered. "Appreciate the business. Call me any time. And thanks for referring me to Amy. She's got a long list of stuff she needs done."

"My pleasure."

"Maybe, I'll change my title to fixer, too. It sounds kinda hip."

"We like you just the way you are, Bernie," Patti said.

"You gals are the best. See ya around. Don't hesitate to call if you need something." Bernie waved and scooted out the back door.

Feeling guilty about poking her nose in Nick's murder case, she texted him. **Any luck with Todd's vandal?**

When no immediate response came, she rummaged through the fridge for a yogurt and an iced tea.

An hour later, Jade was still restless and hungry. "Patti, I'm going to take a walk up the street. Want me to bring you anything back?"

"Nope, I'm good. Thanks. I'll text you if we get lucky with any more bus tours."

"Yes, please," Jade called, slipping out the back.

Today was a day worthy of a picture postcard. A light breeze made the temperatures in the low nineties bearable. She fished her sunglasses out of her purse and enjoyed the walk down the street.

She paused at the corner and crossed when a daycare bus had passed. Todd's parking lot had a couple of cars. Should have been more. It was still lunchtime.

Inside his restaurant, she admired the new window. No sign of the vandalism or the plywood.

"Hey, Jade. What's shakin'?" Todd asked as she approached the counter.

"Your window looks good," she said, pointing over her shoulder.

"Bernie took care of it for me. I saved the plywood for the next hurricane or the next time. What can I get you?"

"How about a Coke and a hot pretzel?"

"Good choice. Be up in a flash."

"Did they find the guy who broke the window?" Jade asked.

Todd shook his head. "Nick said he had a couple of leads and that he's still working on it. Insurance covered it, but I'd still like to get damages from the idiot. And I'd kinda like to know what I did to raise his ire. Here ya go." He handed her a paper plate with a pretzel and a cup. "Careful, that's hot."

"Thanks." Jade dropped all her change in the tip jar. "Let me know what you hear."

Jade found a table on the deck and watched the people in the sand below. Kids, dogs, kites, catamarans, and sun worshippers. Everyone was taking advantage of the summertime weather. She pulled out her phone and posted several online reviews for Hot Diggity Dogs.

As she finished her pretzel, her phone buzzed with a text from Amy. **Working on something new. Wanna stop by tonight?**

Want me to bring dinner? When? Jade replied.

5 and I have BBQ and stuff.

Sweet or Vinegar-based, Jade responded.

How should I know? I just learned about hush puppies. See you at 5.

Jade sent a string of smiley emojis and tossed her trash in the can. "I'm glad I didn't ask if it was chicken or pork," she said to herself. As much as she wanted to stay and watch the seagulls, her office and some unfinished tasks pulled her back to the store like a magnet.

She walked slowly across the street to savor the afternoon sun. Fall would be here before she knew it. Labor Day was always bittersweet because it heralded the unofficial end to summer when all the tourists went home.

Right at five on the dot, Jade climbed the stairs to Mermaid Books. Mr. Darcy, who sat in the front window display, greeted her with a string of mews.

"Hey, fella. Checking out the tourists?"

"That's his new favorite spot. It doesn't matter what display I put in that window, he makes himself a napping spot on top of the books," Amy said. "Come on back. I've got to heat up our dinner."

"What going on in your world?" Jade followed her friend through a maze of bookcases and comfy chairs to the kitchenette in the back.

Amy fluttered around the tiny space, heating up plates of baked beans, macaroni, BBQ, and hushpuppies. She handed Jade the first plate. "There's coleslaw over there if you want it. I have water, tea, and wine."

"Water's fine," Jade said, taking the plate.

"I've heard nothing from our sheriff or any of his staff. I really feel left in the dark about Emory. I keep pouring over the store files in hopes of finding something that will give me a clue as to why she was murdered. I find it hard to believe that it was some kind of random mugging."

"I agree. It has to have something to do with her or the store. It looked too personal. Plus all the voodoo dolls."

Amy nodded, and the pair focused on their dinner.

"This is good. Did you cook?" Jade asked.

"Yup. An old family recipe. Takeout from a BBQ joint near Seaport. The one with the red and yellow awning and the pig statue out front." Amy grinned. "I still don't know what you were talking about with the sauce versus vinegar thing."

Jade laughed. "People take their barbecue and their sauces seriously around here. This has a tomato sauce base, the brown stuff. North Carolina style is vinegar based. That's what I grew up on, but I like both."

"Okay, sorta like the Chicago and New York style pizzas. Got it. So much to learn about living in the south."

"Just wait 'til we get to the desserts or Virginia ham."

Amy rolled her eyes. "I've had Virginia ham." She wrinkled her nose. "I thought something was wrong with it. Way too salty."

"Mmmm. You don't know what you're missing when it's fried and put on a biscuit."

"If you say so. I do like biscuits. Did you hear back from that motorcycle guy?"

Jade pushed her plate forward. "He finally called back. I pretended to be looking for a bike. He's a jerk, but he said he'd call me if he found one. Not sure how he's mixed up in all this, but I know for sure that he broke the Hot Diggity Dogs' window. Poor Todd. The window was just another thing on top of the string of bad online reviews that he's been getting. You haven't noticed anything like that?"

Amy shook her head. "Business has been slow, but it's picking up. I'm hoping the poetry slam and the author readings will bring some more traffic in. I get a little bit of beach traffic. See the trails of sand?"

Jade smiled. "You'll always have that. It goes with the territory."

Amy tapped on her phone. "Now that you mention it, I haven't had that many comments on my weekend event posts."

"I paid a guy to redo my website a while back, and I'm glad I did. I do as much or more business most days with the online orders. The website was a huge investment at the time, but it really helped with sales during the off-season. I can keep part-timers employed year-round now. A lot of the businesses used to board up during the winter when I was a kid. I'm glad most of them stay open now."

"Marketing was never my thing. I managed a call center for an insurance conglomerate. I get managing people, but this is a one-woman show. I work way longer hours than I ever did back home. I like my social media sites, but it's hard to translate that into store traffic. Heck, I do all this publicity and get no response, and then I post a picture of Mr. Darcy, and it goes viral." Amy rolled her eyes and squeezed her napkin into a tight ball.

"Every time I think I have social media figured out, something changes. I try to stay active on my main sites every day to build relationships. Pinterest, Instagram, and Facebook work for my demographics. But I do tweet, too. I try to balance my store sale posts with informational stuff about the beach and the holidays. Chloe and Neville are also the stars. They get more likes than anything I do."

"Hmmm. Maybe Mr. Darcy can post his recommendations. Send me your website guy's information. Emory did nothing with her website. Her last update to it was almost a year ago."

"I do a blog about new products and recipes. That gets me some traction. I also have guest interviews with ornament artists. And I schedule a lot of my social media posts. I studied my analytics to see when my followers were most active. That helped, too."

Amy grabbed a notebook and jotted down ideas. "Thanks. I'm blatantly stealing your ideas."

"I call it inspiration. Try stuff. If it doesn't work, try something else. It also helped me to find my fans. Mine help me spread the word," Jade said.

Amy continued to scribble in her notebook. "As business savvy as I think I am, I've got a lot to learn. And that Tish keeps planting seeds of doubt."

"She just wants to list your property."

Amy blew out a heavy sigh. "I know, but she won't give up."

"That's her. Be flattered that you own a sought-after property," Jade said.

"She gets into my head, and it makes me start questioning if I'm doing the right thing. This is a lot of work for not much to show for it. The pragmatic me says sell it and buy a property somewhere else."

"Yet. You haven't seen the fruits of your labor yet. You will. Give it a chance. And then, if you don't like it, you can sell. The property will always be valuable. Don't let her rush you into anything."

"I know. It's hard. Thanks for coming over. I'm spending a lot on upgrades, and I had five customers today." Amy's shoulders slumped.

"It happens. Here, let's clean up. I want to see what you've done to the place." Jade picked up the paper plates and tossed them in the trash.

"Right this way." Amy waved her arms. "You've seen the kiddie area with my murals. I finished the touch-ups on my dragon. He's my favorite. I painted all those dark bookcases. I'm hoping it makes the back of the store more welcoming. Then I rearranged a lot of the smaller displays into vignettes with chairs and ottomans. That one is my British library look. My mystery corner is over there, and way over there is my tribute to a boudoir for sweet and spicy romances."

"This looks amazing. I would photograph each, maybe with Mr. Darcy, and feature a vignette each day."

"Good idea. I'm thinking of doing a beach pic each day, too. You are a wealth of ideas. Selfie time," Amy yelled. She positioned them in front of the dragon and snapped some candids. "Thanks, My first friend post."

The pair wandered through the store and chatted at the counter and on the front porch before Jade called it a night.

"Thanks again," Amy called behind her. "You're just what I needed."

"We help each other," Jade yelled over her shoulder.

Dusk had fallen on Mermaid Bay, and most of the tourists had headed back to their cottages or hotel rooms. She enjoyed the quiet walk home until a shrill tone emanated from her purse.

Fumbling for her burner phone, she finally located it before the trilling stopped. "Hello."

"Hey, it's me, Vince," he slurred. "I'm over at the Mad Hatters with some guys. Why don't you bring a friend or two and stop by?"

"Oh, thanks so much, but I'm in Richmond. We drove up to look at a bike," Jade improvised.

"Your loss. I've got some great experts here. Hope you don't waste your money or get killed." He disconnected before she could comment.

Jade rolled her eyes. It's a good thing he called when Amy wasn't around. She would have convinced her to check out the biker bar.

Chapter Twenty-Four

J ade's phone buzzed with a text. Thankfully, it wasn't Vince again on the burner phone, but she doubted that he'd be up at six-thirty-two in the morning, unless he was just getting home.

U up? Nick asked.

Of course. What's up?

Sorry I've been out of touch. Wanna meet for breakfast?

What do you have in mind?, she fired off.

Busy Bean in 20?

I'll race ya.

"Come on, Chloe, we've got to get a move on." Jade did a few swipes with the blush brush and packed her work things.

Right on time, Jade and Chloe waltzed through the front door of the coffee shop.

"Good morning," James yelled as Jade looked around for Nick.

She stood in line behind a couple and a twenty-something with her nose buried in her phone. By the time it was Jade's turn at the counter. Someone stepped close enough behind her to block out some of the sun that was steaming in from the window. She turned. "Oh, hi there. Fancy meeting you here."

"Sorry I'm late. Got a phone call. Whatcha ordering?" Nick asked.

"I'm thinking an asiago bagel with cream cheese and an iced coffee."

"Good choice," James said. "What else can I get for you this gorgeous morning?"

"I've got this. Add hers to mine," Nick said. "I'll have the egg and sausage sandwich with the biggest dark roast ya got." He pulled out his wallet and paid for breakfast while Jade gathered utensils.

"Back deck okay?" Jade glanced at the big window and then at the knickknacks on the shelf at the counter.

Nick nodded. "Not too keen on sitting in front of any plate glass windows?" he asked in a low voice.

Jade scrunched her nose and shook her head. "Been there. Done that."

Jade and Chloe found a table on the deck and watched the sandpipers run in the surf until Nick arrived with breakfast.

"Here ya go." He handed her a paper plate with her bagel. "It's nice out here. The calm before my day starts."

"Having any luck on the weirdness around here lately?"

Nick shook his head. "The investigations continue. There seems to be a lot more going on this summer. Usually, it's lost kids and teens drinking beer under the pier. I think big city woes are creeping in."

"Did you find anything on Vince Zimmers?" She smeared cream cheese on her bagel with a plastic knife and waited for Nick to reply.

"Who?"

"The guy in the picture I gave you. The one who ran away from Todd's place and escaped in the big SUV."

His brow furrowed. "We didn't get a match on the partial plate in your photo."

"Todd's part-timer said it looked like Vince Zimmers. She didn't give you his name when you talked to her?" Jade's eyes widened. "I showed her this picture."

A dark shadow crossed Nick's face. "No. Neither of his workers said anything. They clammed up when we questioned them."

"He lives over in Yorktown with his mother, and he does odd jobs. He fancies himself a big, bad biker and a gym rat."

"And how do you know all that?" Nick's lips formed almost a straight line.

"I did some internet searches," she said quietly. *He didn't need to know about the burner phone right now.*

Nick let out a heavy sigh and tapped something into his phone. "Anything else I should know about?"

"I want you to catch this guy. Todd's been having issues lately with bad reviews, and I wanted to see if I could do anything."

He closed his eyes for a moment. "Thank you for sharing the suspect's name. But I don't want you poking around in police work. Leave it to the professionals."

"But he parked on my property. I was curious. Plus, your guys failed to get the name of the suspect at Todd's. I was just trying to help."

"Next time, just call me." He balled up his trash and picked up his coffee. "Sorry. I've got to eat and run. Let's do dinner later this week. I promise it'll be a complete meal, and you'll have my full attention. Work is crazy right now. I'll be glad when Labor Day gets here." He let out a sigh.

Jade smiled. "At least, meals with you are interesting. I never know what's going to happen."

"Glad I can be entertaining. Gotta get to a meeting. And call me if you hear anything else." He gave her a side-eye look and then grinned like the Nick from middle school.

Taking one more bite of her bagel, Jade wiped the cream cheese off her lips. She gave Chloe a small bite before she disposed of the trash. "We should go get our day started, too. Neville might be there today." Chloe's ears shot up, and she danced on the deck. "I don't care how you act. I know you like Neville."

Jade filled a flood of overnight orders and readied everything for shipping by the time Lorelei and Neville strolled in the front door.

"Perfect timing on my part, I see," Lorelei said, winking at her niece. "Wow. Look at all those packages."

Jade dusted her hands off on her jeans. "I'm pleased. We'll be in good shape with our numbers as we head into Christmas season. And if that stays on track, we're in for an excellent year."

Neville made himself at home by hopping on the counter for pats and the possibility of a treat.

"Anything I should know about?" Lorelei asked, stowing her purse in the back room.

"Not really. We've had a few tour buses surprise us recently. Foot traffic is always good. We'll see what today brings. Anything new with you?"

Lorelei pulled up a stool and slipped Neville a treat. "I'll be on the lookout for busses. Hmmm. Not much is going on. I went with some gal pals to an art opening in Williamsburg at the Stryker Center. It was fun. We had drinks afterwards at a pub. Steve and I are going to try a new place in Williamsburg tonight. That's about it. You doing anything besides work?" Her aunt paused and stared.

When Jade didn't respond quickly enough, Lorelei continued, "How's Nick? Is it really a thing, or are you two just buds? It's hard to tell sometimes. You've been friends for so long."

"We had breakfast this morning."

Lorelei's eyebrows shot up, and her eyes widened.

"We met at the Busy Bean. I hadn't seen him in a while, and he's been swamped with work." Jade glared at her aunt. "And it is hard to tell with him sometimes. It's summer, and he's always working. We probably know each other too well." Jade's voice trailed off.

"Missy, you need to figure out what you want to do. Unless you're satisfied with hanging out."

"That from the woman who's sworn off relationships," Jade said.

"Just marriage. I've already done that. And I'm at a point in my life where I want to enjoy my friends. Casual dating is fine. Steve and I make a good team. But we're not talking about me. We're talking about you. You're too young to be a hermit. All you do is work. You need some excitement."

"It takes a lot to keep this store going. And I don't work all the time. Amy and I hang out now. I'm having dinner with Nick this week. I'm nowhere near hermit status. And I could be thinking about getting a motorcycle? Or maybe a tattoo? I got asked out to the Mad Hatters yesterday." Jade winked at her aunt.

"Good for you, but why do I have the suspicion that you're just being sassy." Lorelei rolled her eyes as Jade disappeared into the office. "Can't wait to see the ink," her aunt yelled from the other room.

After scheduling social media posts and working on her next newsletter, Jade wandered through the internet, looking for pictures and friends of Vince. Could he be involved in more than just the vandalism at Hot Diggity Dogs? Right now, he was her only lead.

Taking a deep breath, Jade dialed Vince's number on the burner phone before she lost her nerve. *One-thirty. Hopefully, he'd be awake by now.*

After multiple rings, Jade heard a gruff "What?"

"Vince. This is Tabbi. I didn't buy the bike in Richmond."

"Still on the market then?" He snickered. "I'll ask around. Somebody's always got something they want to get rid of. Can't promise that it will be pink. Give me a couple of days. I've got some stuff to do for work. I'll find you something."

"I heard you worked in Mermaid Bay," she cooed.

"I've got some regular clients there. But I'm in demand a lot. I get around."

"I thought you worked with property managers and big real estate deals. Who told me that? Was it that realtor Tish St. James?"

He took a swig of something and swallowed loudly. "I don't work for her anymore. She's too flippin' cheap. She said something about me? She's always flapping her lips. She needs to shut up. You can't trust that one."

"I can't remember who I heard it from. Maybe I got the name wrong? Maybe it was Jared Carswell. I'm not sure."

"He's a jerk. I don't work for him, either. Gotta go. I'll text you if I find a bike." He disconnected, and Jade stared at the phone.

"So, he does know Tish and Jared?" How could she let Nick know without revealing that she's been snooping again? Maybe his guys would find out the connection on their own.

"Hey, Lorelei, what do you know about Tish?" Jade hollered as she made her way to the lobby.

"Tish the Dish?" Her aunt laughed. "She's been around a while and fancies herself the best realtor within a hundred-mile radius." She cleared her throat. "Seriously though, she's rabid about her business. She crosses the line with what's proper a lot, but she's got a decent sales record. Why?"

"Amy said that she's been hounding her to sell Emory's property."

"That's interesting. Nice oceanfront property next to the hotdog stand. She's always looking for every opportunity for a sale. She's probably already got a buyer in her pocket."

"She's mentioned that I should call her if I ever want to sell, but she's never been persistent with me." Jade straightened the stack of red and green shopping baskets behind the counter.

"Who knows? Maybe she's got a thing for oceanfront property. When she gets a bee in her bonnet, she's like Chloe with a bone."

"Amy found some emails where Emory was adamant about keeping Mermaid Bay as it is. Then there were some about a discussion with Tish and Claude about possibly selling the building. It struck me as odd," Jade said.

"I can't see Emory selling. That shop was her life," Lorelei said. "And she never talked about retiring. She was known for sharing her opinions. I could take her in small doses only. Too abrasive most days when she got on one of her many soapboxes."

"Did you bring lunch?" Jade asked.

"I brought a snack. Steve and I are going for seafood tonight. Gotta save room."

"I'm going to run out and get something. I really need to start packing my lunch, but it's nice to get out sometimes. Want me to bring anything back?"

"Nope. Chloe, Neville, and I will hang out here."

"I've got my phone. Call me if any busses show up." Jade pulled out her sunglasses and walked down the sidewalk on her side of the street. Tish's Lexus sat in front of the real estate office.

Taking a deep breath to quell the jitters, she pulled open the door and stuck her head in. "Hey there," she said to the blond receptionist. "I'm Jade. Is Tish busy?"

The twenty-something giggled. "Tish is always busy but let me check to see if she can break away. Just a sec."

A few minutes later, Tish, in a peach-colored linen suit, followed the blond to the lobby. "Jade, what brings you here?"

"I thought I'd pop in and see how the market's going?"

CHAPTER TWENTY-FOUR

"You thinking of selling?" Tish's eyes sparkled. "Come on back. We can chat."

"Not really seriously. I was curious what my cottage was worth."

Tish let the way to her office. "Can I get you coffee or a Coke?"

"No thanks." Jade sank into the plush purple guest chair.

Tish tapped on her keyboard. "Let's see. Your property has jumped in value over the years. It's not oceanfront, but you can still get a decent price. People are always looking for cute beach houses. Here's my welcome packet," Tish said, pushing a buyer's agreement, a folder, and a pen toward her. "I think you'll make a tidy profit off the cottage. When you sign, we'll do an evaluation, and I'll give you firmer numbers. But here is a rough idea." She handed Jade a yellow sticky note.

Jade picked up the pages on top and flipped through the stack. "I, uh. I need to take this home and go through this. How about if I make an appointment with…"

"Lindsey. She'll be glad to set one up for you. Here's my card. Let me know what works for your schedule. Are you interested in selling the store, too? That's no longer zoned residential, right?"

"No thanks. It's too special to let go right now. And no, it's not in the residential part of town." Jade shoved the papers in her purse and stood. "Oh, by the way, I was talking to someone the other day, and she mentioned that you have a handyman named Vince. Would you be willing to share his contact?"

It looked like a dark cloud passed over the realtor's face. "Vince? Vince Zimmers? I don't know who told you that, but he's not a handyman. And I wouldn't recommend him to my worst enemy." She rolled her eyes. Softening her demeanor, she continued, "I've got to go show a property, but call Lindsey when you want to set up some time to list your house. Ciao."

Jade waved to Lindsey, who had the phone balanced in the crook of her neck. Outside the realty office, Jade almost slammed into Claude Simpkins, who blocked the sidewalk. "Oh, sorry, Claude. I didn't see you there."

"Just looking at my sign here." He pointed to the roof. "I think the sun's starting to fade it. Might have to get someone to come by and look at it."

"Bernie does all of my maintenance work. I heard from somebody that there's a guy in Seaport named Vince who's really handy."

Claude froze for a moment and furrowed his brow. "My guy will take care of it. I trust him." He yanked open the door to his CPA office and disappeared inside.

Jade made a face and continued her walk to Hot Diggity Dogs. With no line inside again, she sidled up to the counter and ordered a soft pretzel and an iced tea. "Hey, Todd. Any word on your vandal?"

"Nope. Hopefully, it was some freak occurrence. Got too much other stuff going on to worry about it. I've been working on my social media sites. We'll see if the happy posts overshadow the bad ones." His voice trailed off.

The front door opened with enough force that caused it to hit the frame. Todd and Jade paused as Claude hustled inside.

With all eyes on Claude, he looked around and said, "Gimme two dogs all the way, chips, and a giant diet drink."

Todd nodded and handed Jade her pretzel and cup.

Claude barreled up to the counter, almost bumping into Jade as she turned. "Todd. I need to talk to you. Can you take a break for a few?" He paused and glared at Jade like she was intruding. "It's important," he whispered.

"Sure. Let me get your lunch, and I'll join you. See ya, Jade."

She nodded and inched toward the door. Claude didn't continue his conversation until she stepped outside. Jade wished she could be a fly on the wall to see what the big secret was all about.

Chapter Twenty-Five

The door rattled. Jade made her way to the front of the store. Looking around, she saw no one in the lobby. She paused and listened. Something rustled in the toy room. *It can't be Neville. She definitely heard the door.*

Wandering into the cottage's former dining room, she looked around at the twinkle lights that flashed in different sequences. She heard footsteps, and her pulse raced slightly. She chided herself for being so jumpy, but too many strange things had happened around here lately. Closing her eyes for a moment, she inhaled deeply and moved on through the rooms to see who her guest was.

More rustling, and then the air conditioning came on and muffled any other noises. Shaking off the eerie feeling, Jade picked up her pace and headed to the front lobby. Maybe it was time to invest in more cameras.

Zipping into the lobby, she almost bumped into a man facing one of the entryway trees. The fifty-something man in the charcoal gray suit turned and stared at Jade. His blue eyes bore into her with laser focus. His athletic build had aged, but he still looked trim with a touch of gray at his temples. *Jared Carswell.*

"Nice doo-dads you have here." He fingered a seashell ornament.

"Thank you." Jade paused, trying to figure out why he was in her store.

After a long pause, he continued, "I've never been in here before. I thought I'd take a look around."

"Welcome," she said, almost whispering. "We've been here since the late eighties."

"I know. Your grandmother was a feisty one. We tangled a couple of times at zoning meetings. I didn't agree with her, but you have to admire her for sticking to her guns. Even if she could be annoying."

Jade smiled. "She was determined."

"I hear you're a lot like her." He raised one eyebrow and stepped closer to the counter.

"Thanks for the compliment. What can I do for you today?" She stared back, determined not to let her voice quake.

"I heard you were at one of my parties. We didn't get a chance to formally meet, so I decided to stop by since I was in the neighborhood. I'm Jared Carswell."

"It's nice to officially meet you. I'm Jade Hicks. You have a lovely place in Seaport. My friend Amy and I enjoyed the view."

"The gal who's trying to run the bookstore. We'll see how that goes. Yep, I enjoy the parties, and the food was pretty darn good, too. But I'm biased. My niece is the caterer." He made a noise that sounded like a cross between a cough and a laugh. "I heard you were looking into Emory's murder. Another spirited one. Though she couldn't ever make up her mind. What a tragedy."

"She was a friend, and I want to know what happened to her." Jade stared at the man's eyes, looking for any hint that his words didn't reflect his feelings.

"She welshed out on the wrong person."

Jade's eyebrows shot up. "Excuse me?"

"She dangled that property of hers in front of too many buyers, but she always chickened out at the last minute. With all her dirty tricks, I'm surprised something didn't happen to her sooner."

Jade furrowed her brows. "I'm not sure what you mean. She loved her store."

"I'm sure she did. But she was always trying to make a buck. She knew that building was worth more than her business, and whenever she got desperate, she'd act like she wanted to sell. It's my business to keep an eye on what's going on with beachfront property."

"I'm sure you didn't come here to talk about Emory today. What can I help you with?" Jade asked.

"You have some nice things here. I'm going to have my assistant contact you. She's always looking for gifts for clients."

"Thank you. We do custom gift baskets, too. Is there anything in particular that I can show you?" She passed several business cards to him.

He shook his head and dropped her cards in his jacket pocket. "I was nearby and wanted to see the property. Always keep your possibilities open."

Jade turned her head slightly. "It's not for sale, but feel free to look around."

"That's what they all say until they see the offer." He turned and strode out the door.

Before Jade could overthink the reason for the real estate developer's visit, Lorelei and Neville breezed in. "Did I see Jared and his big honking Mercedes leave here?"

"Uh huh. He said he stopped in to check out the property."

A puzzled look crossed her aunt's face. "I saw him headed toward Hot Diggity Dogs. You thinking about selling?"

"No, and that's what I told him. The whole visit was weird. And he made a bunch of small talk and some comments about Emory's indecisiveness and how he wasn't surprised at what happened to her."

Lorelei's lips formed a straight line. "Who knows. He's probably got something up his sleeve. He's always trying to work a deal." She set Neville down, and he immediately jumped on the Dutch door and peeked in the office. A guttural growl emanated from behind the door.

"I know, Chloe. It's good to see Neville, huh?" Jade said.

Lorelei laughed and headed for the back room.

Before Jade had time to dwell on the reason for Jared's visit, her burner phone buzzed. It was either someone wanting to talk to her about her car warranty or Vince.

"Hello."

"Katie, Kayce?" a gruff voice asked.

"It's Tabbi." *He can't be that dense, can he?*

"Oh, sorry. This is Vince. I think I found you a motorcycle that you're going to like. It's midnight blue with sparkles in the paint. And it's light. You should be able to pick it up if it falls over. What ya think? Still lookin'?"

"Uh, I guess so. Since I haven't had much luck, I haven't been shopping lately. I got tired of being disappointed. I spent a lot of time looking at bikes that weren't right for me," Jade said.

"Can you meet me to look at it? And bring the cash. The guy who owns it took care of it. You can ride it away today. If you can. You might need lessons." It sounded like Vince was somewhere windy.

"How much does he want for it?" she asked, stalling.

"Twelve grand, but he'll negotiate."

Jade coughed, and after a pause, she said, "That's kinda out of my price range. I was hoping for more in the five range."

"What are you looking for, a scooter?" He yelled in the phone. "Or a moped? You said nine grand last time we talked."

"Now that's an idea. Some of those cute Italian scooters come in cool colors. And I probably wouldn't be scared to ride one of them. I could bop around the beach and to work on it."

"What? Are you serious? You need to go out for a real ride and see how it feels. There's no zipping. Nothing is better than the feel of a motorcycle under you. You can feel it with your whole body. You feel it in your bones."

"I guess so," she stammered, trying to come up with a better response.

"Make up your mind. Scooters are for wimps and old people. Why don't you get one of those trike bikes if you want to look wimpithetic. If you want it, my guy's not going to have the bike for that long. It'll sell fast. He's doing me a favor by not showing it until I talk to you. I don't have all day. Do you want it or not?"

"I don't know. That's a lot of money. How low do you think he'll go?"

Vince snickered. "Everything's negotiable. It depends on what you offer." His laugh sounded like a cartoon villain.

Jade looked at her phone and made a face. "And what if I can't scrape up all the money at one time? I have other stuff I need to pay for."

"Sweetheart, this isn't layaway. Do you want the motorcycle or not? I don't have time for this. I've got to go to work. I'm already late."

"Uh. I don't..."

Before Jade could continue, he snarled. "You need to figure out what you want. Don't bother me unless you're serious. Go buy your pink scooter with the matching helmet. It'll be perfect for your life in Mermaid Bay." He disconnected, and Jade made another face at the phone.

Not that she really wanted to talk to Vince anymore, but she'd probably just burned a bridge. Maybe she should have met him to look at the sparkly motorcycle. But what if he recognized her? Nick would have a fit if he found out that she was nosing around in his investigation.

Chapter Twenty-Six

Around the time Jade was expecting Nick to pick her up, her phone rang.

"Hey, there. It's a lovely day in Mermaid Bay," Tish said with a lilt in her voice. "Jade, I haven't heard from you in a bit, so I was circling back to see if you wanted me to come over and pick up the paperwork to get the ball rolling on the sale of your bungalow. I've got a bunch of buyers in the market for a cute beach home. Strike while the iron is hot, girl."

"Hi, Tish. How are you? I'm still debating. Not sure if I'm in the market to sell right now. I stopped by to see you on a whim. I was just curious."

"The market's on fire right now. Don't waffle too long. You'll be sorry. I'll make a note to check back with you in a couple of weeks." Tish clicked off before Jade could protest any further.

"Great. I opened up a can of worms there."

A rat-a-tat-tat interrupted Jade's conversation with herself. "Hi," she said after opening the door.

"You look nice. There's a new Italian place in Seaport. Wanna try it?" Nick asked.

"Not one of those spaghetti and waffles places?"

Nick laughed. "Nah, but the tourists like those. Sebastian said that this place has a really good menu. That work for you?"

"Italian sounds wonderful." She flipped the porch light on and pulled the door locked behind her. "How's work?"

"Busy. But it's the middle of summer, so what do you expect? I love this season, but by the end of July, I'm ready for some quiet weekends." Nick opened the truck door for her.

"I saw Todd the other day. His window looked as good as new," Jade said, fishing for information as she hoisted herself up into the passenger seat of his truck.

Nick looked over his sunglasses and climbed into the driver's side. "We're looking for Zimmers if that's what you're hinting at."

Jade nodded and stared out the window when Nick didn't add anything else. They rode in silence through Mermaid Bay, over the bridge, and into Seaport. Nick found a parking spot in the crowded lot in front of a megahotel that looked like a giant sand castle.

He took her hand as they walked through the lobby to the restaurant. A hostess in black with an oversized red sash greeted them and led them to a cozy table in the back. "Here are the menus and our drink specials. Your waiter will be right with you."

Jade squinted to read the menu by the flickering candlelight.

Before they had time to look at the specials, a tall waiter with silver hoops in his ear swooped in with water and bread. "Good evening. I'm Rico, and I'll be making your night special this evening. What can I get for you? We have a whole list of fresh appetizers."

Nick looked over his menu at her. "See anything you want?"

"I would like the cheese ravioli with a house salad and Italian."

"Of course, and you, sir?" Rico asked.

"I'll have the lasagna with meat and a house salad with ranch." Nick handed him the menus.

"Anything to drink? We have an extensive wine list."

Nick shook his head.

"Water's fine for now," Jade said.

When the waiter disappeared, Nick said, "We're doing a Crime Stoppers TV spot to run on the local news channels on Emory. I think it airs tomorrow."

"I hope it generates some leads. Folks are on edge with that and the other crazy things that have been going on," Jade said, lowering her voice.

"There just aren't any leads. Sebastian's scoured hours of camera footage and found nothing. I'm hoping we'll get some tips from somebody who might have seen something."

"So, no progress on the dolls, messages, or posters?" she asked, leaning forward.

He shook his head. "It's frustrating. We always get a few kooks who confess to everything. We've weeded those out. My guys are going through Emory's files. We're hoping something's there. And we're not even sure that all the stuff you just rattled off is even related to her murder."

Nick leaned back and closed his eyes for a minute. "My guys are actively looking for Zimmers. Not sure if he ties in with the other shenanigans, but he's definitely a person of interest for the vandalism at Todd's. He's disappeared into the wind, and his momma's not talking. He'll turn back up sooner or later."

The waiter dropped off salads and breadsticks. The conversation faded as the pair dug into their salads.

After the waiter returned with their entrees, Jade said, "The kids at Hot Diggity Dogs said that Vince was a gym rat who did odd jobs and hung around biker bars in Seaport." She lost her nerve about mentioning that she'd talked to him several times.

Nick raised one eyebrow and reached for the parmesan cheese.

After a sip of water, Jade continued, "They said he was a fixer. I asked Tish and Claude about him when Claude mentioned he needed someone to do some work at his office. Neither of them had a glowing recommendation about Vince."

"Jade," he said.

"I was curious, and Claude brought up the topic of needing help."

"Sebastian and I will get to the bottom of this." He rubbed his temple and looked down at his almost empty plate. "Enough about work. What do you want to do tonight? Mini-golf? Bumper boats?"

Before Jade could make a snarky remark about high school dates, Rico appeared at their table. "Can I get you anything? Dessert?"

Jade shook her head. "I'm holding out for ice cream later after go-carts. And I plan to show this guy who the better driver is. But I could use a to-go box."

"Just the check." Nick grinned. "And challenge accepted," he said, pointing to Jade.

After Nick pocketed his credit card and receipt, Jade picked up her box. Nick rested his hand on the small of her back as they walked through the restaurant. She wasn't sure if it was the warmth of his hand or his spicy cologne, but she liked being close to him.

When they stepped out on the sidewalk, a muscular guy in jeans bumped Jade's arm. When he turned around to say something, he froze for a second and stared. Jade locked in on that face. Was this a coincidence? Was he following her? There was no way he could know she was Tabbi.

"Vince Zimmers!" Jade yelled to Nick. Vince took off, dodging people who strolled along the sidewalk. Nick trailed a few feet behind him.

Jade tried to get a glimpse of where they were. Giving up, she jog-walked in her heels after the men.

At the next corner, Nick lunged at Vince, knocking him down. Nick landed on his back. A small crowd had gathered nearby, watching and recording the action.

"Get off of me, man. You got the wrong guy," Vince whined. "And who the heck are you?"

"Sheriff Nick Driscoll. Sit still until we can get this straightened out." Nick handcuffed him and made a call. After an official-sounding conversation with several ten codes and police talk, he disconnected and helped the handcuffed man to his feet. "Do you have some ID?"

"In my truck. But you got the wrong guy. This is all a big mistake. I can explain." Vince struggled to pull away. "What are you doing attacking innocent people? Hey, you all saw what he did. Who's got it recorded?"

"Enough," Nick yelled, tightening his grip. "You'll get your chance to tell your side. What's your name?"

"I don't have to talk to you. And I want the names of everyone standing here. You all are my witnesses. This man attacked me for no reason," Vince yelled. "You all tag me in your posts. It's Vince Zimmers with a 'Z.'"

Nick stared at Vince while some in the crowd held up cell phones to record the altercation. Many dispersed as a Seaport police cruiser, with lights flashing and sirens whooping, pulled up to the curb.

The deputy climbed out and plunked his Smokey Bear hat on his head. "Hey, Nick. You don't have enough to do in Mermaid Bay that you're fighting crime in Seaport?"

"Deputy Carlson. It's good to see you. This is Vince Zimmers, and I have a warrant out for him for destruction of property, vandalism, and endangerment. He didn't want to talk to me a few blocks back, so he decided to run."

"Do you have some ID?"

"Not on me," the large man whined. Vince didn't look so tough with his hands cuffed behind him and his shoulders slumped. "I've got nuthin' else to say until I talk to my lawyer."

The deputy read him his rights and put him in the back of the cruiser.

Nick moved closer to Jade. "Sorry about this. Something always seems to happen when I'm out with you. I need to take you home and then meet them for booking."

"Go with them. Gimme your keys. I'll pick you up at the station."

"Thanks. I owe you." Nick tossed her his keyring and climbed into the passenger seat of the cruiser.

Nights with Nick were definitely never boring.

Chapter Twenty-Seven

Instead of lunch, Jade took a break and walked Chloe while Lorelei covered the store for the afternoon. She hadn't heard from Nick except for a couple of texts over the last two days and was curious to find out what happened to Vince Zimmers. The last time she saw Vince, the gym rat, was sitting in the backseat of the squad car, not looking all that fierce.

Chloe was in no hurry to get back to the store. She'd had enough of Neville's antics today and was enjoying the sunshine. Their walk turned into a stroll. Not much going on at the real estate office. Chloe sniffed the flowers and a bonsai tree in the ceramic pots near the parking lot. "Come on, Chloe. Let's go walk on the beach."

Fascinated with the flowerpots, the little dog balked at moving on. Jade reached down to pick her up and caught a glint of sunlight on the open door. She stifled a squeal that came out like a muffled eek. Vince Zimmers, with a gym bag over his shoulder, strode down the sidewalk and hopped into a black SUV. He zoomed out in reverse and slammed on the brakes. Staring at her over his sunglasses, his lip curled.

Jade hugged Chloe tighter to her, and the little dog wiggled. Before she could say anything, Vince rolled up his window and sped out of the lot.

Willing her heart rate to return to normal, she inhaled and exhaled several times. Still hugging the Frenchie, she pulled out her phone and dialed Nick.

Not even letting him get his full greeting out, she interrupted with, "Nick. It's Jade. I'm at Tish's real estate office. Vince Zimmers just roared out of this parking lot. And he gave me a look that would have curdled milk."

"You okay?"

"Yep. Just surprised. I didn't expect to see him around the beach anytime soon. I thought he was in custody."

"He bonded out this morning. Did he threaten you?"

"No. He startled me when he came out of one of the offices. I almost bumped into him."

"Let me know if you notice anything out of place. He's facing some stiff charges. He better be on his best behavior. If he so much as sneezes wrong, I'll haul him back in."

"He was the last person I expected to see today. So, I guess you weren't able to link him to Emory's murder?" she asked.

"Not yet. We're still investigating. Not many leads. Hey, I got another call. Wanna have dinner later this week?"

"Sure. Movie night?"

"I'll bring a pizza. Call you later." Nick disconnected.

Carrying Chloe across the street, she hustled up the stairs and into Mermaid Books.

"Hey, cutie," Amy yelled from across the room.

Chloe growled at Mr. Darcy, who flicked his tail in her direction.

"Why, thanks," Jade said with a wink.

"I meant, oh never mind, you're cute, too. What brings you both by today?" Amy laughed and climbed down from a wooden ladder propped against one of the tall bookcases.

"Just checking in. Hadn't heard from you. I was out with Nick, and we bumped into Vince Zimmers, the one who broke Todd's window. And Nick apprehended him right there on the sidewalk."

"Wow. Better than binge-watching cop shows on Netflix," Amy said. "One less bad guy on the streets."

"Not really."

A puzzled look crossed Amy's face.

"I spotted Vince on my way over here. Nick said he bonded out for breaking Todd's window." Jade took a deep breath.

Amy fished out her phone and fired off a flurry of texts. "Let's see if the sheriff was able to link him to the destruction of my beautiful car. Thanks to the hit-and-run guy, I'm stuck with a boxy, old thing until the insurance company settles." Amy leaned over and kissed Chloe on the head.

"If he is involved, be careful. Who knows what else he's responsible for. He saw me the day he destroyed the window and again on the sidewalk yesterday. I guess it didn't help that I screamed his name out to Nick."

Amy burst out laughing. "Sorry. That sounded funny. This is all crazy." She bit her lip, and her expression sobered. "Be careful. He sounds kinda dangerous."

"I put some cameras up at the store, and I may have Bernie install some at home, so I'll sleep better. Every little noise makes me edgy," Jade said in a low tone.

"I know what you mean. I'm still stewing about the accident. And I'm anxious when I drive now. I feel like I'm always on high alert, waiting for something to happen. I don't know if it was a chance encounter or whether the driver was targeting me. I'd feel better if it was the former, but there have been weird things going on around here. And you know what happened to Emory." Her voice trailed off. She picked up Mr. Darcy and squeezed him close to her. "And I probably shouldn't leave all the doors unlocked all the time. It feels like Mayberry around here, and I forget to make sure everything's buttoned up." Amy pushed a stray lock out of her eyes. "Let's talk about something else. Something fun. I'm tired of all the creepiness. I'm having a trivia night on Friday. Why don't you stop by and bring Nick?"

"I'll see what his schedule is. He's been doing a lot of OT lately. But I'll definitely be there."

"Get here close to five. We'll divide up into teams. I've got some prizes," Amy said.

"Do you need any more? I can bring two or three gift bags if you want them." Jade set the wiggly Chloe on the floor.

"That would be great. More is always better. See you Friday. And maybe your cute sheriff, too." Amy giggled and picked up a dust rag.

Chloe led the way down the steps, and Amy shut the door behind them. The pair walked back to 'Tis the Season, and Jade glanced over her shoulder several times. No sign of Vince or his oversized SUV.

"You okay?" Lorelei asked when she unclipped Chloe's leash and set it on her desk.

"I'm fine. Why?"

"You sure? That's not what your face is saying. You better not play poker."

Jade dropped into her chair. "That Vince Zimmers guy got arrested for destroying the window at Hot Diggity Dogs. I saw him over at Tish's this morning. He's bad news, but Nick said he can't link him to Emory or anything else that's been going on around here lately."

"Who's Vince?"

"He's some wannabe tough guy from Seaport. He knows Tish and some other people in town. He likes to refer to himself as a fixer."

Lorelei's forehead wrinkled, and a "V" formed between her perfectly manicured eyebrows. "What's he look like?"

Jade scrolled through Facebook and handed her aunt the phone. "Recognize him?

"Nope. He likes biker bars and girls in tiny bikinis. Maybe you should print out that and leave a copy here in case he comes in."

"Not sure we're his kind of store, but okay. He gives me the creeps. Nick said Vince's out on bond and shouldn't do anything to jeopardize that. I hope he's right."

"Keep your guard up. You never know what people are capable of." Lorelei said with a sigh.

Jade texted Nick. **Wanna do trivia night at the bookstore on Friday? Why not.**

Starts at 5, she added.

Pick you up before that?

At my store. She added a string of smiley face and trophy emojis.

As soon as she set her phone down on her desk, it rang. "Hey, change your mind about trivia night?" she asked Nick.

"Nah. But I'm up to my elbows here, and I'm going to have to take some work home. Wanna do dinner after the thing tomorrow night at the bookstore? Sorry that I can't make it tonight with pizza."

"Sure. But bring your 'A' game tomorrow."

"Always the competitive one," he said.

"I'm waiting for Amy to host Scrabble night. I'd be all over that. But for trivia night, you're my secret weapon for questions about sports, cars, and true crime."

He laughed. "Nice to know I bring value. What are we playing for?"

"Bragging rights. And an awesome 'Tis the Season gift bag."

"I can always use the swag. On a serious note, Vince Zimmers had an alibi for Emory's murder. He was at a biker rally in Myrtle Beach. A gal he was shacking up with that weekend corroborated his story."

"Huh? That's not what I expected," Jade said, sinking into her desk chair.

"He's still being charged with a string of serious offenses for the window stunt. And we never got a clear answer from him about why he did it."

"I had the feeling that the posters, voodoo dolls, warnings, the window, Amy's accident, and Emory were all related. Some of them feel like more than pranks."

"Could be. People do strange things. I'm hoping the TV spots on Emory will generate some leads. My guys are working on it with the state police."

"Find the bad guy. I hate this feeling of constant uncertainty," she said.

"Working on it." It sounded like he was drinking something.

"See you tomorrow. Chloe and I are going to study trivia questions tonight."

"Gotta run. Sounds fun. Miss me a little."

"I will." Jade disconnected. A charge of electricity zinged down her spine and caused the butterflies in her stomach to awaken.

Trying not to stress about Nick or Mermaid Bay's crime spree, she checked the recent orders, updated her inventory, and spent the rest of the time scheduling social media posts for the next week.

About five o'clock, Lorelei pulled her purse out of the spare desk and whistled. Neville jumped on the ledge of the Dutch door. She scooped him up and said, "We're headed home. I have to get ready for yoga."

"Have fun."

"We will. Patti has her Simon, and my yoga class has our Lance. He keeps the whole class motivated. Ta-ta."

She winked at her aunt. "Come on, Chloe, let's check on things, and we'll head home, too." She made sure all the windows and doors were locked.

The chubby dog waddled down the stairs as Jade pulled the door behind her. Her phone rang. "Hello."

A shuffling and a muffled voice said, "No. I told you no." Then there was more shuffling and static.

She glanced at the phone's screen. "Hello? Todd, is that you? Todd." When there was no answer, she disconnected and redialed. After several rings, she heard Todd's official-sounding voicemail message. She tried again, and the call immediately went to voicemail.

"That's weird." She dialed Hot Diggity Dogs.

"Hot Diggity. This is Bethany. What can I grill for you?"

"Hi, Bethany. This is Jade Hicks, Todd's friend. Is he there?"

"Uh, no. He said he was going out a while ago. That was about an hour ago. He must have gotten tied up with something. May I take a message?"

"No. I'll check back later." She disconnected "Come on, puppy. That was weird. I wonder if Todd butt dialed me."

Chloe had no comment. She was more interested in the scents around the store's porch. Jade had to give her a little nudge to get her moving.

Todd's weird call crept into Jade's thoughts. On a whim, they crossed the street and she stepped inside the almost empty hot dog stand.

"Hi, I'm Jade. Is Todd around?" she asked the two teens behind the counter.

The male with long blond bangs shook his head.

"Nope. We haven't seen him for a while. He must have run into someone. He's always getting distracted or tied up with someone. You know Todd. He likes to talk," said the female, who was probably Bethany.

"Is that normal for him?"

"Sometimes. He gets involved with other stuff and gets sidetracked. And he's never met anyone that he couldn't talk to. If he's not back by the end of our shift, we'll close up. We've done it before. Can I get you anything?"

"No. But if you see Todd, ask him to call Jade." Something tickled the back of her thoughts and wormed its way forward. Was Todd okay?

Chapter Twenty-Eight

Jade stood and stretched. She'd been sitting at her desk too long. In the middle of a few yoga poses on the floor, Chloe got in on the act. It's hard to exercise with a curious Frenchie.

Grabbing her phone, Jade noticed an overnight alert from the cameras that she had missed earlier. The clips, timestamped around ten o'clock, were dark and grainy. In the first one, two figures, dragging something, shuffled behind the store. Then in another, one guy fiddled with the lock on the shed door until it opened. A few minutes later, two guys exited and shut the door.

Jade's stomach sank. What were they doing in her shed? The lawn mower and weedwhacker were the only things of value out there. And it didn't look like they left with anything.

Trying to keep her voice from cracking, she yelled, "Patti, I'm going out to the shed. Be back in a minute."

"Have fun," echoed from the front of the store.

Pocketing her phone, she picked her way down the back steps and around the building. She hesitated when she spotted the broken lock dangling from the hook. Jade opened the door and peered into the dark shed with the plywood flooring. Dust and grass scents tickled her nose.

She heard a noise and paused to listen. A groan this time.

Taking a deep breath, she stepped back and turned on her phone's flashlight.

Something slumped in the corner groaned again. She stepped closer and shined her light on the pile of clothes. She screamed when she saw a hand.

Fighting the urge to run, she stepped closer and pointed her light in the corner. *An arm with a familiar tattoo?*

"Oh, Todd, are you okay?" She shook him slightly and checked for a pulse. He groaned again. "How did you get in my shed?" Only more groans.

Jade texted Nick and then dialed 911.

"What's your emergency?" Jade's phone buzzed with a call from Nick that she ignored.

"This is Jade Hicks at 'Tis the Season. There's an injured man, Todd Brickman, in my shed. I need an ambulance."

"What's the injury? Is he breathing?" the dispatcher asked.

"He's breathing, but I have no idea what's wrong with him. He's groaning, and I felt a slight pulse. Please send someone. We're in the shed at the back of the property. I probably need the police, too. I have no idea why he's out here."

"Okay, stay on the line," the dispatcher said. "Police and EMTs are on their way. You said his name is Todd Brickman."

"Yes. He owns Hot Diggity Dogs."

"Okay. You should hear rescue soon. They're two minutes out."

"Thank you." Jade took several deep breaths. "I hear sirens. I'm going to hang up now." Jade jogged to the street and waved her arms at the approaching ambulance.

The driver pulled into her side lot as Jade directed him to the shed in the back.

Three EMTs jumped out, and Jade yelled, "In the shed."

Nick's SUV pulled into the lot as she watched the rescue team work on Todd.

"What's going on? I heard the call go out on the radio, and you didn't answer me." Nick jogged over to the open door.

"Sorry. I was talking to the dispatcher, and then it got a little crazy here."

"What happened and start at the beginning," Nick said.

"I didn't notice the camera alerts until this morning. When I came out to check on it, I found Todd in my shed. He was breathing, but I don't know how badly he's hurt. Or what he's doing here. I wish I had seen it last night. I hope it's not too late." Jade rubbed her eyes.

"We'll get to the bottom of this."

A second police vehicle pulled into the lot, kicking up sand. Sebastian slammed the car door and jogged over to Nick. The pair huddled near the shed.

After the EMTs carried Todd out on a gurney, Sebastian and Nick took pictures of the door and poked around inside the shed.

"You're going to need a new lock. This one's rusted, so it wasn't that hard to break. You said you had video from last night?" Nick asked.

Jade tapped in her password and opened the app.

Nick watched the clips several times. "Send these to me, please. Any idea who the guys are?"

Jade shook her head. "It looked like one had on a ballcap. The other had his hood up. The picture is really grainy. I'm disappointed in the quality."

"Anything else?"

Jade looked up and caught Nick's stare. "Todd called me yesterday afternoon, but he didn't say anything. When I called his place, his part-timer said he'd gone out to dump the trash. It didn't seem all that out of the norm yesterday, but now I'm kicking myself for not checking up on it."

"When was that?" Nick asked.

"Uh." She checked her call log. "Four thirty-two. I thought he dialed me by accident."

Nick wrote in a small, black notebook. "When did you come out here?" he asked without looking up.

"Right before I texted you. I wondered what they were doing, skulking around my shed. I wanted to check on things. I thought maybe the two guys took something. Do you think Todd'll be okay?"

"They'll take care of him. He was breathing on his own. So that's always a good sign. I'm not sure how long I'll be tied up on this. I'll call you about tonight's thing. You may have to find another trivia partner."

Jade nodded as her phone binged with a string of texts and email alerts. Everyone in town was curious about the police presence at her store.

She fired off a few texts. "I'm going back inside to check on Patti. Let me know if you need anything."

Nick nodded and returned to the shed.

Jade barely got the back door closed before Patti and Chloe rushed her.

"What is going on out there? We saw lights and all that activity. We've been peeking through the window, but I can't tell all that much. I wish I could read lips."

"I saw something fishy from the cameras last night, so I went to check. I found Todd inside the shed, groaning." Jade sunk into her chair.

"I hope he's going to be okay. Who would want to hurt Todd? He's the most laid-back person I know." Patti's hand flew to cover her mouth.

"I have no idea. There were two guys on the camera feed. Recognize either one?"

Patti stared at Jade's phone. "No, not really. Just that one's short and kinda pudgy. The bigger one is hiding under his hoodie. I'm guessing what they're dragging is Todd. He looks all slumped over. It's hard to tell if it's a person or a large sack of something. Though, I do see legs in that shot."

"It's definitely a person. I wish the video was better."

"And what were they doing in your shed?" Her eyes widened as she peeked out the back window again.

Jade shrugged her shoulders. "I've got some tables and chairs and lawn equipment out there. Nothing super expensive. Now I need to get a better lock and find out how Todd is doing." Her phone continued to buzz and ding with alerts from concerned neighbors and the curious.

A little before four, Jade's phone binged with a string of texts.

Todd's doing okay.

Still got work to do before I can leave. I'll try to meet you at the bookstore later.

Don't worry about it. We'll do something another time. I know you're busy, Jade typed. Her shoulders sagged, and she blew out a puff of air.

I'll make it up to you. Nick added a string of smiley face emojis.

"Well, Chloe, hopefully, I won't be the odd one out tonight. Let's get you settled." She zipped through the store, turning off lights, setting the alarm, and arming the cameras.

At home, Jade changed into jeans and a baby blue camisole with a shrug. She slipped on her matching sandals, hugged Chloe, and let herself out the bungalow's front door for a quick walk to the bookstore. Forgetting the gift bags, she doubled back and retrieved them. Chiding herself for being absent-minded, she continued the dialog in her head about whether walking after dark would be safe with all the craziness lately. Practicality won out, and she hopped in the Wrangler for the quick ride.

She parked next to several cars in the front lot of Mermaid Books, where smooth jazz wafted out the open doors. The cool breeze from the bay mixed with the warm evening and the music to make it seem like the setting for a Hallmark movie. Too bad she didn't have a date.

Jade climbed the steps, and Amy greeted her with a hug. "Thanks for coming." Taking the gift bags Jade offered, Amy continued, "And thanks for bringing those. They'll be a hit. Where's your beau?"

"He's working on a case." Jade pasted on a smile and tried not to look mopey.

Amy hugged her with one arm. "We'll still have fun. Come on back and meet everyone. Here's a nametag."

Jade waved to Claude, Kelly, and Vivian. Claude sloshed his drink when he waved back with his cup.

"Everybody, this is Jade from 'Tis the Season, and she brought three more gift bags. So not only are we playing for bragging rights, we're playing for cool swag from her store and mine. In a few minutes, we're going to count off by threes and form teams. You guys chat amongst yourselves, and there are snacks and drinks on the tables." Amy pointed across the room. "Be back in a sec. You mingle and get to know each other."

Amy returned a few minutes later with a whiteboard on an easel and three hand-held devices. She had the players count off and rearrange themselves to be near their new team. After shuffling and refilling plates with snacks, the group settled in.

Jade's team included Claude and a pale guy all in black named Leo.

"Who's going to ring in for us?" Jade asked, looking at the buzzer.

"I will," Claude said, pulling it out of her hand. "I'll be the team captain. We've got this."

Jade hoped she didn't grimace, and Leo rolled his eyes and yawned. Hopefully, he'll be more talkative during the game.

"Okay, folks. Lisa is going to be our lovely announcer for the evening. She'll read the questions. Click your buzzer to ring in. The computer will tell us who hit the button first, so pick the fastest clicker on your team. Lisa's the judge, and her rulings are final. No arguing. We'll play three rounds and see who's ahead at each. Ready?" Amy threw both of her arms in the air. "Okay, let's go. Lisa, kick us off."

After the first round, Vivian and Kelly's team was in first place. Jade's team trailed the other two because Claude rang in whether he knew the answer or not. *This was going to be a long evening.*

At the end of the second round, Jade's team had moved into second place thanks to Leo pulling the buzzer away from Claude.

"Let's take a quick breather, folks," Amy said. "Grab a drink or some snacks or stretch your legs before the final round."

Leo disappeared into the store with the clicker. Before Jade could get something to drink, Claude grabbed her arm and held it tightly. "Hey, I heard you had some activity at your place. What was going on?"

A creepy feeling crawled over Jade. "Someone broke into my shed."

"Rumor has it that the police found Todd there. He'd been kidnapped and left on your property. Or was he hiding in there for some reason?" Claude stood and looked around to see if anyone heard him. "What's your link to all this?"

"Huh? I don't know the details, but the EMTs took him to the hospital."

"The Mermaid Bay crowd thinks he was mixed up in some drug deal gone bad. I heard he was dealing to save his business." Claude lowered his voice and looked toward the door. You better be careful if the dealers come back."

A shiver went up Jade's spine. Was Todd mixed up in something bad? But what about Emory? Didn't Amy say the bookstore was teetering, too? Did Emory and Todd get involved in something they couldn't control? She shook off the eerie feeling.

Jade couldn't concentrate during the final round. She was grateful when Lisa declared the game over. She fidgeted in her seat while Amy presented gift bags to Vivian's winning team. Thanks to Leo, Jade's team placed second. The last trio, a married couple and their teenage daughter, came in third.

After a few polite minutes to congratulate the winners, Jade yelled her thanks to Amy and waved to the group. "Night all. I've got to check on Chloe. This was fun."

She dashed out the door and down the steps before anyone could suck her into a conversation. She needed to talk to Nick.

Chapter Twenty-Nine

After flipping on the floodlights, Jade and Chloe slipped out the side door and hiked toward the beach. They had a clear view of the white shell path and the sand. Several dots of light bobbed on the bay as the waves rocked whatever ships were moored there for the evening. She inhaled the ocean air and let it out slowly. *Deep breaths of sea air. Good for whatever ails you.*

Jade had been on edge all day since they found Todd, and for some reason, Claude gave her the heebie-jeebies tonight. She couldn't quite pinpoint it, but she wanted to talk to Nick. She was disappointed when she got his voicemail twice.

The little dog, happy to be outside, trudged toward the beach. "Come on, puppy. It's getting dark. Let's head back." The Frenchie sniffed everything in her path and stopped to listen to every new sound. It took a few tugs to coax Chloe toward home.

After a bit of nudging, Chloe reluctantly headed toward the bungalow. Jade paused when a cracking sound jarred her from her thoughts. Not hearing anything else, she picked up the pace. She thought she heard footsteps as she put the key in the door. Picking up Chloe, she closed the door and doused the interior lights. She peeked out the window for a while to see if there was any movement. It took a few moments to calm her racing heartbeat. Nothing moved outside.

Chiding herself for being so jumpy, she pulled out her phone and called Nick.

"Hey," he said after a few rings. "How was trivia night?"

"We missed you," she said, unhooking the leash. Chloe trotted off to her bed. "It was fun, but Claude was on my team."

"Ha. So, I take it you didn't win. I didn't think he came out of his CPA cave much. He usually keeps to himself."

"You owe me. I was on a team with him and a guy named Leo, who at least helped us to second place. Any word on Todd?"

"He should be released sometime tomorrow. He didn't recognize his captors. He said a guy approached him near the dumpster for a light. Then the next thing he remembered was being in the back of a big van. He didn't remember anything about your shed."

"Maybe the video will jog his memory."

"He didn't seem to recognize it or himself when I showed it to him. The doctor said he may regain some memories as time passes. We'll see," Nick said, crunching on something.

"I hope so. I'm going to call him tomorrow to see if he needs anything. Claude was saying some disturbing things."

"More than normal?"

"Uh-huh. He hinted that Todd was mixed up in some drug deal, and I needed to be careful in case the dealers come back to my store."

"Doesn't sound like Todd, but I'll check into it," Nick said. After a pause, he continued, "Not sure what nights I'll be around for dinner this week, but when I have a better idea of my schedule, I'll text you. I need a do-over for trivia night."

"Dinner sounds good, but you missed your one and only shot to see Claude in action."

Nick laughed. "What a shame. I'll call ya later. Night."

Jade hung up and hugged the phone.

Thunk. Thunk thunk thunk. Jade opened one eye and tried to figure out where she was. The living room? She and Chloe had fallen asleep on the couch. Pop music still streamed from the TV. It took a minute to register where the noise came from. Chalking it up to the TV, she clicked it off and stretched. "Come on, kiddo. We need to go to bed."

Thunk thunk thunk thunk. Jade stiffened and listened. Not the TV. Then she hurried to the window. Nothing looked amiss outside. But she definitely heard weird noises. Was it a drip somewhere?

She did a circuit through the bathroom, kitchen, and laundry room. No odd sounds and, thankfully, no leaks.

When she thought she heard the noise again, she paused in the living room, listening for any other sounds. Chloe growled and skittered to the front door.

Dowsing all the interior lights, she moved from room to room to peer out the windows. Nothing moved, and no more sounds.

She took several deep breaths to calm the jitters. "Come on. It's night night time." She and Chloe hopped in bed, but she left the lamp on her nightstand on.

After a lot of tossing and turning, Jade opted for a quick breakfast and an early morning start to her day. She made a call to the hospital's information desk and gathered her things for work. As soon as Patti came in, she'd head over to see Todd.

Pulling the front door to the bungalow closed, Jade spotted small rocks on the porch and sidewalk. She hadn't had anyone throw rocks at her window since bad boy Nick had tried to get her to sneak out to parties in Seaport in her junior year of high school.

Probably not Nick this time. Not having time to clean up the mess, she snapped a picture and headed to the store. At least she knew what the weird noises came from. But why would someone pelt her stoop with rocks? Could it just be pranking kids?

They trekked down the street, and Jade checked her camera feeds on her phone. Not noticing anything out of the ordinary, they climbed the steps.

"There," she said, flipping the switch. "The lights make all the difference in the store. And Christmas is magical every day."

Jade pulled out a basket and gifts to take to Todd. Remembering the food ornaments in the toy room, she trekked through the store. Rummaging through the peach basket at the base of the tree, she found a hotdog decoration and a pretzel one that she'd add with a mug and holiday swag to the basket.

By the time she was struggling to hold the plastic wrap and tie a festive bow, Patti zipped in. "Oh, here. Let me get that for you."

"Thanks. Sometimes, I can't walk and chew gum at the same time."

"There. That looks nice," Patti said.

"I'm going to take it over to Todd in a few minutes. Hopefully, he'll be released today."

Patti shook her head as she started the coffee maker. "The gossip mill is revved in high gear about the, uh, shed incident."

"About Todd?" Jade fluffed the bow and moved the basket to her desk.

Patti nodded. "Rumors are flying about mafia and drug connections that want to put him out of business." Patti lowered her voice and looked around.

"Why are we whispering?"

"I don't know." Patti let out a laugh that sounded like bird's twitter. "You don't think he's mixed up in something nefarious, do you? Nor our Todd. He's always so nice."

"I wouldn't think so. We've known him and his family forever."

Patti shrugged one shoulder. "You never know. I hope it's not true. He's always been kind."

"I'm going to run over to the hospital to try to see him. Be back in a few. I didn't get to the online orders this morning."

"No problem. I'll be glad to dive in and see what came in. Chloe will help."

When she heard her name, the dog opened one eye and looked around like she was half-asleep.

"Be back in a flash. Call me if you need me."

"We'll be fine. Tell Todd I hope he's feeling better. What an ordeal," Patti said.

Jade picked up the basket and patted Chloe on the head. "Will do. See ya."

The classic rock station and the beautiful summer day made the perfect backdrop for a quick road trip. Jade found parking and walked what felt like miles to the hospital's front entrance.

"Good morning," she said to the receptionist. "What room is Todd

Brickman in?"

"Hello. What a beautiful basket," the woman with the silver bouffant said. She pulled up her glasses, dangling from a sparkly, beaded chain, and typed something in the computer. "Brickman. Ah, here he is. He's in room 403. You'll see the nurses' station as you exit the elevator on the fourth floor."

"Thank you. "The basket's from 'Tis the Season in Mermaid Bay." Jade's sneakers squeaked on the tile floor. The more she tried to suppress the noise, the louder it seemed to get.

When the elevator doors dinged and opened, Jade bypassed the nurses' station and found room 403. She rapped lightly with her knuckle on the door. After a "Come in," Jade slipped inside. "Hey, how're you doing?"

"Hey, Jade. Thanks for coming all this way. Is that for me?"

Jade smiled. "I hope you're feeling better." She handed him the basket. Todd, in a green hospital gown, sat propped up on a pillow.

"Cool." Todd tore off the bow and plastic and pulled out the mug, hot chocolate, candy, and ornaments. "Love these. They're going on the store tree this year. And thanks for finding me in your shed."

"What happened? You butt dialed me, and when I called you back, the kids in your store said you'd had taken the trash out."

Todd's grin faded. "I remember going out to the dumpster. I got a call from Tish while I was vaping. She was annoying as usual. When I hung up, some guy in a hoodie approached me. A hoodie in summer. Very weird. Anyway, he asked for a light, and I held up my ecig. We chatted for a while, and then he whipped out a metal rod and konked me. The next thing I knew, I woke up in the back of some kind of van or panel truck. They drove around for what seemed like hours."

Jade pulled out her phone and scrolled through her calls. "See. You called me." She pressed the button to play the weird message.

"That must have been at the dumpster? I don't remember. Sorry."

"Then I have you on camera with two guys in the wee hours," Jade said. "Well, I think they were dragging you."

Todd pinched his eyes closed for a moment. I remember being in the vehicle for a long time. We'd drive and stop and drive again. My head pounded, and I was queasy. It was hard to think straight. Sometime after dark, the guy dragged me out, and there was a second guy. We were somewhere with a lot of trees. And both guys had masks on. And I remember being thirsty."

Todd ran one hand through his already disheveled hair. "They asked if I had had enough and was ready to sell the hotdog stand." He paused. "I thought it was some kind of joke. I laughed, and the big one kept hitting me. They shoved me back in the van for me to think about what I wanted to do. I kinda remember the rescue squad and Nick and Sebastian. It seemed like a dream. One long, weird dream."

"Did you check your phone to see if you had any other calls?"

He reached for his phone and scrolled through it. He smirked. "Looks like just the calls to Tish and you. No photos or texts either."

"Tish call often?"

"I must be on her lead list. She calls every few weeks. She pretends to chat, but she really wants to see if I want to sell. She said she has a beachfront buyer."

"Amy said Tish was calling her, too. Did the kidnapper guys give you any clue as to who they were?"

"Nope. The shorter one was kinda quiet. He only whispered to the muscular one. For some reason, I got the impression he was older. But that's just a guess."

"I'm so sorry this happened. Do you need anything?" Jade asked.

He shook his head slightly. "I'm hoping they'll let me get out of here today. The food's terrible. And I need to check on the shop." He paused and braced the side of his head with his hand. "I probably shouldn't move my head too much. Ouch."

"Please be careful. Someone's targeting you. Think it's related to Emory?" Jade asked.

"Maybe by coincidence? She and I didn't have much in common." He snickered again. "We didn't quite run in the same circles."

"I'm concerned someone's targeting our business owners." Jade shuddered.

"I don't think so. I just had the window incident and some bad reviews.

And I have no idea where those are coming from. Well, and the kidnapping… What about your store?" he asked.

"Just the note and voodoo dolls. And my property isn't beachfront like yours, and Emory's" She paused and stared at Todd. "First, Emory, then you, and now Amy."

His smile vanished. "I'll call Nick later." He lay back and closed his eyes.

"Can I get you anything?" she asked.

"No, thinking about it gives me a headache."

"I'm sorry to get you upset. I'm going to head out," Jade said.

"It's not you," he said with his eyes still closed. "My gut tells me to never sell. I love my life here. But my brain says to be practical and get out before I'm ruined." He blew out air like a deflated balloon.

She patted his tattooed arm. "Let me know what I can help with."

"Will do. I need to figure out what I want to do. Never in my worst nightmare could I have imagined any of this."

Jade slipped out the door, a gloomy feeling descending on her. *I came here to cheer him up, and I think I made it worse.*

Chapter Thirty

Jade woke up at three-thirty with no hope of going back to sleep. She paid all of her bills, did a week's worth of laundry, and cleaned out her refrigerator. When the sun rose, she and Chloe hiked down to the Busy Bean for breakfast and coffee, though she probably didn't need any more caffeine.

Chloe sniffed the air in the coffee shop. The pastry scents made Jade's mouth water, too.

"Hey, gals. What brings you out this early?" James asked. "And what can I make for you on this bright morning?"

"Good morning. I'd like a small, iced mocha and a butter croissant. How's life around here?"

"Perfect. Summer is our favorite season. It'll be right up in a sec." James slipped Chloe a doggy treat.

Jade paid for her order and took her breakfast out on the deck. She found a good spot to watch for Todd's arrival next door. His Facebook post from last night stated that he was headed back to work after a short hiatus. She only hoped he wasn't coming back before he was fully healed. The breeze from the bay rustled Jade's curls. She held onto the croissant's paper wrapper, not wanting to chase it down the beach. Chloe, though, would have been fine if all or part of the croissant had landed on the deck.

Jade watched the morning beach visitors and seagulls from her vantage point on the deck. If she didn't have a whole pile of work things pulling her back to the store, this would be the perfect day to lounge in the sand with a good book.

Finishing the last few bites, Jade looked up as Todd hopped out of his blue FJ Cruiser and crossed the lot in five or six steps. He disappeared inside the hotdog stand. Jade dumped her trash and led Chloe down the back steps. The little dog had to jog to keep up with Jade, who hiked over the small dune to the parking lot next door.

When she yanked on the glass door, it didn't budge, and it jarred her.

Todd appeared on the other side and unlocked the front door. "Hey, what are you doing here so early?" He held the door open as he talked.

"We were out for a walk, and I wanted to check to see how you're doing. I saw you drive up."

"All better. I'm a little sore, but I should be back to normal in a few days," he said.

"Does the doctor know you're back at work?" Jade asked.

"Thanks, Mom." Todd rolled his eyes.

Jade gave him a side-eye, and he fidgeted.

"No, but you're a small business owner. You know that if you're not there, stuff doesn't get done."

Jade nodded. "But you're sure you're okay?"

He nodded and braced his head with one hand.

Jade bit her lip and swallowed her sassy comment.

"Come on in. I've got to get set up, or I'm going to be behind when I open. And if I start out behind the eight ball, I'll never catch up."

Jade scooped up Chloe and followed Todd inside. He paused and locked the door.

"Can I help you with anything?" she asked.

"Nah, I've got it down to a routine. Keep talking. I can hear you as I work. Want something to drink?"

"I'm good. Thanks. Did you happen to remember anything else about the two guys?"

He shook his head again and caught himself. "I've got to stop doing that. Nah. The guy at the dumpster didn't look familiar. He was stocky and youngish. The hoodie was really weird in warm weather. I wonder what he was hiding?"

"What about the other guy?"

"I don't remember actually seeing the other guy's face. I got a sense he was older. I do remember the stocky guy talking to someone in the van. And I think we stopped in some spooky, wooded area. I remember seeing water and big cypress trees. Then I woke up in the dark next to a lawn mower.

"Did they talk to you while they were driving you around? Or did you overhear anything? Something that might help ID them?"

"You working for Nick now?" Todd asked with a grin.

"No, but you were found in my shed." She raised both eyebrows.

"Sorry. I'm still not back to my loveable self yet. I may need a nap later. Hoodie guy talked a lot. The other one kept telling him to shut up. Let's see. We drove around for what felt like hours. Hoodie kept saying that I should make up my mind and sell. Wait. Wait. When we were in the woods, they both told me that I needed to get out of the restaurant business, and they were there to persuade me. They asked if I agreed. I said something snarky, and Hoodie punched me in the stomach. That went on for a while until I don't remember what happened. Oh, and they told me not to talk to that lapdog Tish. I have no idea what that meant. They said I needed Claude, the CPA, to make this all work out to my advantage."

"That's odd. Not to be Captain Obvious, but Tish is the realtor."

Todd shrugged his shoulder. "None of this makes any sense. I'm not fond of Tish or Claude."

"Did they mention any other names? Or did they slip up in any way?"

"Nope. And now I'm more determined than ever to make the restaurant work. I've got to check my supplies in the back before I prep for lunch. Can I get you anything?" Todd asked.

"Thanks for chatting. Please let me know if I can do anything."

"I appreciate your concern. My focus is to make it through this summer and to regroup over the off-season."

"You've got the grit to do it." Jade tugged on Chloe's leash, and the little dog headed toward the door.

"Just tell your friends to eat a lot of hotdogs," he yelled over his shoulder.

Jade smiled. "Of course." She and Chloe hurried across the street to open her own store on time.

As she gathered the inventory to fill the overnight orders, her thoughts kept flashing back to Todd. Why would the two guys tell him to contact Claude? It would make more sense if it were a realtor or developer. And why were they trying to put him out of business?

She boxed and addressed all the orders and had them ready for Simon by the time Patti, dressed in a lime-green Grinch sweater, floated in.

"Cute sweater," Jade said.

"I never wear this one. I decided to give it a whirl this morning. It matches your Jeep." Patti greeted Chloe and headed for the kitchenette. "How're you doing?"

"Good. Everything's ready to go for Simon."

Patti's blue eyes sparkled, and she smiled, showing off her rosy, apple cheeks. She selected a pod of coffee. "I started a weaving class at the art studio."

"Sounds fun. Clothing or other stuff?"

"Right now, we're learning how to do placemats. It takes me forever to string up the loom. It's fun once you get going. Not sure if this is going to be a permanent thing. They're offering a stained-glass course next. That sounds like something I'd enjoy. Plus, if I get good at it, I could make Christmas suncatchers."

"That does sound fun. I need a hobby."

"I'll text you the registration information. We can be art buddies." Patti smiled and pulled out her phone.

"I'm going to walk down and see if Claude is in. I'll be back in a few."

Patti wrinkled her nose slightly. "No biggie wiggie. Chloe and I'll mind the store."

Jade slipped her phone in her back pocket and jogged down the back steps. The sun warmed her face during the short walk. Thoughts of her marketing calendar jumped around in her head and overpowered the bliss. She'd add the promo work to her long list of to-do items for later.

As she passed the realty office, the door flew open. Tish stuck her head outside. "Jade. Hey, Jade. Howdy. Have you thought more about selling your adorable little bungalow?"

"Hi, Tish." Jade smiled, probably showing more teeth than was considered friendly. "No, I think I'm going to stay put for a while. I've been watching HGTV, and I think I'm going to tackle some DIY projects first. I like being so close to work. And it's full of family memories."

The realtor's face didn't change, but she seemed to talk through her teeth. "Oh, fun. Well, if you change your mind, promise that you'll call me first."

"Will do. You're the only realtor in my contact list."

"Don't tell Farrah or the others." Tish winked. She turned on her lemon-yellow stilettos and disappeared inside.

Jade dodged the uneven spots on the sidewalk and stopped in front of the CPA's office. The inside looked dark except for a few stray sunbeams full of dust mites. She pulled on the door, and a musty gym locker smell smacked her in the face. Her nose twitched as she stepped inside and got a whiff of the stale air.

The receptionist's desk looked abandoned, with a stack of mail teetering on the edge.

"Hi, is anyone home?" Her voice echoed through the suite.

"Uh, hello, Jade. Interested in another trivia night?" Claude stepped through a doorway in the back. "I was getting coffee. Would you like some?"

"No thanks. I can't stay long. I stopped by on my walk. I popped in to see Todd, and he mentioned you. His captor kept telling him he should work with you. Any idea why? There's been a lot of unusual stuff going on around here lately."

It was hard to tell in the room, lit only by natural light from the windows, but Jade thought she saw Claude flinch.

Standing up straighter, the older man replied, "It's a shame that Mermaid Bay is going downhill. I may have to reevaluate whether I want to keep my business here. There's been way too much crime lately. It's not like it used to be." Claude paused, and his mouth trembled slightly. "I don't have a clue about Todd's issues. And I'm not sure how I could even help him unless he needs accounting services." He seemed to force himself to half-smile. "And now I'm getting endorsements from kidnappers. Just what I need." He pursed his lips and stared at Jade.

"It is odd. Todd didn't remember much, so he couldn't put any context to it."

"Maybe he's suffering from a concussion or he's hallucinating. Hope he's not on drugs." If he was waiting for Jade to comment, he was disappointed. "Anyway, maybe it's time I relocate." He sighed loudly. "I've got to get back to work. It's been nice talking to you, but I've got quarterly taxes to take care of. I'm glad Todd's doing better. If you hear any more about me, let me know. Though I'm not sure I really want to get involved."

When he retreated to his office, Jade retraced her steps and let herself out. Not ready to give up yet, she crossed the street and wandered into Amy's store.

Waiting for her friend to finish with two customers, Jade browsed the stacks near the counter. Amy had rearranged all the shelves like bookstagram displays. The store definitely looked more welcoming and interesting than it had in the past. A table featuring upcoming events caught her attention. Lots of author events on the calendar. Jade smiled.

"Hey, long time no see. What's shaking?" Amy closed the register drawer.

"Been out visiting this morning. Did you hear about Todd?"

"Scary stuff. I'm always looking over my shoulder when I go to the dumpster or my car. I didn't feel this jumpy when I lived in the city. Do you find yourself sizing up customers?" Amy's eyes widened.

Jade laughed. "Most of mine are women over fifty or moms with little kids. But yes, I do a lot more checking out my surroundings lately."

"Rumor has it that Todd was found in your shed. Weird, huh?"

"And I have no idea why. He said there were two guys. One approached him at the dumpster, and after a tussle, they shoved him in a van and drove around until they left him at my place. He said they warned him about selling his property and that he should talk to Claude."

"Claude from the other night? No sense of humor, Claude? Why?"

"Yep. That one. Todd had no idea. And Claude wasn't as chatty today as he was last Friday. He said that he was thinking about moving his business."

Amy's smile faded. "I am constantly checking and rechecking my doors to make sure they're locked. And I'm always listening for weird noises. This whole Todd thing gives me the heebie jeebies. What if I'm next? But so far, nothing else has happened. I'm hoping things calm down. This isn't how I wanted to spend my first summer at the beach. Hey, I need a day off. We should play hooky tomorrow afternoon and go to the beach."

"Sounds fun. I can close up around four," Jade said.

"Cool. Meet me here and bring whatever you want to drink. I'll bring sandwiches and a blanket."

"It's a date. See you then." Jade waved over her shoulder and hustled back to the store. Everyone in town seemed to be on edge. Maybe a day at the beach would be a relaxing change.

Chapter Thirty-One

"I feel like something different this morning," Lorelei announced. "I'm going to the Busy Bean. Want anything?"

Jade shook her head. "I'm good. I've been working on next month's newsletter, and I need to get some social media posts done. Did the packages get picked up?"

"Nope, not yet. Looks like Simon's running late. I'll be back in a bit." Lorelei hummed her way out.

Jade stood and stretched. Chloe opened one eye and decided to go back to sleep. "I know. We need to liven this place up, girl. I hate slow, draggy mornings." She changed the streaming music to a peppier playlist and wandered through the store.

In the toy room, she checked the inventory. The novelty ornaments were selling well this season. She made a mental note of items to add to the next order sheet.

She paused when she heard a noise. No bells, so it probably wasn't the front door. "Stop being so jumpy," she said, picking up a dog ornament that looked like Chloe.

A scraping sound made her pause. Not hearing anything else, she tiptoed toward the doorway. Something rustled behind her. A peach basket moved, and Neville strutted out like he owned the place.

"Neville, you devil. You scared me." She picked up the cat and nuzzled him close to her neck. "It's good to see you back. How's life at Lorelei's?"

The tuxedo cat tolerated a few minutes of cuddles, and then he wiggled until she set him back on the floor. Jade made her way through the collectibles and rainbow room, where each tree had a color theme. She could make the lights and colors pop in some evening photos, perfect for her Instagram account. She'd drag out her tripod and lighting kit to take some new photos soon.

Rounding the corner into the local artisans' room, Jade noticed that something moved down the hallway. Probably just Neville again. Chiding herself for being so skittish, she checked the displays.

Chloe barked. As she turned to check on her dog, something moved behind her. A shadow crossed her path, and someone covered her mouth. The leather glove smelled smoky.

Jade stomped hard on the guy's foot, and he loosened his grip for a moment, long enough for her to wiggle free and run toward the storage room. Slipping and regaining her balance, she tore through the store for the back room and slammed the door. She locked it and looked around for something to block it with. She rolled Patti's inventory cart, full of boxes in front of it, and slid a chair under the knob.

Patting her pockets, she had a moment of panic when she remembered her phone was on her desk. "Wait. Office phone." She hurdled over a small table and punched in 911 on the desk phone as her attacker slammed into the door.

"What is your emergency?" the dispatcher asked.

"This is Jade Hicks at 'Tis the Season. Someone is trying to break into the backroom of my store. Help. He attacked me, but I was able to get away."

The pounding on the door continued. Then there was a loud crack, and she could see the guy's elbow and then his arm through the door.

"He's breaking down the door. Hurry!" Jade screamed.

The guy punched again, and more of the door splintered. A head with sunglasses and a ballcap appeared where part of the door used to be. One more kick. The door splintered off its hinges. Jade could hear Chloe barking in the next room. She said a silent prayer that she'd be quiet and that this guy would leave her precious dog alone.

He stepped over the remnants and swung an arm with a gun around.

"He's got a gun!" Jade yelled and ducked under the desk. The receiver dangled on the cord next to her. Jade tried to make herself as small as possible. As he stormed through the room like Godzilla, she looked for another hiding place. She was a sitting duck.

"Come out," he bellowed. "I know you're in here." It sounded like he was shuffling around the room.

Jade took a deep breath and let it out slowly. *It's now or never. Hopefully, the 911 operator was still listening.* Crawling behind the desk to the nearby counter, she flattened herself behind it and peeked around the corner. The guy, all in black with motorcycle boots, seemed to wreak havoc in every direction.

When his back was turned, she lowered her head and zoomed over the debris and out the doorway. It didn't take long until she heard pounding footsteps on the floor behind her. In the hallway, she headed to the lobby and the front door.

Dashing behind the front counter, she heard footsteps moving away from her. She paused. *Are the police on their way?*

She stood and darted toward the front door at the same time the guy appeared in the doorway. "Freeze."

Jade's heart leapt to her throat and pounded like a bass drum at a high school football game half-time. Not ready to surrender, she plowed on toward the door.

The guy grabbed her hair with one hand and yanked her backward. He twisted one arm behind her and pulled it up over her head.

Jade winced as pain shot through her arm and up her neck.

"I've had enough of you. Stay still. You keep butting in where you don't belong. I'm going to teach you a lesson. And your cop friend's not here to help you this time."

He half dragged her across the floor to the office. Setting his gun on the corner of her desk, he shoved her in a nearby chair.

"Be quiet. You've caused enough trouble," the guy snapped.

Bile welled up in the back of Jade's throat. How was she going to get away from this guy?

Something moved in the hallway. Footsteps caused them both to stare at the broken door.

A wave of relief flooded over her when Claude stepped into the room. "Help me. He's got a gun! Do something!" Jade yelled.

The CPA's lip curled, and his facial features tightened. Jade stared at the older man, and a sudden recognition flashed across her thoughts. *This was why the guy told Todd to work with Claude.* Fear flooded through her body and made her heart race. The CPA wasn't here to help her.

"Tie her up," Claude snarled. "Then we have to figure out what to do with her. It's going to be hard to get her out of here in broad daylight without somebody noticing."

The guy in black grabbed her shoulder and zip-tied her wrists in front of her.

"We could leave her here and come back later," the guy offered, wiping his brow.

"What if someone comes in before we get back?" Claude's glance darted around the room.

"Then they release her. No biggie."

"She can ID us, Vince," Claude said, smacking the guy on the head. "Don't be stupid."

"Me? You're the one using our real names," the guy said, adjusting his ballcap. "Gimme a minute to think of a way to get rid of her."

Jade had to stall until someone else showed up. Lorelei. No! She panicked at the thought of her aunt walking into an ambush. And where was Chloe? Jade's stomach burned, and her head started to throb. She had to stay calm and think of a way out of this mess.

"Go lock the doors while I think about this," Claude ordered.

Vince shuffled out while Claude paced in the hallway. Jade glanced at the gun on the desk and wiggled her wrists. Wait, she saw something on TV once about getting out of zip-ties. What did the guy say to do?

It's worth a try. She didn't have too many options at the moment. She sat tall in the chair and raised both arms over her head. With one good heave, she dropped both arms and pulled her wrists apart as far apart as she could.

Pop. The plastic broke, and she jumped up, lunging for the gun.

Grabbing the gun, she pointed it at Claude, hoping her voice didn't quake. "Get up against that wall and don't move. I'm a little frazzled from wrestling with your pal, so my trigger finger may be a little twitchy, and that won't work to your benefit."

"Vince, you frickin' idiot. You left your gun in here," Claude yelled.

They heard shuffling and footsteps. Then silence.

"Vince!" Claude bellowed again. "Vince, where are you?"

The back door slammed.

"Looks like he left you high and dry," Jade said. "Why are you even here, Claude?"

"You wouldn't let it go. You couldn't leave well enough alone. We had a plan, and now it's all ruined." Claude slid down the wall and rested his head in his arms. "First Emory, now you."

An icy sensation crept down Jade's spine and landed in her stomach. "What did you do to Emory?"

"Nothing. It was Vince," Claude sniveled. "She and I had a partnership, but she weaseled out. The plan was for us to buy Todd's place too, and we'd have quite a nice corner to develop with a perfect entrance to the beach. With that much real estate, we could attract big money. We were going to hold onto it until we could change the zoning. Nobody would have paid any attention. We could have made a killing." He paused when he realized what he said. "We would have made a bundle." Claude's voice trailed off. "I would have been set for retirement."

"What?" Jade asked, stepping closer. "That's no reason to kill someone."

"Emory got cold feet. She started being all nostalgic and didn't want to hurt the kids over at the Busy Bean, so she backed out. Then she got all high and mighty on me. Always rubbing salt in wounds. Then she came after me. She started council discussions about making the zoning even stricter. This was going to be my goose and golden egg."

"So, you killed her?"

"No," he whined. "I sent Vince over to talk some sense into her, and next thing I know, she's dead. I told him to scare her. Vince is crazy. And now I'm cleaning up his messes."

"What about the posters and the other stuff? And the spooky suitcase with the bones?"

Claude lifted his head, and a slight grin crossed his face. "That was my idea. Keep 'em on edge. If people didn't visit, our economy would suffer. And if people didn't feel safe, they'd move. I wanted to create a buzz and for people to question whether or not Mermaid Bay was safe. Plus, the property values might have dropped. It was working, too, until Emory's niece showed up, and you started poking around. We had a great deal that we could go to the developers with. Mermaid Bay would never be the same."

Jade heard a noise, and her gaze shifted toward the door.

Claude didn't seem to notice. "It was a great plan until it fell apart. I should have waited and not called Vince." He spat out the younger man's name like it was bad sushi.

"It looks like he jumped ship and left you hanging in the breeze," she interrupted.

"Who knows? He's not really dependable. I never should have gotten mixed up with him. This is all his fault." He buried his head again in his arms. "Why did I ever trust him?"

Was Vince still creeping around her store? Jade's heart pounded. She took a few steps backward, making sure she had a good view of the doorway and Claude. She felt better with her back almost against the wall.

Straining to hear any indication of approaching footsteps, the adrenaline coursed through her. All she heard was Claude's sniffing and her heart pounding in her ears.

After what felt like an eternity, there was stomping, and "Police!" echoed through the store.

"We're back here, and I have his gun," Jade yelled.

Nick stepped over the rubble of the ruined door.

She handed Nick the gun as he stared at Claude.

"You okay, Jade?" Nick asked. The voice was stern, but his eyes brimmed with concern.

Jade nodded, trying to calm her nerves. "But the other guy got away."

Stomping and scuffling interrupted them. Sebastian shoved a handcuffed

Vince through the doorway.

"He didn't quite make it," Sebastian said. "Sit in that chair, and don't move until we get this sorted out."

A rumpled Vince dropped into the office chair and scowled.

Sebastian took a deep breath. "He came flying out of your back door. I caught up to him just east of the pier. The sand slowed him down."

Vince sneered. "I would have made it if I hadn't tripped over your stupid dog and fallen a couple times in the sand."

A slight grin crossed Sebastian's face.

"Chloe!" Panic washed over Jade.

"She's fine after her adventure. She's outside with Lorelei," Sebastian said.

"Thank goodness." It felt like a load of bricks had been lifted from her shoulders. Jade blew out a long breath and leaned on the desk. "I was worried that Lorelei was going to walk in on all this." Jade closed her eyes for a moment.

"We heard everything that happened here." Nick replaced the receiver on the phone. "Claude, what were you thinking?"

"It was supposed to be a way to bankroll a lot of cash. Emory and I had a deal until she wormed out. But I didn't kill her. That was him." He nodded his head toward Vince. "He did all the violent stuff. I was just trying not to go bankrupt. You've got to believe me," he wailed as Sebastian took him into custody. "He did all the bad stuff!"

"Claude, you're so full of it. You knew exactly what was going on. You helped me plan the meeting with the crazy lady and the hot dog guy. You're not pinning this on me. I'll cooperate if I have to. You're going down for this." Vince squirmed in his chair and stared at Sebastian. "Officer, I'm ready to make a statement."

"Shut up!" Claude shouted. "And I want to make my statement. I want to talk to my lawyer. Vince, you're making it worse."

"Not sure how it could be much worse," Vince said. "You bumbled everything."

"Both of you be quiet," Nick snapped. "Get him out of here. Take him to the station for booking. When forensics gets here, I'll get Claude transported."

CHAPTER THIRTY-ONE

Sebastian pulled Vince to his feet and guided him out.

"Oh, wait, I need to check on Neville. He was in the store too. I hope he didn't get loose." Jade rushed through the store to find the cat curled up on the front counter. "Oh, Neville. I'm so glad you're okay." She scooped up the black and white cat and hugged him until he squirmed.

"Your aunt is in the back parking lot. Forensics is going to have to go through this place. Do you need anything out of your office?" Nick asked.

"My phone and purse."

"Do you have some paper nearby? I need you to describe what happened while it's still fresh."

Jade climbed over the debris and pulled out her purse and a legal pad from the bottom desk drawer. She spent the next half hour writing out her narrative. After looking over her scribbles that she hoped the police could read, she signed and dated the bottom and tore off the five pages.

"Here." She handed the pages to Nick.

"Thanks. Forensics is on the way. I'm hoping we can turn this back over to you this afternoon. But it may be late tonight. Where are you going to be?"

"Nearby, I guess. I want to check on Lorelei, and my phone has been blowing up. Maybe I'll get something to eat. Want anything?"

Nick shook his head. "I'll text you when we're done."

She smiled faintly. "Thanks. I'll be outside if you need anything." She picked up Neville and looked around at the damage.

Chapter Thirty-Two

Jade dodged three forensic techs as she stepped out on the back stoop into the bright sunshine.

Lorelei rushed over and hugged her with Chloe in her arms. The little dog snorted when she was sandwiched between them. And Neville wasn't pleased with all the feels either. "Are you okay? I got back, and the police wouldn't let me go in. And then I found Chloe out back by herself. And I couldn't reach you. This is just crazy." Lorelei handed her Chloe and reached for Neville.

A crowd of neighbors with hundreds of questions surrounded them.

"I'm fine. Sorry to frighten you. Vince did a number on our office door. And he scared the crap out of me when he busted in with that gun."

"Jade, we're so glad you're okay. Is it true it was Claude?" Vivian asked, her breath ragged after she rushed over. *Did she run all the way over here from the library?*

Jade nodded, not sure about how much she should say, especially since Nell was skulking around. "I'm sure the sheriff will give a statement when they're done inside."

Nell looked like she was about to ask a question. After a pause, she clamped her mouth shut and walked around the perimeter of the crowd.

"You captured Vince and Claude? You go, girl." Amy fist-pumped the air and hugged Jade. "I'm so glad this is over."

Remembering their plans, Jade said, "Me too. And I think I'm going to have to take a rain check on our beach day. Not sure how long forensics going to be here."

"No worries, but you have to promise to call me as soon as you can. We need to catch up. I want deets. I gotta head back but call me if you need anything." Amy waved over her shoulder.

Jade smiled as her friend dodged gawkers who clogged the sidewalk. Standing outside her store, Jade and Lorelei watched the crowd ebb and flow. When the police action died down, more folks wandered off.

Lorelei pulled out two chairs from the shed, and they sat in the only shaded spot they could find next to the store. Jade responded to a flurry of texts and email posts. It felt like everyone in Mermaid Bay had contacted her.

A shadow fell over the pair, and Jade looked up. Todd offered two boxes. "Hey, y'all. I brought over lunch when I heard what happened. You okay?"

"My scrap with Vince wasn't as bad as yours. I just have a couple of scrapes and bruises." Jade opened the cardboard box. Chloe and Neville became interested in the hot dog smells.

"And according to Vivian, you wrestled his gun from him. Way to go. Nick should hire you." Todd handed each of them a Coke.

"Jade's our hero. She solved this whole thing and figured out who killed Emory." Lorelei pulled out a paper napkin and spread it across her lap.

"Claude spilled everything when I had the gun. He said Vince did all the bad stuff. He was plotting with Emory to buy up property for a big development deal. He claimed it was all business. And then Vince started to talk when Claude ratted him out. And, of course, he blamed Claude for everything."

"I guess that makes what Vince said to me make more sense. He kept telling me to sell and to call Claude. I hope this is the end of my problems. Thanks to you, I had a huge lunch crowd today." Todd pushed his long bangs out of his eyes. "It'll be nice to get back to beach normal."

"Who was doing all the posters and voodoo mumbo jumbo," Lorelei asked. "Vince?"

"No, that was Claude's way of spooking people and getting them riled up. He said he and Emory were in cahoots at first, and then she turned on him. It wasn't clear if she knew about the pranks. Then he brought Vince in as muscle, and things turned bad."

"You think you know someone, and then bam! Never in a million years would I have predicted that Claude was in on all this." Lorelei rolled her eyes.

"Vince broke my window, and I'm sure he was the guy at the dumpster who took me on that not-so-joyful joy ride. I'm glad it's all over." Todd patted Jade's shoulder.

"Claude was singing like a canary when they hauled him out of here. He was screaming that he was framed, and it was all Vince's fault." A smile almost crossed Lorelei's deep, red lips. "He caused quite a scene."

"Nick should have fun sorting this out. I hope it doesn't affect the rest of our season," Jade said.

"People have short memories," Lorelei replied. "They'll be onto the next shiny thing that catches their eye. By fall, this will be just a sad memory."

Todd nodded. "I gotta get back. Text me if anything exciting happens. Maybe we can have dinner sometime." He winked at Jade.

Jade's eyes widened, and Lorelei poked her in the ribs. *Did he just ask me out?* When she realized that she hadn't replied, she said, "Thanks for lunch. A hot dog never tasted so good."

About an hour later, Nick followed the forensic team down the back steps.

"You want to check the place out before I leave?" Nick said to Jade.

"I've got the chairs and the critters. Go ahead." Lorelei stood and gathered the remnants from lunch.

Jade followed Nick on a quick tour of the store. She took some pictures of the door in case she had to file an insurance claim. "It looks like more of a mess than anything. The door and the frame are the only things that need to be replaced, thankfully. It won't take me long to clean up. I'll get Bernie on it tomorrow."

Nick turned and folded her into a deep hug. "I'm glad you're okay. I freaked out when I heard the call come in, and the operator couldn't get you back on the line."

Jade hugged back. It felt warm and safe, and she had to fight back the tears that were welling up in her eyes. When she was sure her voice wouldn't quake, she added, "Thanks. It happened so fast. I was stunned when I realized

CHAPTER THIRTY-TWO

Claude was part of it."

"You did well. You had the sense to stay calm and not to egg them on."

"I'm glad this is all over." Jade turned slightly. His holster jabbed her in the rib cage. "Ouch, I guess that's one of the hazards of hugging a cop."

"Tonight's going to be a late one. How about dinner tomorrow?"

"A real date?" she asked, pulling back and staring up into his green eyes.

"Yes. A real date. It's about time we quit dancing around the obvious. We need to make this official."

He kissed her, and she felt a warm tingle move its way down her spine.

"So, I can change my status from 'it's complicated'?" Jade smiled and snuggled in closer.

"About time," Lorelei said, bustling in with Chloe. Catching her eye, Nick didn't back away, wrapping his arm tighter around Jade instead. Lorelei gave him a nod of approval. Then to Jade, "Neville and I need to hit the road." Her grin widened. "I think we've all had enough for one day. Don't you?"

Patti's Chocolate Peppermint Bombs

Ingredients:

- 1 cup butter, softened
- 1 cup sugar
- 1 large egg
- 1 teaspoon peppermint extract
- 2 1/3 cups of all-purpose flour
- 1/3 cup cocoa powder (for baking)
- 1 teaspoon salt
- 1 teaspoon baking soda
- 1 package (12 oz.) milk or dark chocolate chips
- 1 cup marshmallow cream
- 1 cup crushed candy canes (or peppermint candy)

Directions:

Mix butter and sugar in a large bowl. Beat in the egg and the peppermint extract. Then add flour, cocoa powder. Salt, and baking soda. Mix all ingredients well.

Drop the dough by tablespoons about 2-3 inches apart on a greased baking sheet. Bake at 375 degrees F for 12 minutes. The cookies are ready when the tops start to crack. Cool cookies on wire racks.

In a microwave-safe bowl, melt the chocolate chips.

Drop a teaspoon of marshmallow cream into the center of each cookie. Then carefully dip half of each cookie into the melted chocolate. Let the excess drip off. Top each cookie with the crushed peppermint candy.

Peanut Butter Kiss Cookies

Ingredients:

- ½ cup granulated sugar
- ½ cup brown sugar (packed)
- ½ - 1 cup creamy peanut butter
- ½ cup softened butter
- 1 egg
- 1 ½ cup of all-purpose flour
- ¾ teaspoon baking soda
- ½ teaspoon of baking powder
- Additional granulated sugar
- 36-40 Hershey's Kisses Brand (Unwrapped)

Directions:

Preheat your oven to 375 degrees F. In a large bowl, mix a ½ cup of the sugar, brown sugar, butter, peanut butter and eggs with an electric mixer (medium speed). Make sure the mixture is well blended. Add flour, baking soda, and baking powder.

Shape the dough into 1-inch balls. Roll the balls in the remaining granulated sugar. Put the balls on an ungreased cookie sheet about 2 inches apart.

Bake for about 10 minutes until the edges are a light golden brown. When you pull the cookies from the oven, press a candy in the center of each cookie. Cool the cookies on a rack.

To add some festive decorations, before baking, you can roll the cookies in sparkling sugar or decorating sugar instead of the granulated sugar.

You can also use different kinds of chocolate candies in place of the Kiss to mix up the flavor.

Lorelei's Holiday Cookie Bars

Ingredients:

- ¾ cup of butter (softened)
- 1 cup granulated sugar
- ½ cup of brown sugar (packed)
- 2 large eggs
- 2 teaspoons of vanilla extract
- 2 cups of all-purpose flour
- ¾ teaspoon of baking powder
- ½ teaspoon of kosher salt
- 8 Oreo cookies (crushed)
- ½ cup of holiday M&Ms candy
- ½ cup of semisweet chocolate chips
- cooking spray

Directions:

Preheat the over to 350 degrees F. Grease a 9x9 baking pan with the cooking spray. In a large bowl, mix the butter and all sugars with an electric mixer on medium. Add the eggs and vanilla and continue to mix.

In another bowl, mix together the flour, baking powder, and salt. Combine the contents of both bowls and mix until thoroughly combined. Add the cookies, candy, and chocolate chips.

Press the batter into your pan and bake for 25 minutes until the middle is slightly soft. After the cookies cool, slice into squares.

You can substitute any baking chips, candy, and the cookies to change up the bar's flavors.

Mermaid Bay Gingerbread

Ingredients:

- ½ cup unsalted butter
- ½ cup dark brown sugar
- 1 cup of molasses
- 1 large egg
- 1 teaspoon vanilla extract
- 2 ½ cups of all-purpose flour
- 1 ½ teaspoon baking soda
- 1 teaspoon ground ginger
- 1 teaspoon ground cloves
- 1 teaspoon ground cinnamon
- ¾ teaspoon salt
- 1 cup boiling water
- Topping: whipped cream

Directions:

Preheat the oven to 350 degrees F. Grease a 9x9 baking pan.

In a large bowl, mix the butter and brown sugar. Use an electric mixer to combine until creamy. Add the molasses, egg, and vanilla.

In another bow, mix the flour, baking soda, cinnamon, cloves, ginger, and salt. Combine the contents of both bowls. Stir in the boiling water.

Pour the contents into your baking pan. Bake for 40 minutes. Use a toothpick to test the center of the dessert.

Cool and slice. Don't forget the whipped cream.

Virginia Peanut Brittle

Ingredients:

- 2 cups of sugar
- 1 cup of corn syrup
- ½ cup water
- 2 cups of roasted, salted peanuts
- 2 tablespoons butter
- 1 ½ teaspoon of baking soda
- 1 ½ teaspoon vanilla

Other Supplies:

- Medium Saucepan
- Parchment Paper
- Sheet Pan
- Candy Thermometer

Directions:

Line a sheet pan with parchment paper.

Mix peanuts, butter, baking soda, and vanilla. Set aside.

Mix sugar and water in a saucepan and stir well. Add the corn syrup. Use medium heat. You don't want to heat it too fast. Stir until the mixture comes to a gentle boil.

Attach your thermometer to the pot. Cook until the temperature reaches 250 degrees F.

Add the peanuts and stir until the temperature reaches 300 degrees F.

Remove the candy from the heat and add butter, baking soda, and vanilla.

Pour the hot mixture in the pan. Be careful. Use a knife to spread the mixture evenly.

Allow the candy bake for 30 minutes.

Break the candy apart. You can store the candy when it's cooled in an airtight container.

Eggnog Snickerdoodles

Ingredients:

- 1 sugar cookie mix (you'll need eggs and butter for most of these)
- 1 teaspoon ground nutmeg
- ½ teaspoon rum extract
- ½ teaspoon cinnamon
- ¼ cup sugar
- 1 ½ cups white baking chips
- waxed paper

Directions

Preheat your oven to 375 degrees F. Mix the cookie mix, egg, butter, ½ teaspoon of nutmeg, and rum extract. Make 36 balls from the dough (about 1 ¼ inch).

In another bowl, mix sugar, cinnamon, and remaining nutmeg. Roll the dough balls in this mixture. Place them on an ungreased cookie sheet (about 2 inches apart).

Bake about 9 minutes until the edges are set. Cool and remove from the cookie sheet to a rack. Let them cool for about 20 minutes on the rack.

In a bowl, microwave the baking chips on medium power for 1 minute. Stir. Continue to heat in 15-second increments until the chips are a smooth liquid.

Dip each cookie halfway into the melted vanilla chips. Let excess drip off. If your chip mixture cools, reheat to liquify it. Let cookies stand for 30 minutes before serving.

Bernie's Orange Treasures

Ingredients:

Cookie:

- 1 cup shortening
- 2 cups sugar
- 2 large eggs, separated,
- 1 cup buttermilk
- 5 cups of all-purpose flour
- 2 teaspoons baking powder
- 2 teaspoons baking soda
- Salt (pinch)
- Juice and grated zest of 2 navel oranges (medium)

Icing:

- 2 cups confectionary sugar
- ¼ cup orange juice
- 1 tablespoon butter
- 1 tablespoon orange zest (grated)

Directions:

Preheat your oven to 325 degrees F. In a bowl, mix the shortening and sugar. Beat in egg yolks and buttermilk. Sift in the flour, baking powder, baking soda, and salt. Then add the orange juice and zest. Add egg whites and beat until the dough is smooth.

Drop cookie dough (teaspoon-sized mounds) onto an ungreased cookie sheet. Bake about 10 minutes and cool cookies on wire racks.

Combine the sugar, orange juice, butter, and orange zest in a bowl and beat until smooth.

Once the cookies have cooled, frost them with the icing. This recipe makes about six dozen cookies.

Amy's Cranberry Jar Cookie Kits

Ingredients:

- 1 cup all-purpose flour
- ½ teaspoon baking soda
- ½ teaspoon salt
- ½ cup of rolled oats
- 1/3 cup sugar
- ½ cup dried cranberries
- ½ cup white chocolate chips
- ½ cup chopped pecans
- 1 teaspoon vanilla
- Quart-sized jars (Mason jars work well)
- Paper, fabric, or ribbon to decorate the jars

Directions:

Make sure the jars are clean and dry.

Combine the flour, baking soda, and salt. Separately, mix the sugars. Add half of the flour mixture, followed by the oats. Then add the rest of the flour mixture. Top with the sugar mixture, cranberries, and white chocolate chips. The last layer should be the chopped pecans.

Decorate the jars for the holiday season. Ribbon, tulle, or twine make good bows. Create a gift tag with the instructions for baking:

Preheat oven to 350 degrees F. Grease a cookie sheet. Mix the ingredients in the jar in a medium bowl with ½ cup of unsalted butter, softened and 1 beaten egg. Drop the cookies on the sheet about an inch apart. Bake for 12-14 minutes. Cool the lightly browned cookies on a wire rack.

Acknowledgements

I want to thank my family and friends who provided all the wonderful support for me and this book: Stan Weidner, thanks for being the key part of my writing life, my parents who instilled in me a lifelong love of reading, Cortney Cain for being my texting buddy at five a.m., Meagan and Jocelyn Cain, my social media gurus, and Bill Cain for always keeping everyone entertained. And I appreciate all the encouragement, love, and support from my Bethia UMC family.

I am so grateful for my talented Sisters in Crime, Guppy, Virginia is for Mysteries, International Thriller Writers, and James River Writer friends. Your support is invaluable! Jayne Ormerod, Mary Burton, Sherry Harris – You all are so gracious with your support!

Many, many thanks to my fabulous agent, Dawn Dowdle for all her help and hard work. And a huge thank you to Shawn Reilly Simmons and the infamous Dames of Detection, and everyone at Level Best Books for letting me share life in Mermaid Bay with y'all.

Many thanks to Dom, Jennifer and Ms. Bruin Bear Cristello for all of your expert advice on French bulldogs.

Pluto Living (Pluto, may you rest in peace)

Pluto was the inspirational Schnauzer and her talented crew who kept me in stitches and reminded me of hope during the pandemic and for giving me the idea for a mortal cat enemy for Chloe. Neville the Devil cat is based on your frien-emy.

About the Author

Through the years, Heather Weidner has been a cop's kid, technical writer, editor, college professor, software tester, and IT manager. *She writes the Delanie Fitzgerald Mysteries, The Jules Keene Glamping Mysteries*, and *The Mermaid Bay Christmas Shoppe Mysteries.*

Her short stories appear in the *Virginia is for Mysteries* series, *50 Shades of Cabernet, Deadly Southern Charm,* and *Murder by the* Glass.

She is a member of Sisters in Crime – Central Virginia, Sisters in Crime – Chessie, Guppies, International Thriller Writers, and James River Writers.

Originally from Virginia Beach, Heather has been a mystery fan since Scooby-Doo and Nancy Drew. She lives in Central Virginia with her husband and a pair of Jack Russell terriers.

She earned her BA in English from Virginia Wesleyan University and her MA in American literature from the University of Richmond.

SOCIAL MEDIA HANDLES:

Website and Blog: http://www.heatherweidner.com

Twitter: https://twitter.com/HeatherWeidner1

Facebook: https://www.facebook.com/HeatherWeidnerAuthor

Instagram: https://www.instagram.com/heather_mystery_writer/

Goodreads: https://www.goodreads.com/author/show/8121854.Heath
er_Weidner

Amazon Authors: http://www.amazon.com/-/e/B00HOYR0MQ

Pinterest: https://www.pinterest.com/HeatherBWeidner/

LinkedIn: https://www.linkedin.com/in/heather-weidner-0064b233?tr
k=hp-identity-name

BookBub: https://www.bookbub.com/authors/heather-weidner-d6430
278-c5c9-4b10-b911-340828fc7003

TikTok: https://www.tiktok.com/@heather_weidner_author

YouTube: https://www.youtube.com/channel/UCyBjyB0zz-M1DaM-r
U1bXGA?view_as=subscriber

AUTHOR WEBSITE:

http://HeatherWeidner.com

Also by Heather Weidner

The Jules Keene Glamping Mysteries
Vintage Trailers and Blackmailers
Film Crews and Rendezvous

The Delanie Fitzgerald Mysteries
Secret Lives and Private Eyes
The Tulip Shirt Murders
Glitter, Glam, and Contraband
Male Revues and Subterfuge

The Mutt Mysteries (Novellas)
To Fetch a Thief
To Fetch a Scoundrel
To Fetch a Villain
To Fetch a Killer

Short Stories
The *Virginia is for Mysteries* Series (Volumes 1-3)
Murder by the Glass
Deadly Southern Charm
50 Shades of Cabernet

Nonfiction
The Secret Ingredient, The Mystery Writers' Cookbook